CW01642875

A Little Christmas Panto

Angela Britnell

Choc Lit

Where heroes are like chocolate – irresistible!

Published 2022 by Choc Lit Limited
Penrose House, Crawley Drive, Camberley, Surrey GU15 2AB, UK
www.choc-lit.com

EPUB: 978-1-78189-044-8
PRINT: 978-1-78189-076-9
PRINTED AND BOUND BY AMAZON.

To the St Stephen Pantomime Company where I once trod the boards in the Junior Chorus! They exemplify the wonderful British tradition of village pantomimes and after being forced to take a break during the pandemic will be back performing in the New Year for their seventy-sixth production – Robin Hood and the Babes in the Wood.

Acknowledgements

I'm grateful to my friend and super fan, Rae Lynn a New Orleans native, for sharing her family's Christmas traditions with me so I could use them here and one day I hope to see those Christmas Eve bonfires!

As always, thanks also go to the Tasting Panel readers who said yes to the manuscript and made publication possible: Jenny Mitchell, Zoe Rippon, Liana Vera Saez, Mary Alpern, Michele Rollins, Laura Sumner, Janice Butler, Julie Lilly, Lorna Baker, Alan Roberton, Emily Smeby, Fran Stevens, Honor Gilbert, Joanne Elliott, Lynda Adcock, Gill Leivers, Bee Master and Jo Osborne.

Chapter One

Rosey stared at the packet of chocolate biscuits in her hand. If she couldn't come up with an idea soon for Aladdin and Jasmine's first act duet she'd be in trouble. It was the middle of October so pantomime rehearsals had been underway for a month already and her mother was starting to get agitated about her lack of progress.

'Excuse me, ma'am, is this the right kind of flour for bread making?'

She gazed up into a pair of disturbingly familiar electric-blue eyes.

In the fragment of her brain that wasn't struck dumb, she decided Zach Broussard was even more handsome in person than on the big screen. He loomed over her, which admittedly most people did as she was only a shade over five feet tall on a good day, and his thick black hair accented his sculpted face. Combined with the dark stubble peppering his square jaw, it was easy to see where the description of him having the face of an angel with the aura of the devil came about.

Everyone in Polcarne – one thousand, five hundred and thirty-six inhabitants at last count – knew the Oscar-winning Hollywood actor was renting Joe Warren's holiday let, The Old Hay Barn, on the outskirts of the village. He'd been there for the last month or so, but until now no one had seen him venture into the village.

'Uh, sorry … were you talking to me?'

He threw an exaggerated look around the otherwise empty shop and held out a bag of flour.

'I don't suppose you've got any clue if plain flour is equivalent to American all-purpose flour?'

Hearing his signature deep, rich drawl sent a hot flush creeping up her neck. 'Yes, you're absolutely right, although I'd recommend this one if you're making bread.' She selected a bag of strong plain flour off the shelf and held it out to him with a smile. 'I know England is a little behind America, and some people say the Cornish are even slower, but we do have pretty decent already-sliced packaged bread.'

The hollows deepened in his cheeks and the smile lines fanning from the corner of his eyes faded.

'I have time on my hands.'

She could kick herself. Everyone knew the reason behind his empty days. Thanks to the press, she was all too aware that two years ago he'd withdrawn from public life after his young wife's fatal climbing accident on Mount Everest became headline news. The tabloids and social media milked the tragedy for all it was worth, especially because Laura Broussard was pregnant at the time with their first child.

'Home-made bread does taste so much better though,' Rosey babbled on, extolling the virtues of it in a way Paul Hollywood would have been proud of. She pretended to check her watch. 'Oh, is that the time? I must be off or I'll be late …' Her voice trailed away and a trace of Zach's smile returned. No doubt her non-existent acting skills clued him in on the outright lie. 'Good luck with the baking. Bye for now. I'm sure I'll see you around.'

'It's a small place.' His dry response made her blush all over again. 'Thanks for the help.' Zach tilted a heart-stopping smile her way. 'By the way, do you have a name?'

'A name?' Rosey could sense her voice turning shrill.

'Yeah, you know one of those things parents give their kids when they're born?' His famous dimples emerged and her ability to think dwindled even further. 'I'll give you an example. Mine's Zach …'

'Well, of course I know that! I can hardly pretend I don't know who *you* are. Even the politest of British people would find it hard to pull *that* off.'

Oh God, would she never learn to think before she spoke?

Zach clamped his lips together to stop his laughter breaking out but was forced to give up. He knew he should explain that he wasn't laughing *at* her but he'd forgotten how damn good it felt to find anything funny about life. The harder he laughed, the more confused the petite redhead staring at him appeared. After the overly made-up, groomed-to-the-nth degree Hollywood women he was used to, Zach found her clean-scrubbed look immediately appealing. There was nothing out of the ordinary about her regular jeans, thick moss-green jumper and black ankle-boots, but her long, straight, red-gold hair caught his eye. She'd probably tied it back in a neat ponytail to minimise its attention-grabbing qualities, but if so that was a complete failure.

'Sorry.'

They apologised simultaneously. A wonderful peal of husky laughter erupted from her and a flare of bright pink illuminated her pale, freckled skin. Close up, it turned out that her eyes weren't dark blue as he'd assumed but a rich, velvety shade of violet reminiscent of a young Elizabeth Taylor. Something else stirred inside him that had lain dormant for the last two years and a flash of panic seized him by the throat. Zach tossed the bag of flour back on the shelf and strode out of the shop, leaving the door wide open in his haste.

'Stop, please. I'm sorry for whatever I said wrong!'

In his head Zach heard his mother's reprimand. Marie Broussard was a southern lady through and through who'd drummed good manners and consideration for other people into her children. He turned back around.

'I'm the only one who needs to be sorry. I don't know what came over me.' A lie but he couldn't admit the truth.

'It's Rosey, by the way.'

'What is?'

'My name. Rosey Teague. You did ask.'

'I sure did.' Zach collected himself and stuck out his hand. 'It's a pleasure to meet you, Rosey Teague, and as you already know my name, we should be all good now.' A hint of pink returned to her cheeks. 'If you don't have anywhere to be in a hurry, how about—'

'Yoo-hoo, Rosey love!' An Amazon of a woman with waist-length white hair was headed their way. The red cape that topped her swirling red and gold caftan caught in the breeze so she resembled one of Wagner's Valkyries emerging onto the opera stage. He almost felt obliged to applaud.

'Oh God, it's my mother,' Rosey muttered.

The woman nodded at her daughter before switching her attention to him. 'Well, if it isn't Zach Broussard at last. How're you settling in, my 'andsome?'

'Uh … fine, thank you, ma'am.' Her local accent was much stronger than her daughter's but he got the gist of what she was saying.

'I'm not the Queen! If this one won't introduce me, I'll do it myself. Kids these days don't have any manners.' A rumble of laughter broke free. 'I'm Anna Teague and

Rosey's mother for my sins. I was only saying to someone the other day we haven't seen anything of you around Polcarne yet. It don't do a body any good to hide away, you know? We're all some sorry about what happened to your poor wife but no one's going to bother you here so you take as much time as you like to get yourself to rights again.' Anna nodded at her daughter. 'It's worked for you hasn't it, my lover?'

He sensed Rosey's unease. More than most people he knew the horror of having his private life become public property. Whatever the older woman was hinting at, he didn't need it flung in his face in this way.

'Mum. We should go.' The snapped warning stopped Anna Teague in mid-flow. 'Bye, Zach.' Rosey hooked her arm through her mother's and almost dragged her away.

He sighed, turned and set off for a long, solitary, wet walk back to his rented accommodation. Without his flour.

Chapter Two

Silence was Rosey's best weapon as a stroppy teenager so she employed the same method now. Anna was bound to crack first because her mother hated an unfilled space in the conversation.

'I only wanted the poor soul to feel he's not alone in his troubles.' The wheedling tone indicated her mum knew she'd been out of line.

'Mum, you can't compare my failed marriage and career to Zach's wife plunging to her death on Mount bloody Everest.'

'I know that, my love, but—'

'But nothing.'

'I've had an idea.' Anna's eyes brightened.

Rosey flung up her hands. 'I don't want to hear it. It's bound to be crazy and inappropriate and—'

'Oh, for heaven's sake, get the stick out of your bum. How I gave birth to such an unimaginative daughter, I'll never understand.'

Her mother's words stung.

'I'm sorry, my sweet. You know I love you to bits.' Anna gave a nervous giggle. 'Your dad used to call me his "Drama Empress" because he swore "Drama Queen" wasn't enough to do me justice.'

She suspected it probably hadn't been said as kindly as her mother chose to remember. After all, Will Teague had done a runner when Rosey was a toddler and was last heard of living in Birmingham with his fourth wife.

'One of us has to be sensible and I'm afraid you got stuck with the job. It was a daft idea anyway.'

'Go on. You might as well tell me.' She heaved a sigh and dropped down on the sagging red velvet sofa. She already knew this would be *War and Peace* rather than a short story.

'You said yourself Zach seemed to be looking for ways to fill his time. I shouldn't think baking will be much help but the pantomime might do the trick.' Anna flourished a triumphant smile.

'Are you mad?' Rosey burst out laughing. 'Even if you set his problems to one side, do you seriously think an Oscar-winning Hollywood actor wants to get involved in our little village show? What do you think he's going to do? Put on fake boobs, a dress and garish wig and prance around as Widow Twankey?'

'It may be "little", but need I remind you that we won the Best Small Village Pantomime in the South-West Region Award last year?' Anna bristled.

This was delicate ground. Her mother's loud, confident manner covered a sensitive heart when it came to any criticism of the pantomime. Anna had started off in the junior chorus at five years old when her own mother was the producer and progressed through the ranks. She routinely bragged that her last acting role as Principal Boy in *Puss in Boots* was still regarded as a performance for others to emulate.

'I thought he might like to help with the scenery or the lights. Being around theatre people might lift his spirits,' her mother continued.

Rosey kept to herself that calling amateur actors like Demelza Rowe, the local hairdresser, "theatre people" might be a stretch. 'You're absolutely not to ask him. I'm sure Zach came here seeking peace and quiet so we're staying well out of his way. I can't waste any more time on this anyway. I'm due up at the Hall at one o'clock.'

'How's Lady Muck coming on? Going to star on the concert stage soon, is she?'

'Don't be unkind. Amanda is a sweet person.' Rosey couldn't help smiling. 'I've got to admit though she has the musical talent of a block of wood.' These days, giving piano lessons was her bread and butter. Most of her pupils were children but she had an increasing number of adults who'd been denied the opportunity when they were young. It was a complete contrast to the years she spent as a concert pianist, both as a soloist and working with orchestras. At first she'd thrived under the pressure but the never-ending demands that came with performing at a high level and the constant travel involved had begun to negatively affect her. The last straw came when her challenging career became a major factor in the break-up of her brief marriage. Now she strove to keep a better balance in her life and was healthier for it, emotionally and physically.

'I suppose she doesn't have anything better to do with her time,' Anna scoffed. 'His Lordship wouldn't want her picking up a duster or cooking a meal.'

'You know very well Perry isn't that way. He's totally down to earth. They do most of the work themselves. There's no big staff these days. Anyway, I'm going to make a sandwich. Do you want one?'

'I suppose so.'

She retreated to the kitchen and grimaced at the sight of her mother's breakfast remains strewn over the table. There was no time for day-dreaming about what Zach Broussard was about to say when her mother had interrupted them. He was an Oscar-winning heartthrob. She was as ordinary as it was possible to be. The flicker of connection she thought she'd sensed between them had undoubtedly been nothing more than the figment of her over-active imagination.

Rosey started to pick up the dirty dishes. She'd put Zach out of her mind and concentrate on real life.

Zach trudged back in through the gates of Warren Farm and headed for the old barn. He unlocked the door and pulled out his phone as soon as he stepped inside to check his messages. Six more pleading texts from Cody, his agent. Calls from worried friends. Plus his mother's daily greeting. It ended, as always, with a veiled suggestion that he give her a ring to put her mind at rest. Every few weeks he succumbed to guilt and phoned her, but these days their conversations were brief and stilted. After Laura's death he was too ashamed of the bitter anger entwined with his grief and closed in on himself. His parents' loving sympathy was too much to bear.

He stared around the cavernous living room with its high vaulting oak beams and stark whitewashed walls. It had been madness to rent a place big enough for a large family because it only emphasised his solitude. When he'd got off the train in Cornwall and given the taxi driver the address of Warren Farm, the grizzled old man had chuckled.

'What be 'ee wanting to go there for, boy? There's nothing for visitors to do in Polcarne.'

That was precisely why he'd picked Joe Warren's farm out of what seemed like a million Cornish holiday cottages. The converted barn's remoteness on the edge of the bleak and rugged Bodmin Moor had been appealing, as was the promise that visitors would only find one small food shop, a pub and a few other struggling businesses on the doorstep. Whether he'd stick out the full five months of his rental was still up for debate though.

He knew it was only a matter of time before the press tracked him down but he'd deal with that when it happened. Zach had never been a publicity-hunting celebrity but he hadn't shunned it either, regarding it as a necessary evil and part of the job. Since he'd arrived in Polcarne a month ago, he'd avoided going into the village in order to delay the inevitable curiosity that his appearance would spark. He'd taken regular long, solitary walks in the surrounding countryside and even risked jumping on a local bus a few times to venture further into Cornwall, purposely avoiding the most popular tourist spots. He had managed to go unrecognised so far by wearing an old grey hoodie tugged up over his head and dark-rimmed glasses with plain lenses – both tricks he'd used back in LA for the same purpose. The rugged beauty of this remote part of the country had taken him by surprise and it had worked as a balm to his bruised senses. This morning, he'd finally gathered up the courage to venture into Polcarne and had conflicting feelings now about the way it had turned out. The main reason for that was his encounter with Rosey Teague.

She'd shown the typical mixture of curiosity and embarrassment when she'd first recognised him but at least she hadn't pleaded to take a picture with him or begged for an autograph. What had come next was the scariest part. Rosey's kindness and subtle everyday beauty had drawn him in and made him crave something he'd assiduously avoided for the last two years. Thanks to the media, the general assumption was that Zach remained alone because he was still grieving for the love of his life, but the truth was far less palatable. The sad state of his marriage when Laura had died made him reluctant to risk his heart again.

Zach retreated to the kitchen, his favourite room. The old-fashioned black range steadily percolated its warmth, gleaming copper pots hooked to a swinging dark metal frame hung over the unpretentious oak table, and the same slate-grey tiles used throughout the cottage were softened in here by colourful woven rugs.

Another long day stretched out in front of him, and before his mind could drift towards a dangerous place he jumped up and headed for the door. His Hollywood cronies would laugh to see him kick off his sheepskin slippers and shove his feet into an old pair of Joe Warren's rubber boots. Before he arrived, he'd dreaded finding himself with an inquisitive host but the taciturn young farmer wore a permanent frown and said little beyond the bare minimum. Zach got the distinct impression that converting the old farm building into a holiday let was Joe's last-ditch attempt to hold onto his family land. Deep down, he clearly hated the intrusion and Zach stayed well clear of Joe's dilapidated farmhouse.

The rain had stopped so he'd go for another long tramp across the fields. Perhaps when he got back he'd work some more on the new project he'd started last year.

Best to steer well clear of the village and Rosey Teague ...

Chapter Three

'We're always looking for extra help if bread making isn't taking up all of your time.' Rosey tapped Zach on the shoulder. She'd caught him outside the shop, a plastic bag of groceries in one hand, staring at a pantomime poster. A week ago it'd been disconcerting to come face to face with him for the first time and still only felt marginally less so today. She'd met a number of fairly famous people during her music career away from Cornwall but they paled in comparison to Zach.

'What?'

'Sorry, I didn't mean … it was a joke.' By his horrified face, it seemed she'd put both feet in a pile of cow dung. Now he'd assume she found it funny that he wasn't acting any longer. The inevitable happened and she didn't need a mirror to know her face resembled a boiled lobster.

'I'm guessin' you're involved with this? I see your mom's the producer.' He pointed to Anna's name at the bottom of the poster. 'Don't tell me. You're the leading lady?'

'Good grief, no!' Rosey grimaced, but was secretly glad she didn't seem to have completely offended him. 'Mum forced me into the junior chorus when I was six and I hated every moment. I kicked up such a fuss she never made me do it again. I'm the pianist.'

'Oh right. I've heard of your English pantomimes but never seen one. They sound strange.'

'I suppose they are. The whole thing is a very British tradition, although it has its roots in the Italian "*Commedia dell'Arte*" and the early Elizabethan and Stuart *masques.*' Rosey chattered on about the first acknowledged pantomime in 1721 based on the characters of Harlequin and Columbine, and caught Zach's amusement. 'Sorry, I didn't mean to bore you. It's a fascination of mine and I tend to forget not everyone shares it.'

'Don't apologise.' He rested his hand on her arm, and despite the sharp wind blowing in off the moors, she felt the press of his warm fingers all the way through her coat sleeve. 'The history of the theatre is one of my passions too.' A shadow passed over his smile. 'I should say it used to be.'

'It will be again.'

'Maybe.'

Rosey left it there, afraid of patronising him. 'Perhaps you'll come and see the show. Will you still be here in January?'

'I'm not sure.'

'Last time we met you started to ask me something. What was it?' A frown settled between his eyes. 'I'm sure it was nothing—'

'I wondered if … can we get a coffee in the pub, or is there a café maybe?'

That was the last thing she'd expected.

'It's okay. Forget it, I—'

'Don't say that.' He'd misinterpreted her silence. 'I'd love a coffee but the only place to go is the pub, and if we're spotted there it'll stir up gossip you might not want.'

Zach nodded.

'If you don't mind drinking cheap instant coffee, I'm happy to stick the kettle on back at my place? Don't worry, my mum's not there. She's at a meeting with the woman who's in charge of making the pantomime costumes.' She suddenly realised how that might sound. 'I wasn't … I mean … it's just coffee.'

'Yeah, I get that.'

Rosey was furious with herself. It shouldn't have crossed her mind for a single second that he might misconstrue her offer. Zach was a Hollywood superstar and, when he was ready to look beyond his grief, he'd no doubt have a parade of hot women throwing themselves at him. An average-looking, verging-on-middle-aged divorcee whose own mother called her dull and sensible wasn't likely to interest him.

'I could do with a friend,' he suddenly said.

'Me too.' She managed a bright smile. Her mother wasn't the only actress in the family.

Zach heard his cynical agent's warning ringing in his ear.

Everyone's after a piece of you. Women want you as a notch on their bedposts, and although the men will claim to be a genuine friend, at the end of the day they're all hoping your influence and money will help them worm their way into Hollywood.

'Let's get that coffee.' Saying those few words felt as courageous as taking his first step on the stage thirty-four years ago. Flashbacks of himself as a scared five-year-old, dressed in a robe made from an old bath towel with a gold paper crown on his head as one of the three wise men in his kindergarten Christmas play, came flooding back. The knot of nerves in his stomach. A fleeting urge to throw up. At his teacher's urging, he'd trotted out with the equally terrified Noah Warner and brash Ross Milburne, but as the bright lights bathed his face something vital changed inside Zach. He *was* Melchior. Shoulders back, full of his own importance as a wealthy, sumptuously dressed king, he'd swaggered forward – at least that was how his amazed mother described it afterwards. Then, when Ross had frozen and couldn't say his lines, Zach had spoken up, smoothing over the hiccup like a practised actor. That was it. He was hooked.

Rosey's smile blossomed. 'Our place is around the corner from the old church. Come on.'

He fell into step beside her. 'I'm guessin' you grew up here?'

'Oh yes. Is the small town in Tennessee where you were born similar?'

Zach was startled.

'I can't pretend I don't know stuff about you.'

'Yeah, I get that and I should be used to it but…' He shrugged. 'Laura hated that side of our life together. The fact we couldn't go out for coffee on a Sunday morning or browse around a shop like normal folk.'

'Not even in Los Angeles?'

Where did he begin to describe the crazy hamster wheel of Hollywood life to this down-to-earth woman? A place where tourists with cameras lurked around every corner so a celebrity always had to be "on" unless they wanted to be plastered all over the tabloid rags and social media slopping around in old sweats with bed-hair and a scowl on their face. This was a major reason why so many celebrities dated and married other celebrities so they didn't have to explain their curious way of life to complete outsiders.

'Nope.' Zach shook his head. 'You were right though. Collin's Run is even smaller than this place. It's barely on the map. No stoplights and only a small gas station and convenience store. The nearest town is half an hour away but there's not much there either.'

'Your family still live there?'

'Yeah. My mother is Tennessee born and bred but my father isn't. The Broussard family go back generations in Louisiana on the Gulf coast. After my grandparents' house was flooded three times, they'd had enough and packed up and moved to East Tennessee. That was long before Hurricane Katrina.' He fell silent and appreciated that Rosey didn't press him. The aftermath of Katrina was one of the few times he'd been in a place where no one cared who he was. He'd simply been another volunteer helping people get back on their feet. 'My dad met my mom in high school and they've been together ever since.'

'That's something these days.' She sounded wistful. 'My dad left when I was a toddler so I've no first-hand experience of that sort of long, loving relationship.'

'No man's tempted you enough to give it a try?'

'One did but it didn't last long.' There was a forced edge to her smile. 'This is my road. Buttercup Lane. It sounds more picturesque than it is. They're all former council houses.' A long terrace of uninspiring grey concrete homes stretched in front of them. She stopped outside the end house – distinctive from its neighbours with a bright purple door, narrow front garden crammed with colourful flowers clinging on from the summer, and a tiny fish pond in one corner guarded by a jaunty red and white plastic gnome. 'Mum doesn't do ordinary.'

'I've worked that one out already.' Zach stood close enough to catch a hint of Rosey's delicate perfume: something floral overlaid with a punch of spice. The autumn sunshine brought out the fire in her hair and he stared at the stain of deep pink gloss emphasising her generous mouth. An intense need surged through him but it shrivelled as shock bloomed in her eyes. 'Sorry.' He pulled away. 'I got …' Before he could make a fool of himself any further, he hurried off.

Rosey considered calling after him but had second thoughts. The fleeting pull of desire between them had come from nowhere, like a bolt of lightning. She'd been acutely aware of the line of dark stubble along his square jaw and his fresh, minty breath. But if they'd given in to the impulse, it would have destroyed their tentative friendship.

She pulled out her house keys and unlocked the door then headed straight for the living room to sit at the piano. On autopilot, she warmed up with a few scales to start with and then a couple of Chopin etudes to limber up her fingers. Although she'd given up playing professionally – despite her mother's insistence to the contrary, she didn't count the pantomime – Rosey hadn't abandoned the habits drilled into her over the years. Every month she challenged herself by selecting an unfamiliar piece to work on but she wasn't in the mood for October's Rachmaninov. She needed the familiarity of Mozart. As a child she'd been introduced to the magical world of the piano and the formidable Maude Lander had nurtured her talent. The desire to make music her career took her away from Cornwall, and although she'd had a certain amount of success, she'd never reached the dizzying heights Maude predicted. When playing became a hardship rather than a joy, she'd had few regrets about leaving her concert career behind.

Now she lost herself in the Andante, the second movement of Mozart's Piano Concerto Number 21.

'What's wrong, my love?'

'Mum! I didn't hear you come in.' Anna and her mother were poles apart in most ways but they still knew each other through and through.

'And don't try to tell me you're all right because we both know that's rubbish.'

Rosey rested her hands on the keyboard to hide any tell-tale shaking. 'Oh, it's nothing really. I bumped into Zach again and he was coming in here for a coffee but he lost his nerve. I must've frightened him off.'

'You'll have to be patient, my 'andsome. I'm sure you didn't do anything except be your own sweet self.' Her mum's face creased in a warm smile. 'No wonder he ran off. He'll get there.' Optimism was a cornerstone of her mother's ebullient personality. 'How about a nice cup of tea? We'll sit down and make a plan.'

'A plan?'

'If we're going to help that poor boy, we need a plan.' A mischievous twinkle lit up her eyes. 'By Christmas we'll have him smiling again and with any luck sharing your bed. It'll do you both a world of good.'

'Bloody hell, Mum! My sex life or lack of it is none of your business. For heaven's sake, forget whatever nonsense you've got in mind.'

'It's all right, dear. You can thank me later.' Anna swanned out of the room.

Rosey rested her head on the keyboard and groaned. This would not end well.

Chapter Four

'You're just the man I need. It's lucky I spotted you walking along.' Rosey's mother pounced on Zach in the middle of the street. Today she was channelling a fifties' vibe with her red and white polka dot dress, scarlet leather jacket, white kitten-heel shoes and stiff bouffant hairstyle. 'If you're free, could you lend me some muscle power?'

'Uh, sure, what d'you need?' He'd been heading back to the shop for more flour. Bread making was proving more exacting than he'd expected, and so far his efforts had produced the baking equivalent of concrete blocks. It had obviously been a false assumption on his part that being a decent enough cook when it came to feeding himself would carry on over to baking. Zach had quickly discovered that the two things were as different as night and day.

'It's the OAPs' bingo at two o'clock and the tables need setting up in the hall.' Anna fluttered long fake eyelashes that could do double duty as spiders. 'Rosey normally helps me but she's running late. Her pupil didn't turn up on time for his lesson.'

'No problem, I'm happy to help.'

She squeezed his bicep and smirked. 'I bet you could pick up the tables in one hand with these.'

'Maybe.' Zach wriggled out of her grasp.

'We're over there.' Anna pointed to a dark, rain-stained building where a bright red door stood wide open. She must have been lurking behind it watching for someone to accost. 'Come on.' She set off with a purposeful stride and he hurried to catch up. 'This used to be the church hall. When the congregation dwindled, they closed the church and the council bought the hall for a community gathering place. It's where we stage the pantomime. The second week of January. The thirteenth, fourteenth and fifteenth. People need a bit of cheering up after Christmas.' She gave him a shrewd look. 'You'll still be here so I expect to sell you a ticket.'

The planned length of his rental must be public knowledge, he realised grimly.

'In here.' Anna led him through a small lobby and pushed open a set of swinging doors.

'Are those what you need getting out?'

Long wooden tables were folded up against the wall closest to them and stacks of grey plastic chairs stood at either end. She looked surprised by the question and he got the distinct impression she'd forgotten the reason they were there.

'Oh … yes. Six should be plenty plus three chairs on each side and one on the end facing the stage. Don't put any on the other end because they'd have their backs to me and a lot of the old dears don't hear well. They need to see me calling the numbers so they can lip read.'

Before she talked him to death, he hauled one table to the middle of the room and started to unfold the rickety legs.

'I told you I'd make it in plenty of time to … oh … what're you doing here?' Rosey gawped at Zach.

'Don't be so rude!' Anna chided her daughter. 'This sweet young man offered to help a poor old lady.'

If he'd been eating or drinking, he would have choked. For a start, *she'd* dragged him in off the street … and "poor old lady"?'

'You don't need both of us, so I'll—'

'Don't be daft. You stay and help Zach set up. I, um … need to go to the shop for biscuits.'

He suspected if he snooped around the kitchen, he'd discover more biscuits than the bingo group could eat in a month.

'I won't be long.' Anna swept out in a cloud of musky perfume.

Talk about awkward. He'd known they couldn't avoid meeting again for the next three or so months, but it'd only been three short days since he'd made a complete fool of himself – nowhere near long enough for the sting of embarrassment to subside. It would be easy to claim he'd reacted the way any single man might to a beautiful woman but that wouldn't be fair on Rosey.

'She strong-armed you, didn't she?' Rosey sighed. 'I'm sorry. I didn't put her up to it if that's what you were thinking.'

'Oh, I guessed that. You looked horrified when you saw me.'

'It wasn't horror!' Her stomach sank. No doubt this was all part of her mother's so-called plan – the plan she wanted nothing to do with and had ordered Anna to forget.

'What was it then, Rosey?' Zach's syrupy drawl sent her into meltdown. 'Why don't I start off by apologising?'

'Apology accepted. I must admit that was a first for me.' She grinned. 'I know you're used to grander things than Asda's own brand instant coffee but you only had to say so. You didn't have to run off like a scared cat.'

'It wasn't that. I'm no coffee snob.' He tilted her a shy smile. 'I was telling the truth when I said I really needed a friend.'

‘So was I.’ Rosey picked out her next words carefully. ‘My marriage didn’t end happily so I’m not comparing it to your loss but—’

‘You don’t understand. No one does.’ Exasperation oozed out of him. ‘Laura and I were at odds with each other when she died and parted in anger.’

Rosey knew the media often got things wrong, but there’d never been any hint that his marriage was less than perfect. Didn’t those sort of things always leak out? ‘But surely the two of you were ecstatic about the baby? I can’t imagine the pain you suffered losing them both.’

His face turned to stone. ‘You have no idea.’

‘No. I’m sure I don’t. Alan and I had put off starting a family … although we both wanted one.’ She hesitated. For some reason, she found herself needing to be more honest with Zach. ‘That’s not quite true. He wanted a family right away but I convinced him to wait because I wasn’t ready to take a career break.’ Rosey couldn’t help sighing. ‘Now I see all my friends with their children, who are all growing up so quickly and starting school and everything, and I wonder if I’ve missed the boat.’ Something altered in his expression and she wondered if her confession was a step too far. After all, they barely knew each other. ‘I’m terribly sorry … I didn’t mean to make this about me.’

‘Don’t apologise. It’s fine.’

‘No, it’s not. It was thoughtless of me.’ She tried to think of something else to say. ‘Do you think you’ll ever go back to acting?’

‘No way. I can’t.’ Zach’s gruff whisper echoed around the empty room. He jabbed a finger towards the stage. ‘My acting career played a huge part in destroying me and Laura. Goin’ back to it isn’t happening. Ever.’

She should have kept her mouth well and truly shut. 'Mum will be back soon so maybe we'd better get on. If you finish setting up the tables, I'll do the chairs,' she said quickly.

Zach realised he'd had no right to fling Rosey's kindness back in her face when all she'd done was attempt to comfort him. She didn't know that the one confidence she chose to share, about her longing for a family of her own, made him even more aware that he shouldn't pursue her in any way, shape or form. That avenue was closed to him and, although he'd somewhat come to terms with it, the sting never quite went away.

'Tables, Zach.'

'Oh yeah, right. Sorry.'

'I know you've officially given up acting, but could you try to give the impression everything's fine? Mum picks up on stuff and you don't want her interfering. Trust me on that.' A wry smile lifted the corners of her mouth.

He could indulge her this one small thing. 'Sure.'

They set the last chair in place as the door opened and Anna swanned back in.

'Run along and fill up the tea urn, Rosey, there's a dear.' She zeroed in on Zach. 'I've got one more teensy favour to ask you.'

Behind her mother's back, Rosey mimed a broad smile before she hurried off to the kitchen.

'Do you have any plans for the next couple of hours?'

'Nothing special.'

'Perfect.' She beamed. 'In that case you can stay for the bingo. At the interval you can help take the teas around, then I'll get you to hand out the prizes at the end. It'll make the old folks' day.' Anna clapped her hands as Rosey returned to join them. 'Can you believe this kind man offered to hang around this afternoon? He didn't like the idea of us taking all these tables down on our own.'

'Like we do every other time you mean?'

He caught the bubble of amusement in her voice.

'I s'ppose we do manage but it's a struggle.' The grudging concession was as far as Anna would go.

'Well, there's no need for it today. I'm happy to have the chance to flex these and impress two beautiful ladies.' Zach's dramatic bodybuilder pose made them laugh.

'Vera. Pauline.' Anna breezed across to two elderly women who'd shuffled in. 'Come and meet our lovely American guest. His name's Zach Broussard. You'll have to watch out though, he's a charmer.'

In for a penny, in for a pound, he thought. 'Now ladies, why don't I find you the best seats in the house and y'all can tell me about yourselves?' Zach bent down to take their arms and saw Anna's unbridled glee.

The hall soon filled up and Rosey's mother took centre stage – literally – to call the numbers. Bingo was a mystery to him and he'd expected a gentle, good-humoured game, but these people took it seriously. Anna even stepped in to separate a man and woman who simultaneously claimed to have won the afternoon's star prize – a bottle of whisky. To prevent bloodshed, Zach offered to run down to the shop to buy a second bottle.

'Wow ... that was interesting.' He flopped down on one of the chairs and shook his head at Rosey as her mother shooed the last people out of the door. 'How often do you do this madness?'

'Every fortnight.'

'You must be saints.' He leaned forward to brush away a strand of silky red-gold hair that had escaped her high, tight ponytail, then pulled his hand back as if he'd been stung. 'Sorry. I—'

'It's just hair, Zach. Don't make too much of everything.'

'Do I?'

'I get the impression you think people are judging you all the time.' Sadness crept into her velvety eyes. 'Maybe it's like that in your world but we're not like that here. I didn't read anything more into your effort to tidy my appearance than simply that.'

Then you're not as smart as I thought you were. Anything else he might have been reckless enough to add went unspoken because Anna re-joined them. He should have been grateful for the rescue.

Chapter Five

Rosey struggled not to wince as Amanda massacred 'Away in a Manger', the simple Christmas carol she'd been practising for a fortnight with no appreciable improvement.

'Perry thought it would be lovely if I could play a little when his children come for the holidays. I do so want to make it a happy time for them.' A worry line feathered Amanda's smooth brow.

Rosey felt for the young woman. Being thrust into the role of step-mother to twin six-year-old girls, who apparently wrongly saw her as the reason they weren't living with their father any longer, couldn't be easy.

'I'm sure it will be. Christmas is a magical time for children.'

'I know it *should* be that simple, but—'

'I didn't say simple.' Rosey leaned on the piano – a beautiful, gleaming black Steinway baby grand she would give her eye teeth for. 'Life isn't that way very often.'

'We'd love a baby of our own but Perry says we need to wait until the girls are a little older so they'll accept it better.'

She doubted Amanda's step-daughters would be happy to be usurped at any stage but kept that to herself.

'No one would think I used to run the HR department at a major London bank but perhaps nothing could've prepared me for this.' Amanda gestured around the cavernous ballroom, its faded splendour an echo of years past. 'It's like living in a bloody time warp. The villagers either resent me or kowtow to me and both extremes make me miserable.' Her shoulders slumped. 'And don't suggest

I ask Perry for help. The poor man is almost at the end of his rope trying to keep this place going. Lanhay Hall is in constant need of work and the struggle to maintain it is relentless.' She lowered her voice. 'Sometimes I wonder if it's worth the effort but I'd never say that to him.' A weak smile lifted the corners of her mouth. 'I'm sorry to dump all my worries on you. You'll have to start charging double for the counselling help.'

'Help?' She laughed. 'I can't imagine what help you think I am.'

'You listen and that's priceless.' Amanda shook her head.

'Can you paint?'

'Paint? Does that count?' She pointed to a large picture hanging over the fireplace. The ornate gold frame set off a Mediterranean landscape so vivid that Rosey could almost smell the summer heat rising from the white-walled buildings and the scent of bougainvillea in the air.

'Is that yours? Seriously?'

'I have a degree from the Royal College of Art. That was before I came to my senses and studied business instead to pay the bills. What made you ask about painting anyway?'

Rosey wished she'd kept her mouth shut. 'It doesn't matter. I'd be insulting you—'

'Rubbish. I want to hear.'

'Okay, but feel free to say no. If you're keen to make friends in the village we're always in need of help with the pantomime. Fred Cann is in charge of the scenery, but he'd be the first to tell you himself that he's no artist.'

'Oh gosh, I'd love to.'

'Seriously?'

'Yes, it sounds like fun.' Amanda grinned and closed the lid of the piano. 'No offence, Rosey, but quite frankly anything would be more fun than this. We both know I'm wasting your time and mine. I'll download some Christmas carols on my iPhone for the girls rather than torment them with my playing.'

Rosey's face flamed. 'Please don't think I've let you go on taking lessons because I'm desperate for the money. I honestly thought I might be able—'

'You're an absolutely brilliant teacher and if anyone could overcome my complete lack of musical ability, it's you.' Amanda fidgeted with her wedding ring. 'I've kept you coming because I needed a friend and paying for lessons seemed like a small price for that.'

'You don't have to pay for my friendship.'

'I know that now.' She straightened her shoulders. 'Tell me more about this pantomime and what you need me to do.'

Zach sniffed at the tempting aroma filling the kitchen and regarded the two loaves of crusty wheat bread cooling on the counter with satisfaction. He'd finally cracked it and made something worth eating. His mother insisted he'd inherited his stubbornness from the Broussard side of the family but his father wasn't the only bull-headed one. Marie had defied her parents, one a doctor and the other a lawyer, to marry a man who made his living as a plumber. In their eyes Pierre Broussard wasn't a suitable match for their college-educated daughter. Zach rather thought that his parents' fortieth wedding anniversary last year was confirmation that they'd been wrong.

To prove his success, he'd take a loaf of bread down to Rosey. There were a million reasons why he should stay well away from her but none registered right now. His navy sweatshirt boasted a liberal dusting of flour so he made an attempt to rub it off, then negated any improvement by wiping his hands on his jeans. The weather had improved over the last week, and apart from the occasional shower, they'd had a run of clear blue skies and mild temperatures. Mild was a relative term though because it was certainly nowhere near as warm as early November usually was in sunny southern California, so Zach still shrugged on his ancient black leather jacket. He selected the best shaped loaf, wrapped it in a clean tea towel and headed out.

It was a brisk fifteen-minute walk from Joe's farm to Rosey's house but he bumped into his new bingo friends Vera and Pauline outside the hairdresser's shop. They peppered him with a barrage of questions from what Americans typically ate to what he thought of Cornwall. After he managed to extricate himself, Zach hadn't gone a hundred metres before Anna materialised in front of him. Today she rivalled Cruella de Vil in a sweeping floor-length black coat complete with a flamboyant white fur collar and matching patent leather boots. A black velvet hat perched coquettishly on her striking white hair, swept in an elegant chignon.

Does the woman have a spy camera set up to follow me or has she put a tracking device on my phone?

'Hello, my 'andsome. Were you looking for my Rosey?'

As soon as he said yes, Anna's smile broadened to smug satisfaction.

'She's in the church hall working on a song for the pantomime.'

'Oh right, she did say she was the pianist.'

Anna tutted. 'She's not one to brag on herself. Rosey's the musical director.' Maternal pride oozed out of her. 'She composes a lot of original songs, and for others – particularly the chorus numbers – she takes recognisable modern pop songs and writes her own lyrics. Rosey's got a wicked sense of humour and enjoys throwing in some local colour and political humour.' Anna chuckled. 'We enjoy poking fun at the idiots up in London.' She eyed up what he was carrying. 'Got something for her, have you?'

'Yeah.' Zach sensed Anna wrestling with her conscience and waited to see which side would win – the one that itched to satisfy her curiosity, or the other which clung to good manners. 'I'd better be off.' He made a quick escape before she could offer to come with him.

A woman's pure, clear voice drifted out as he crept into the building and he closed the outside door behind him with a gentle click. He hesitated by the coat racks then tiptoed over to the half-open door leading into the hall. The piano itself was nothing special but the person playing it certainly was. Only when everything went quiet did he push the door open and step inside.

Rosey jerked around and turned bright red.

'Your mom said I'd find you here. This is for you.' He held out the package. 'I think I've cracked the bread making at last.' Their hands brushed as she took it from him and a shot of electricity ran through his fingers. 'I tapped the bottom and it sounded hollow like the YouTube video said it should.'

'If all else fails, take to the internet – right?' She unwrapped the towel and sniffed appreciatively.

'Hey, it worked. If you haven't had lunch, perhaps we could taste-test it at your place?'

She tilted her head with a quizzical smile. 'Are you going to run out on me again if I say yes?'

Her tone might have been light but Zach sensed the question behind her words was anything but. He mentally tossed a coin. Was it safer to keep this particular door closed? Of course it would be, but then she fixed her soft violet eyes on him, making the choice pretty much inevitable. 'No. I promise I won't.'

'Okay. I need to pack up my music first to bring with me. I'm wary of leaving it here because we've had a few things go missing recently. Nothing valuable. I'm only talking about a packet of cheap pens and a new paint brush Fred needed for the scenery, but I don't want to take any chances.'

'Could it be down to bored kids in rehearsal maybe?'

'I suppose so but we've never had any trouble with them before.' Rosey shrugged. 'Anyway, I won't worry about that for now. Let's go eat.'

'By the way, you sounded great when I came in. I didn't realise you could …' No way could he patronise her by asking why someone with her obvious talent was teaching beginners' piano lessons and helping with a village pantomime.

'Play piano at a professional level and have a half-decent voice?' She rested her hands on the keys and it drew attention to her long, shapely fingers. 'I studied music in London, and up until a few years ago I made a good living as a soloist at minor venues and with various orchestras around the country and Europe.' The straight line of her lips and flint-like eyes told Zach he'd ventured into dangerous territory. 'After things went wrong, I came home.'

'Sorry, I didn't mean to pry.' Zach risked a brief smile. 'But if we're goin' to be friends …' He wasn't being fair, because if he demanded more of her then she had every right to do the same in return and that terrified him. If he told her all the depressing details about his marriage, it might mean sharing one particular secret that, outside of his parents, he'd only told one other person – and that was Laura. Despite all of her promises to the contrary, in the end it was one of the things that broke them.

'I think that's a pipe dream, don't you?' A tangible wistfulness ran through her soft voice. 'Let's forget lunch. I've got lots to do before the rehearsal tonight.' She turned her back to him. 'I'll get something to eat later and enjoy your bread then.'

He knew when he was beaten.

Chapter Six

This was lining up to be another frosty breakfast time and Rosey wasn't talking about her bowl of cereal. Usually her mother's sulks lasted no more than twenty-four hours but she'd kept it up for two days now since Thursday night's rehearsal.

'So are you going to explain why you didn't tell me you asked Lady Amanda to help with the scenery? Anna blurted out, bursting with indignation. 'Poor Fred Cann got the shock of his life when she turned up at the hall.'

'I can't imagine why he'd be surprised because I told him she'd be there. Amanda's an extremely talented artist and she said she thoroughly enjoyed herself.'

'That's all very well but who's running this pantomime?' Anna twisted a linen napkin into knots and flung it on the table. 'Everything is supposed to go through me.'

'Oh Mum, don't be such a diva.' She slathered a thick layer of marmalade on her toast – the last slice of Zach's incredible bread. If he wasn't an out-of-her-reach Hollywood star, she could hardly imagine a more perfect man – handsome, intelligent, quick-witted *and* he could cook. 'You're usually happy to drag anyone in to lend a hand, so what's the problem? Is it because *I* thought of asking Amanda instead of *you*?'

'You're a rude, ungrateful child.'

'In case you'd forgotten, I'm thirty-eight. Hardly a child.' The spiteful reminder made her mum glower. Anna never revealed her own age to anyone unless forced to.

'Will you be at the rehearsal tonight?'

'Why wouldn't I? It is Saturday.'

Anna rose from the chair and rearranged the various purple garments she was draped in today. 'I don't know what's got into you recently.' Her eyes glittered. 'Or *not* as the case might be. You had a handsome man drooling over you, but—'

'That's enough. I've had it.' Rosey sprang up. 'Zach's not interested in a relationship with me or anyone else.' That wasn't strictly true because they had teetered on the verge of flirting before she'd bridled at Zach's unspoken questions, tucked behind his compliments about her musical abilities. There'd been a lot of wild rumours flying around the village when she'd come back home three years ago. They ran the gamut from her having a nervous breakdown in the middle of a performance to the multiple lovers she'd supposedly had all around the globe. At the time, she'd been too bruised to defend herself but now she was in a better place and knew everything that had happened was for the best. Why she hadn't had the guts to explain that to Zach instead of flying off the handle was beyond her.

'But I saw sparks flying between the two of you. Don't deny it. I'm sensitive to these things.'

'Neither of us is dead from the waist down but he's clearly still grieving for his wife and I …' She reined in her emotions before they got the better of her. 'Forget it. Please.' Maybe her begging tone did the trick because something altered in her mum's expression. 'I'm going for a walk.'

'A walk? It's only eight o'clock.'

'So? Am I only allowed walks between certain designated times these days?'

'Don't be so daft.' Anna shooed at her. 'Off with you and don't come back until you're in a better mood.'

That might be sometime next month or next year. Rosey stomped out to the hall and dragged on her boots. She knew she should fetch her fleece from upstairs because the weather had cooled off again but couldn't bear to stay in the house a minute longer. She marched through the village with her head down, only lifting it once to greet an elderly man out walking his dog. If she kept on in this direction, she'd go right past Joe Warren's farm with the possibility of being spotted by Zach. Logically, she had every right to walk where she liked but Rosey made an about-turn anyway and trudged back the way she'd come. Albert Rundle was bent over in the shop window setting up his Christmas display. He was stacking gift sets of scented toiletries alongside boxes of mince pies and tins of Quality Street. Nothing to arouse her interest.

'What's the long face for, my 'andsome?'

'Oh, hello Fred.' The old man had come out of the shop while Rosey's mind was elsewhere.

'I s'ppose Christmas will be on us before we know it. Don't seem possible. The year's flying by.' He rolled his eyes. 'Wendy's already started buying loads of stuff the kids and grandkids don't need. I'm partial to singing a few carols but don't care tuppence for the rest of it.'

'I'm with you but I think we're in the minority.' Rosey's jaundiced view of the holidays came from her mother. There'd been no spare money when Rosey was little so that kept their celebrations simple, and now Anna used the excuse that, with the pantomime starting three weeks after Christmas, she didn't have time for a lot of fuss. To her mum, the holidays were an irritating disruption to the rehearsal schedule.

'Wouldn't do if we were all the same.' A smile creased Fred's weathered face. 'That Amanda you sent over to help me is a good woman.' He coloured up. 'She told me to call her by her first name. Said she didn't want any of the Lady Amanda nonsense. A real blessing she is.'

He'd been in charge of the pantomime scenery for decades after being dragooned into helping by his wife, one of Anna's stalwart group of costume makers.

'Some clever with a paintbrush, she is. You should see what she's done with Aladdin's palace. Bloody marvellous 'tis.'

'Could I come back with you now and take a look?' Fred did the initial work in an empty barn on his farm before bringing things down to the hall.

'Of course you can, my lover.' He lifted the newspaper in his hand. 'Wendy likes to do the crossword with her first coffee of the day so I always get it for her of a morning.'

A pang of envy rolled through Rosey. Those sort of small gestures of love were more touching to her than bouquets of roses or expensive jewellery. They'd been lacking in her own marriage, and recently she'd come to the conclusion that it wasn't fair to lay all the blame at Alan's feet. She'd been shocked to discover his infidelity and more so when he claimed she only had herself to blame because he felt neglected and relegated to second place after Rosey's career. It didn't excuse his behaviour but she saw now that relationships were like plants and needed nurturing to thrive.

'You sure you'm all right?'

'I'm fine.' She managed to smile. 'It's a bit cold, that's all.'

'Tis nearly the middle of November, you know? Bound to be nippy first thing.' Fred shook his head. 'Why you young people never think to put a coat on is beyond me.'

She'd let him think she was scatty rather than explain why she'd stormed out of the house under-dressed. 'Actually, I ought to go home and do a few things before my first piano lesson. How about I pop up to the farm this afternoon instead?'

'You do that.' Fred tipped his cap. 'Tell Anna I said hello.' He bustled off.

Before she did anything else Rosey needed to put things straight with her mum. Not that she believed an apology was in order on her part, but she didn't care for them being at odds with each other. She'd go back home and smooth things over to keep the peace.

'You don't have to do this you know, mate?' Joe frowned over at Zach.

'Yeah, but I needed a workout and there's no gym in Polcarne. Anyway, the job needs doin' right?' He grinned and wiped the sweat away from his brow.

'You're a paying guest not cheap farm labour.'

'I offered.'

After another restless night, he'd been sitting on the patio behind the old barn sipping a mug of coffee when Joe had trailed out of the farmhouse. The grey-faced young farmer looked as tired and worn down as Zach. His host's flash of annoyance was quickly replaced by a tight smile when he called over to say hello and Joe trudged across for a chat. He explained his plan to renovate another of the dilapidated buildings dotting the property for a holiday rental which was when Zach offered to help. They'd spent the last couple of hours dragging out old pieces of machinery ready for the rubbish tip and clearing years of accumulated dirt off the concrete floor.

'You gonna do all this remodelling yourself? It's a big job.'

'I'll manage. I've got a fair amount of experience in construction work. I can't keep my head above water with what the farm makes these days so I do that and odd jobs for other local farmers to pay the bills.' Joe kept his eyes fixed on the ground.

'Must be tough.'

He shrugged and shoved his hands in his pockets.

'What was this place anyway?' Zach asked. The walls of the stone building were solid and the roof timbers looked in decent shape but blue sky was visible through gaps in the slate tiles.

Joe's grey eyes took on a faraway look. 'My mum's buttery. If you ask any of the older folk in the village, they'll tell you she made the best butter and cheese in the days when we still had cows.' He picked up his shovel. 'I reckon we've done enough for today. How about I buy you a pint down the pub?'

'Sounds good to me.' Zach pulled a cobweb out of his hair. 'Don't know about you but I reckon a shower's in order first.'

'I suppose.' A faint smile lifted Joe's habitually dour expression. 'Don't they say women like a working man to look a bit rough?'

'Yeah, but there's rough and there's smelly and dirty. I'm pretty sure we're verging on the latter. I'll meet you out front when I've scrubbed up.' He set off for the barn, lighter in spirits than he'd been in a long time.

An unexpected stab of nerves hit Zach in the gut as he followed Joe into the pub. He caught a few sly looks flung in his direction but didn't spot any phones being whipped out to take photos. Every morning when he stepped outside, he expected to find paparazzi on the doorstep and still struggled to believe he'd been able to stay under the radar this long.

'Pint of Tribute? It's the best local ale.'

'Yeah, thanks.' He'd walked past this place before but never ventured inside. The Trelawney was a meeting place for the locals. Dark wood tables and chairs, scuffed with age, were dotted around a swirly patterned carpet of indeterminate colour and vintage. There was no ancient fireplace surrounded by gleaming horse brasses, only an everyday gas fire with fake logs. The pool table in the back had been hogged by a gaggle of youths and two grizzled old men were playing darts on the opposite side of the room.

'You hungry?'

'I guess.' Zach hadn't given food any thought since his frugal breakfast of fruit and yogurt. 'Do they serve meals here? You want me to fetch us a menu?'

Joe grinned. 'You've got a choice of pasties or sandwiches. Take your pick.'

'Pasties are a Cornish thing, aren't they? I'll give one a try.' He'd heard of the local meat pies but hadn't sampled them yet. In his A-list actor days, all high-fat, carb-rich, sugary foods were off limits. The type of roles he played demanded he stayed fit and he'd had his own nutritionist and personal trainer. There were certain aspects he missed from his old career but not everything. 'I'll get us a table.' He settled for one facing the door.

'Here you go.' Joe set down two frothy pints. 'Beth's bringing the pasties over in a minute.'

Sure enough, the attractive young woman with glossy, short, dark hair and sparkling blue eyes he'd noticed serving behind the bar soon appeared with their food. She paid little attention to Zach but treated Joe to a dazzling smile as she placed the plates in front of them. His friend's cheeks turned ruddy and he hunched over the table without speaking. Beth's face fell and she scurried off again.

'Cute girl.'

Joe grunted something he couldn't catch and picked up his pasty, a massive half-moon-shaped pie that hung over the edges of the plate, before taking a hefty bite.

'I reckon the buttery will make a decent one-bedroom cottage when you're done.' Zach decided to change the subject, taking a long draught of the full-bodied beer and wiping his mouth. 'It would've been big enough for me.'

'That's the idea.'

Now he sampled the pasty and exhaled a soft moan. The combination of the hot, flaky pastry and savoury filling were unbeatable. No wonder the things were on sale everywhere. 'That's pretty damn good.'

Joe twitched the hint of a smile. It didn't last long. Next thing he glowered towards a noisy crowd of people who'd swarmed in. 'Oh hell, we won't be able to hear ourselves talk now they're here. Bloody pantomime lot. Come here after rehearsal, they do.'

He spotted Rosey's eye-catching hair and wondered if she'd seen him yet. Unless she deliberately walked out of the way, their table was slap bang in the middle of the most direct path to the bar.

'Zach, my 'andsome, how're you?' Anna, a vision in fluorescent pink, was suddenly hovering next to them.

'Very well, ma'am – and you?'

She wagged her finger in his face. 'It's Anna, remember? Ma'am makes me sound like an old woman.'

Behind her shoulder he noticed Rosey struggling to keep a straight face.

'I sure am sorry. Let me buy you a drink to apologise.'

'You're a sweet boy but we're all here together.' Anna waved her hand in the air and almost stabbed him with her manicured purple talons. 'Someone else might take you up on the offer though.' She nodded at Rosey.

'Mum, for goodness sake, let's leave Zach and Joe in peace.' Rosey hitched her arm through Anna's and dragged her mother away.

'Cute girl.' Joe's thick Cornish accent was laced with mischief. 'We're a useless pair, aren't we?'

'Yeah. So what're we goin' to do about it?'

Chapter Seven

'Oh wow, that's amazing.' Rosey gawped at the stunning representation of Aladdin's palace hanging from the barn rafters. Last week she'd been too busy to come to see it as she'd promised, but when one of her pupils had cancelled that afternoon, she'd seized the opportunity to get out from under her mum's feet.

'It has turned out fairly well.' Amanda's shy smile blossomed.

'Fairly well? I'd say it has. Our audience is in for a treat.' She remembered Fred was standing there too and hurried to backtrack. 'Not that your scenery isn't always stellar.'

'Don't you worry about hurting my feelings.' The old man chortled. 'I've never claimed to be an artist and I'm right glad to have this one here.' He patted Amanda's shoulder. 'All I've got to do now is talk her into taking charge next year and I can go into semi-retirement.'

'I only came along to help, not do you out of a job!' Amanda protested.

'Perhaps your other half … I mean his Lordship … wouldn't like it?'

'Oh, it's absolutely not that. Perry is thrilled I've found something I enjoy in the village and extremely relieved that I'm not torturing the piano any longer.'

Rosey stifled a giggle.

'Well, let's see how this year's show goes and we'll talk afterwards.'

‘Perfect.’ She mustn’t forget to pass all of this on to her mum later so Anna wouldn’t get bent out of shape again. ‘Now show me the rest.’

The palace backdrop was a superb riot of over-the-top colour and spectacle but Rosey’s personal favourite part turned out to be the garden of the royal palace where Aladdin and Princess Jasmine had their first meeting. Everything about it caught her imagination from the exotic flowers to the rose-covered arbour perfect for a secretive assignation. The beginnings of a tune stirred in her head and the longer she stared at the incredible painting, the more of it came to her.

‘You’re a genius, Amanda.’ Rosey squealed with pleasure. ‘I’ve been struggling with Aladdin and Jasmine’s duet for weeks but now I can hear every note. I’ll have to go. If I don’t get it written down right away, I might lose it again.’

‘I’m glad to have helped even if it wasn’t deliberate.’ Her friend’s hazel eyes shone. ‘I’m the same when I’m stuck on a painting. When the lightbulb finally goes off, all I want to do is paint night and day to get it down.’

‘Off you go, my ‘andsome.’ Fred shooed her away.

She raced down the road, debating whether to head for home or the church hall. At home she’d have her music manuscript paper and sharpened pencils, but she needed peace and quiet to focus and the costume group were probably still there. Even if they’d finished with their official meeting, Anna, Zoe and the other people who helped with the mountains of sewing were doubtless all sitting around drinking tea and gossiping. Rosey sighed and fished the hall key out of her handbag.

The heat was never turned on unless the building was being used and she shivered when she went in, but as soon as her fingers rested on the keys she forgot her discomfort. The music poured out and, miraculously, the lyrics began to emerge too, which didn't always happen.

Rosey lost herself in the music.

Zach's restlessness returned with a vengeance. He'd worn himself out physically helping Joe every spare minute of the previous week but still couldn't get Rosey out of his head. His imagination ran riot, conjuring up how her lips would taste if they kissed and he guessed they'd be reminiscent of the ripe summer strawberries he loved to pick fresh from his mother's garden. It was ridiculous to tell himself she'd given no hint of returning his interest – he definitely hadn't been the only one flirting with the idea of flirting.

He spied Joe ambling across the farm yard and lifted his hand in greeting. In the pub the young farmer confessed he'd dated Beth, the barmaid, when they were both teenagers but the relationship fell apart because she hadn't appreciated coming second to the farm in his attentions. Zach pointed out that it didn't take a genius to see they were still attracted to each other. Just because a decade ago they weren't mature enough to work through their differences, that didn't mean if they tried again it was doomed to failure too.

Zach blamed his own disclosure about having a crush on Rosey on the two pints of Tribute he'd drank in quick succession. The truth was he'd needed to share it with someone before it drove him crazy.

'It's bloody obvious now you've said so, mate,' Joe had said. 'You went all weird when she was around and the poor woman turned red as her hair. Do you know she were a proper pianist like? The word going around when she came back home said her husband dumped her and she got tired of all the travelling. I haven't heard any gossip about her having any boyfriends or nothing like that either, and it's hard to keep things quiet around here.'

None of this helped with his indecision.

Zach grimaced when his mobile jangled to life. 'Hi, Mom. What's up?'

'What's up? I'm calling to see how my son is because *he* never calls *me*.'

'I do!'

'Not very often and you know it.'

He couldn't argue with the truth.

'For starters, you can tell me what're you up to this weekend. Nothing much, I suppose?'

'I've actually got a date on Saturday night.' *Where did that come from?*

'With a woman?'

'Yeah. Is that a problem too?' He instantly regretted his sharp tone. 'Sorry, Mom.'

'I know. Your papa says I should leave you be. He reckons you'll sort yourself out in your own time but it's been two years now and I hate knowing you're so unhappy.'

'I'm okay … things are better here. I promise.'

'That's what I like to hear. Now who's the lucky lady?'

Very reluctantly he shared Rosey's name and how they'd met.

'A musician. Another creative person. She sounds perfect for you.'

'Don't make too much of it, please.'

'I must go tell Pierre.' She blithely ignored him. 'He'll be over the moon.' After a quick goodbye she hung up and Zach dropped his head in his hands. He was still hunched in the same position when he heard footsteps and glanced up to see Joe making a beeline for him across the yard.

'Is something wrong, mate?' Joe stood there, frowning.

'Yeah, you could say that.' He blurted out the whole crazy story.

'I s'ppose you'd better ask Rosey out then, hadn't you? Can't be telling lies to your mum.'

Trust Joe to be right.

Chapter Eight

'You're a clever girl. I've no idea how you came up with that but it's brilliant.' Anna smacked a kiss on Rosey's cheek. 'I'll resist the temptation to say I was beginning to wonder. You know as well as I do that three-times-a-week rehearsals start on Monday so we don't have oodles of time to waste.'

They'd just finished listening to Aladdin and Princess Jasmine's first run-through of the new duet. When they'd done the first read through and auditions back in June, her mother sunk into her usual panic over casting, but partnering Demelza Rowe with Samira Key had been inspired.

Demelza had grown up in the pantomime family, working her way up from a timid five-year-old in the junior chorus to small speaking parts as an adult. It took a lot of cajoling on Anna's part to talk the nervous local hairdresser into taking on the role of this year's Principal Boy. Rosey had been dubious but her mother overruled her, seeing something in the young woman no one else had. On the other hand, Samira was a complete unknown and an even bigger risk. The rather serious barrister, who'd only moved from London to Polcarne earlier in the year, surprised them by turning up to the auditions. As soon as they heard her strong soprano voice and she demonstrated she could act and dance, the part of Princess Jasmine was hers. It was a bonus that Samira's Iranian heritage meant her stunning dark beauty suited the part down to the ground. Rosey had caught a few rumbles of discontent from Mike Blamey, their long-time pantomime dame, and some of his cronies about Samira's casting. To their narrow minds, the fact she wasn't born and bred in Polcarne went against her. As far as Rosey knew, those complaints had all died down when they saw how good Samira was on stage though.

'Right, everyone, that'll do for tonight.' Anna clapped her hands. 'Same time on Monday. We'll need to work hard for the next month or so until the Christmas break but it's starting to shape up nicely.' They'd already dismissed the little ones so they wouldn't get overtired. 'I think we deserve a celebratory drink.' She peered at Rosey. 'You look a bit pale, love, have you got a headache?'

All day she'd struggled, and failed, to find a way to drop into the conversation that Zach had asked her out for dinner tonight. 'No, I'm fine … but I'm not coming to the pub—'

'I knew it! You've got a date! Who is he? You've been ever so secretive and you even ironed a couple of dresses yesterday and we both know you never iron.' A broad smile lit up her mum's face. 'Oh my God! It's Zach, isn't it?'

'Shush.' She dragged her aside. Anna was clueless how far her voice carried and the last thing Rosey needed was this becoming public news. 'Yes.' She felt her face heat up. 'It's dinner. That's all. Don't start imagining … whatever your fevered brain is thinking, and don't you *dare* breathe a word about this after you've had a few glasses of chardonnay at the pub.'

'Anyone would think I can't keep a secret.'

It amazed Rosey that her mother's nose didn't sprout to Pinocchio-like proportions. 'You can use the standard headache excuse for me if you like.'

'Where's he taking you?' Anna begged for more information. 'Somewhere nice, I hope?'

‘I’m not sure.’ Zach’s out-of-the-blue phone call had surprised her so much she hadn’t got around to asking. ‘He’s picking me up at seven.’

‘You’d better get on home and pretty yourself up then. I know everyone says you can’t go wrong with a black dress but that’s not true in your case. It drains all the colour from you. Put the pale green one on, it’s much more flattering, and use some make-up for a change! Remember, he’s used to glamorous women.’

‘Mum, I am not attempting to compete with the Hollywood stars he knows. If Zach wanted that, he clearly wouldn’t have asked *me* out.’

Anna threw up her hands in disgust. ‘If you won’t make an effort to impress a handsome, charming man who’s interested in you, it’s your loss.’

She refused to rise to the challenge. ‘I’ll see you later.’

‘Much later, I hope.’ She gave a knowing wink. ‘Maybe even tomorrow morning.’

‘Oh God, don’t you ever give up?’

‘Of course not. You’re my little girl and I want to see you happy again.’

The sharp retort she’d almost made died on her tongue. The tears in her mum’s eyes and the hitch in her voice couldn’t be attributed to brilliant acting because Anna wasn’t *that* good. ‘I should go or I won’t be ready on time.’ Rosey touched her mother’s cheek. ‘I love you.’

Outside the hall she took a few gulps of cold air to settle her nerves but it didn’t do much good. Zach had made it abundantly clear he wasn’t in a good place to date again, so what had prompted the sudden turn around? It’d taken her from the ground up when he rang to ask her out, especially after the way they’d left things when they’d last properly spoken. Apart from anything else, women like her didn't go on dates with celebrities – although that probably wasn't fair of her because Zach never behaved as if that mattered. Rosey marched off down the road and didn't stop until she reached the solitude of her bedroom. After her second shower of the day, she slathered on the expensive lilac-scented body lotion she reserved for special occasions then slipped on a new set of blush-pink lace underwear – purely to boost her self-confidence, of course. At least that's what she told herself.

Her reflection in the mirror when she was through dressing brought back uncomfortable memories. In a last-ditch effort to save her marriage, she'd made reservations at Alan's favourite London restaurant and had bought this same green dress because she knew he'd admire its thigh-skimming wrap-around style. But the evening was a dismal failure from the moment she stupidly answered a call from her agent while Alan was scanning the menu. His tight mouth and sour expression made his feelings clear and things went downhill from there.

Rosey ripped the dress off and tossed it in the back of the wardrobe. If the slim-fitting black shift with its matching jacket, a leftover from her concert days, washed out her pale skin so be it. She finished her minimalistic make-up with a slick of bright scarlet lipstick as the church clock struck seven. So much for her intention to do something sophisticated with her hair; all she had time for now was to shake it out from the ponytail and give it a vigorous brush. The doorbell rang and she hopped to the top of the stairs while wriggling into a pair of black high heels to yell down at Zach.

'Come in. The door's open. I'm almost ready.'

She rushed back to the bedroom and threw a few essentials into a small black clutch bag. All of a sudden, the advice her piano teacher had given her before her first recital flooded back.

Take your time. They'll wait for you. Rest your hands at the base of your stomach and take six deep, steadying breaths. Fix on a bright smile. Now go out there and amaze them.

Fingers crossed it worked tonight.

Zach struggled not to make a complete fool of himself as he gawked at Rosey. 'I guess we're not used to seein' each other in our Sunday best.'

'You didn't say where we were going, so I wasn't sure how much to dress up.' Her violet gaze swept over him. 'I love the suit. Armani?'

'Yeah, it's the only one I packed.'

'Don't apologise for looking … good.' The hairs on the back of his neck tingled when she ran the tip of her tongue over her pouting scarlet lips. 'I'm surprised you aren't wearing your leather jacket though. I don't think I've ever seen you without it.'

'It was a twenty-first birthday present from my folks because I needed something for going to auditions. So far it's worked every time I've worn it; it's become a sort of good luck charm.'

'I bet it could tell some stories.'

'Oh yeah.' Zach checked her out again. You look fine yourself.' *Fine*? Could he really come up with nothing more flattering than that? 'Vintage Chanel?'

'Aren't you a man of mystery? I wouldn't have put you down as a fashionista.' A tiny frown furrowed her brow. 'Oh … I tend to forget you're rich and famous.'

'Rosey, I simply had what the world describes as success doing something I loved. It was a blessing at first then not so much.' He hated it when his so-called celebrity status put a barrier between himself and everyone else. Some days it seemed like he'd never be able to leave it behind.

'I understand, at least a little, and I'm sorry I mentioned it. Let's save the soul-baring for later. I don't know about you but I'm starved.'

'Let's go eat then. I warn you now the ride isn't fancy because Joe lent me his old Land Rover and it's had a hard life. Hopefully the restaurant will make up for it. On his recommendation I booked a table at Rick Stein's in Padstow.'

'Sounds good to me.' A smile lifted the corner of her mouth. 'I'm not laughing at you, but it's amusing to me that an Oscar-winning Hollywood heartthrob is taking advice from a man who, as far as I know, hasn't had a date in forever.'

'That's something you might be able to help with.'

'I'm not going on a date with Joe Warren too!'

A warmth spread through Zach's veins. 'I'm pleased to hear it. I'll tell you Joe's story over dinner. He needs a fairy godmother.'

'I'm afraid we're doing Aladdin this year so no fairy godmother, only a genie.'

Her smart quip made him grin. 'We'll make it work.'

'Just answer one thing before we go … I'm curious as to why you asked me out tonight after I was so rude to you the other day?'

'You weren't rude. I was … tactless and not very honest either. I expected answers from you but I wasn't willing to reciprocate.' Zach was terrified she'd press him but she simply nodded. 'It's all mixed up with the Joe story. C'mon. We've a lot to talk about while we eat.'

Alarm bells tolled in Rosey's head. Everything about the evening so far was perfect. *Too perfect?* In between bites of the most delectable lemon butter scallops she'd ever eaten, she revelled in the company of this handsome, funny, sexy man. Their table overlooked the harbour and the stars in the dark night sky vied with the twinkling fairy lights which illuminated the boats bobbing around in the still water. She reminded herself that fairy tales were for children's stories and pantomimes, not real life.

'Don't look so worried. If you can't think of a way to give Joe and Beth a little nudge, I'll keep workin' on it myself.'

Rosey allowed him to think that was what was wrong. She'd almost shed a tear when Zach explained the pledge he'd made to help Joe Warren. She knew very little about the young farmer's failed relationship with Beth ten years earlier because she'd moved away from Polcarne by then, but apparently Joe still carried a candle for his first love and Zach was sure Beth felt the same way. In his opinion, they just needed a nudge to get them back together again. 'Joe's good with practical stuff, right?'

'Yeah.'

'Gerry Tremayne is in charge of the pantomime lighting but he's started commuting to Exeter four days a week for work so he can't always make rehearsals. If we can talk Joe into being Gerry's deputy, he'll be thrown together with Beth a lot because she's our assistant stage manager. She's lucky that Jock, the pub landlord, manages to juggle her shifts so she doesn't miss many practises.' Rosey felt pleased with herself. 'After that, it's up to them.'

'You're a genius.' He sprang up and dragged his chair around to sit next to her. It made her tantalisingly aware of the heat and energy pulsing off him and the tease of his warm, woodsy cologne. 'That's better.' Zach's smile took her breath away. 'It's not romantic to put couples on opposite sides.'

'Are we a romantic couple?' Rosey's voice trembled.

'We could be … if you'd like.'

'Like?' She wasn't sure how to respond. Her mother always complained that she should live more in the moment and not worry so much about what the future might bring. *Time to give it a try*. 'Okay. Yes.'

'Just yes?' Zach gave her a quizzical smile.

'For now.'

'Perfect. How about I pay the bill and we get out of here?' His drawl thickened.

Somehow Rosey managed to nod. The moment was almost spoiled when they stood up ready to leave and a young woman on the next table also sprang up from her chair and accosted Zach. It impressed her when he betrayed no hint of annoyance, signed the menu for the excited fan and smilingly posed for a picture. By now everyone in the restaurant was staring at them.

'Aren't you afraid she'll post that online?' she asked quietly when Zach's attention returned to her.

Zach shrugged and draped his arm around her shoulder. 'I can't hide for the rest of my life. I'm done with that.'

A surge of joy ran through Rosey. Perhaps in her own small way she, and Cornwall, were helping him?

The thirty-minute drive from Padstow to Polcarne felt like three hours. He'd abandoned his jacket and red silk tie and unbuttoned the cuffs of his crisp white shirt, rolling them up so she was drawn to watch the play of his muscles while he drove.

'You look mighty pleased with yourself, Ms Teague.' His free hand slid over to rest on her knee. 'I sure hope you still look that way tomorrow morning.'

'Tomorrow morning?'

Zach frowned. 'I'm assuming too much?'

'Assume away.'

Chapter Nine

'You're already regretting this, aren't you?' Zach should have guessed it was too good to be true when he woke up with his arms wrapped around Rosey. Warm. Naked. Snuggled into him. Everything he'd been dreaming about.

'No! Why on earth would you say that?' Layers of hurt stretched through her voice.

'The look on your face.'

'I'm a realist, Zach.' Rosey shifted from his arms and pulled the covers back up. 'You're only here for another couple of months so let's enjoy ourselves while we can and not worry about the rest.'

He was a realist too. More than she knew. There were things she deserved to know if they were to get serious about each other, but he was thankful now he'd held his tongue. Hell, he'd won a couple of Oscars; if he couldn't put on a good enough act to convince Rosey they were in complete agreement he should be ashamed of himself. 'Sounds like a plan.' Zach yanked the covers off her. 'I reckon enjoyin' ourselves again right now is a great way to kick start the day.' He resolved to hold something of himself back but that crumbled when he stared into her deep violet eyes, heavy with desire and framed by long golden eyelashes fluttering against flushed cheeks. Rosey's lush pink lips were swollen with his kisses. The last trace of his self-control dissolved when she touched him, stroked him. Zach caught her throaty gasp in an all-consuming kiss and buried himself inside her. His heart shattered into a million tiny pieces, and afterwards he clung to her, silent against her heartbeat.

'I'm really sorry but I ought to go.' She broke the spell. 'I've got a pupil coming at nine o'clock, and I need to shower and stuff first.'

'Oh yeah, right.' Zach rolled over. 'How about I cook dinner for you tonight?' A wary look crept into her smile. 'I didn't mean to assume that we … I mean …'

'Don't get weird, okay?' Rosey pleaded. 'I'd love nothing better than have you show off your skills in the kitchen but I've got rehearsal tonight so I won't be done until close to nine. We're practising three times a week now, plus I do extra sessions with some of the principals.'

'You won't keep that up next month over the holidays surely? Doesn't your mom give everyone a break then?'

'Every year there's a battle over the schedule between the die-hard obsessives like Mum and those who put celebrating the holidays with their families first.'

'Where do you fall on the spectrum?'

Rosey shrugged. 'I get stuck trying to keep the peace. Are you a Christmas person?'

'Not really these days. Laura grew up with parents who were strict Jehovah's Witnesses so they didn't celebrate Christmas. Although she broke away from that later, she was always ambivalent about the holidays so we stayed in LA, and apart from going to a few parties we didn't do anything special. When I was a child, Mom and Dad made a big deal of the holidays. There were always tons of family around and enough food for a small nation. My favourite memory was when I was about fifteen and we went to New Orleans for Christmas. The Broussards come from the area known as the River Parishes and there's a tradition going back centuries of lighting bonfires all along the levees on Christmas Eve. It's a spectacular sight when they give the signal at seven o'clock and all of the bonfires are lit simultaneously.'

'It sounds amazing.' A smile played around her lips. 'I bet you know every bit of the history behind it too.'

'Yeah, I know a bit. Nowadays it's popular to believe it's a Cajun tradition and the bonfires are to light the way for Papa Noel, the Cajun Santa Claus. That's got to be wrong because the early Acadian exiles from Nova Scotia followed the French tradition of giving children gifts on New Year's Eve, not at Christmas. It really started in the early 1700s when French and German colonists recreated the traditional bonfires they built on special occasions throughout the year and it's grown from there. After the Second World War was when it really exploded.' The memories flooded back in full force. 'My cousins were in one of the so-called bonfire clubs. They construct the bonfires from willow cut from along the river banks. I joined them a couple of days before Christmas Eve and we walked miles in search of fresh cane reeds. You put them in and around the structure so when it's lit, the reeds make a popping sound like fireworks. We'll have to see it together one …' His voice trailed away. He had no right to make that promise so he quickly changed the subject. 'What about your childhood Christmases? Good memories?'

The last thing Rosey wanted was his pity but being dishonest about yet one more thing wasn't an option. It'd torn her up after the wonderful night they'd spent together to suggest they look on their relationship as a temporary thing, but she'd done it to protect herself.

'We don't have to talk about it if you don't want. I get it's a painful time for some folk—'

'Oh no, it's not that. Honestly. When I was little, we did all the normal things but after my granny died and Mum took over the pantomime, we sort of stopped bothering much.' Rosey caught Zach's frown. 'I promise we're not like Scrooge. On Christmas Eve we cook a festive lunch for the bingo club, and in the evening a crowd of us go over to St Merryn for their carol service. Mum and I eat whatever we fancy on Christmas Day but we don't bother with gifts.'

'There's nothing wrong with all that.' He swung his long legs out of the bed and grabbed a pair of jeans off the chair. 'I'll borrow Joe's car and run you home.'

'There's no need. I'm fine to walk.'

'You won't make it far in those ankle-breakers.' Zach pointed to her high-heeled shoes. 'Anyway, do you wanna be seen leaving here and walking through the village in last night's dress?' His smile faded. 'I assume you'd prefer it if no one finds out about us sleeping together?' Zach yanked a baggy dark blue jumper over his head and shook out his hair.

Talk about making it hard to focus her mind. Rosey dragged her gaze away because even rumpled, unshaven and sleepy-eyed, he was seriously gorgeous. 'It's probably for the best. We'll be gossiped about in the village shop and smirked over at pantomime rehearsals. I'm not keen on that and I doubt you are either. Plus what happens if it gets out on social media? Surely you've had more than enough of that?'

'I suppose you're right.' He sighed.

Rosey shimmied into her wrinkled dress. She avoided her reflection in the floor-length mirror as she sidled around the bed. 'I don't suppose you've got a rubber band?'

'What for?' His bright blue eyes gleamed. 'Is this some new sex game I haven't heard about?'

'You're incorrigible.' She lifted a lank strand of hair. 'It's to get this mess out of my face.'

'We could ask Joe.' Zach stroked his hand over her tousled hair. 'You're gonna look like Rapunzel on my spiral staircase.'

Rosey snorted and followed him out of the bedroom. 'I love these barn conversions and Joe did an awesome job with this one. It's the high ceilings and sense of space.' It was on the tip of her tongue to say that buying one would be top of the list if she won the lottery, but she was uncomfortably aware some people would call her hooking up with Zach a better bet. 'I suppose your house back in Hollywood is massive with a pool and everything?'

Zach didn't reply until they were outside the old barn and he'd locked the thick oak door. 'I haven't set foot in the house since Laura died. My mom cleared out all our personal effects and put them in storage for me. I've rented it out since then.' His shoulders sagged. 'I should cut my losses and sell up because I'll never live in it again. I bounced around between different hotels at first but it was impossible to shake off the paparazzi, so I ended up renting an apartment in a run-down area of LA. It suited me and no one there ever seemed to pick up on who I was.' He set off across the gravel yard and she hurried to catch up with his long strides.

'Sorry. I shouldn't have asked.'

'Don't apologise. You've every right to ask anything you want. If I don't or can't talk about it, I'll say, okay?'

'Okay.' Rosey considered adding to that, but the farmhouse door opened and Joe stuck his head around it.

'You want these?' Joe held out a bunch of keys. 'Good meal last night?'

'Yeah, really great. I'm in a rush to get this one home because she's got work to do but then I'll be back and we'll talk. Rosey's got a neat plan to get you and Beth back on track.' Zach swiped the keys and walked away.

'Oh God, did you see his face?' She groaned. 'The poor bloke was mortified. I'm pretty sure he didn't want us discussing his private life. You could've passed the idea off as coming from you.'

'He'll get over it.' Zach swept her in his arms and his mouth found hers, leaving her breathless.

'Is your offer of supper still open? It'll have to be late and—'

'I'll cook at midnight – 2 a.m. – doesn't matter.' He caressed her cheek. 'Text me when you're done with rehearsals and I'll come pick you up.' His famous heart-breaking smile, the one adored by his legions of fans, rested on her. She should have resisted his offer because the more she got used to Zach being a part of her life, the worse it would be when he left.

She'd love to believe they were like the stars of the pantomime, who went through their dark moments when they appeared to be doomed before vanquishing the evil baddie – in their case, common sense – by the finale when love would always win the day. Rosey was in serious trouble if she thought that was possible.

She kissed him again. At least he hadn't turned into a frog yet …

Chapter Ten

'How did I bloody well let you talk me into this?' Joe groused.

'Because you want to convince Beth you're a great guy who deserves a second chance.' Zach grasped the sleeve of his friend's muddy wax jacket and dragged him towards the hall. Over the last ten days, when he wasn't busy romancing Rosey, he'd cornered Joe every chance he'd had and badgered him about her bright idea. He suspected the young man caved in to shut him up.

'Well, aren't you two a 'andsome sight?' Anna scurried across the road and planted herself in front of them. 'Come in with me and we'll introduce you to everyone. Of course, they're all familiar with Joe, and they'll *all* recognise *you.*' She smirked at Zach. 'Rosey told me to expect Joe tonight but you're a bonus.'

'I'm not staying. I came to make sure this guy doesn't lose his nerve and bolt.'

'Don't 'ee be so silly. We can always use another pair of hands and surely you can't turn down the chance to see Rosey?' He should have guessed the sharp-eyed Anna would work out that he was the reason behind Rosey's frequent absences. Since they'd spent their first night together, they'd slipped into an unspoken routine. They often went for long walks or took off in her car to check out some of the quiet beauty spots she knew around Cornwall. So far, the isolated coves and remote coastal paths had proved ideal for avoiding other people. His new favourite place was Cape Cornwall, which Rosey assured him was as beautiful as Land's End but without the crowds and over-commercialisation. The evenings, when they ate dinner together, always ended up with them going to bed, but, except for the first time and even after giving herself to him over and over again, she still insisted on going back home to sleep. Zach found himself impatient for more and it was taking every ounce of his self-control not to challenge Rosey on whether she'd changed her mind about keeping things casual between them. He pushed the nagging thought that he should have the sense to leave it well alone to the back of his mind.

'Well, yes, ma'am … I mean Anna … but—'

'But nothing.'

'Yeah, but nothing, mate.' Joe sniggered behind her back.

He'd make his friend pay for this later. Zach stepped inside the crowded hall and stopped dead. The familiar atmosphere jabbed like a stake through the heart. It didn't matter if it was an amateur production or a multi-million-dollar film set, the same palpable sense of excitement and anticipation filled the air. He spotted a striking, dark-haired young woman hunched over a script with her lips moving as she silently practised her lines and a harassed older lady struggling to stop half a dozen lively little girls intent on racing around the room.

'You all right, mate?' Joe clapped a hand on his shoulder.

'Yeah, it's just …' His mouth dried up.

'I get it. About five years ago, Mum nagged me to get off the farm and do something more reliable to bring in a steady wage. I took a job in a bank in Truro. Lasted a week I did and hated every minute.' Joe shrugged. 'Our work is a way of life. It's who we are.'

'But I can't handle it any longer.'

'You will.'

Zach wasn't as sure.

'Listen up, everyone.' Anna clapped her hands for silence. 'We've got two new recruits. Young Joe is here because he kindly offered to help Gerry with the lighting, and you all recognise Zach even if you haven't met him face to face yet. He's come along because he knew his expertise would be invaluable to us.'

He caught a group of teenage girls gawking at him and whispering behind their hands. Zach flashed them a brief smile which made them giggle even harder.

'Oi, we're not going to stand for some bloody fancy Hollywood bloke taking over.' A brawny middle-aged man with bad skin, tight jeans and an appreciable beer gut glared down from the stage. 'We've got enough bloody outsiders around here as 'tis.' He threw the dark-skinned woman Zach had noticed a few minutes ago a meaningful look.

'Don'ee be so rude, Mike Blamey.' The fierce response made the man colour up. 'Samira, love, you ignore him.' She gave the woman an apologetic smile. 'He don't always think before he speaks. And Zach, you don't need to take no notice of him either. We're glad you're here to help.'

'I'm happy to provide another pair of hands but I don't want to step on anyone's toes.' He projected his voice so they'd be able to hear him at the furthest end of the room.

'We don't have time to waste so let's get on.' Anna's pencilled-on eyebrows shot up into her hairline. 'The little ones know their Advent calendars started today, so if it's the first of December, that means we've only got a little over six weeks until opening night.' She puffed a resigned sigh. 'And Christmas and New Year come slap bang in the middle of it, of course.'

Zach suppressed a smile.

‘We’ll start with a run through of Act Two, Scene Two. Aladdin’s Palace. Senior chorus, let’s try to look as though you’re carrying boxes full of valuable treasures and not the weekly food shop from Asda tonight.’ She turned back to him. ‘Fred needs some heavy things shifted around so you can put your muscles to good use backstage.’

‘Sure.’ He left Joe getting his marching orders and made a detour to Rosey at the piano.

‘She nailed you, didn’t she? I should’ve guessed she would. I’d say sorry but …’

‘Don’t worry, I’ll get my own back.’ For a second, he almost leaned in to kiss her but resisted the temptation.

‘Might be something to look forward to.’

‘Rosey, dear, please pay attention.’ Anna’s strident shout broke up the moment. ‘The chorus is ready and waiting.’

‘Yes, Rosey. Pay attention.’ Zach chuckled. ‘Back to the salt mines for you. I’ll go see what trouble I can get into backstage.’

‘I’m sure you’ll find some.’

With a wink, he sauntered off.

Rosey’s first flash of pleasure at seeing Zach trail in behind Joe dissipated when she registered his stricken expression. As far as she knew, he hadn’t been near anything connected to acting since his wife died and now her mother had forced him to face it again. But then he’d brightened up enough to joke around and flirt with her, so the jury was still out on whether Anna had been thoughtless or wise.

‘Let’s do the “Wash Day Blues” and try to keep it on tempo this time.’

She didn’t waste her breath by pointing out that the piano would be in perfect time but she couldn’t promise the same of the chorus. Miracle worker she wasn't. They kept at it for an hour until she noticed the youngsters start to flag. 'That's enough for tonight, Mum.'

They had an unwritten agreement that, as music director, she had the final say on anything connected to the pantomime score. If Anna tried to weasel around it, Rosey would remind her that, like everyone else involved, she was a volunteer and volunteers could un-volunteer. That would throw the pantomime back to the mercy of Roland Stephens, the violin teacher who'd been in charge of the music for over twenty years before Rosey's return. Competent but unimaginative was the politest way to describe his tenure. He wasn't best pleased when Anna offered him the consolation prize of deputy music director and hadn't darkened the doors of the production again. If they saw each other in Polcarne, he made a point of crossing the road to avoid talking to Rosey. Any disparaging remarks going around the village about the show were regularly traced back to him, but they couldn't do much about it.

'We could work on Aladdin and Jasmine's secret garden duet next?' The suggestion made her mother sniff, but Anna dismissed the chorus with dire warnings of additional practises if they didn't improve by the following week.

The next half hour reminded her why she loved this job. Demelza didn't have the world's strongest voice, but it was clear and true, and paired with Samira something magical happened. She could tell they'd been working on the song on their own and taken the suggestions she'd made at the last rehearsal to heart.

'Wonderful!' Rosey's praise made the shy hairdresser blush and even the confident Samira beamed. 'Mum, shall we call it a night now?'

'I suppose so.'

They'd be there until midnight if someone didn't draw a line. While she packed up her music, she noticed Zach deep in conversation with Gerry and Joe, pointing up to the lights.

'You know what they say about getting back on after you've fallen off a horse? It's working already.' Anna sounded smug. 'He's loving every minute of this.'

'I was concerned when you dragged him in, but now I think you might've been right.'

'Ooh, I don't hear that very often. Are you two coming to the pub or are you off to …?' The unfinished sentence came with a suggestive elbow nudge.

'Oh God, Mum. I don't know. Shush, will you, please? I don't want my personal life splashed all over Polcarne, thank you very much. You know as well as I do it's never going to turn into anything serious.'

'You'm a daft girl sometimes. That sweet man thinks the sun shines out of you. Anyone can see it.'

Rosey's face heated. 'I don't care what other people *think* they see. We've talked it through and we're in complete agreement about where we stand.'

'Really?' Her mum's eyes narrowed on her. 'I'll say one more thing, then I'll shut up. If you honestly think you can let him walk away when his time's over here then you're a hard-hearted woman and I don't believe that for one second. I know you too well.'

Rosey struggled to get her emotions back under control as she spotted Zach heading straight for them.

'Hello again. Mum wondered if we were going to the pub with everyone else?'

'Sure.' Zach came to rest an arm on the piano. 'Unless you don't want to?'

'No, that's fine.' She realised it might smooth the path with Mike Blamey and others wary of Zach's intentions.

'You two can run on. I'll lock up.' Anna shooed them away.

'Should we wait for Joe?' Rosey asked.

'I'll go with a no on that.' Zach nodded towards the stage door where Beth stood laughing at something Joe was saying to her. 'Let's leave them to it.'

'Do you still think it's going to work? Isn't Joe still set on holding onto the farm?'

'The land, yes, but when we were having a chat yesterday, he said he's realised he needs to find a way to make it work for him rather than the other way around. He's head over heels for Beth and is determined not to screw up this time.'

'Let's hope so.' She linked her arm through his. 'Come on, I'll buy you a drink and you can meet the gang properly.'

'I don't care what your mom thinks, I'm not interfering with the show.' His drawl thickened. 'I'll haul scenery or whatever, but that's it. I mean it, Rosey.'

'I know, and don't worry – I'll protect you from the demon producer.'

'Are you pair going to stand there all night? It'll be bloody closing time if we don't get a move on.' Mike pushed out past them.

'He's a piece of work.' Zach shook his head. 'Don't tell me – he plays the evil magician?'

'You won't believe it but he's the dame and has been ever since I can remember. This year he plays Widow Twankey.' Rosey tried to be fair. 'He's actually brilliant. Mike has great comic timing and no one carries off fake boobs, outlandish costumes and garish make-up better. He's won several awards for his performances.' She wrinkled her nose. 'It's a shame he's an idiot.'

'There's one in every production. I could tell you stories about some …' His face suddenly became expressionless. 'Sorry. Laura hated it when I showed what she called my "bitchy Hollywood side".'

How am I supposed to respond? Treading on eggshells would be easier than knowing what to say when anything connected to Zach's late wife came up. Rosey almost took hold of his hand as they wandered along the street then thought better of it. 'It's natural to talk about the people we work with and not necessarily bad. Her comment sounds a bit judgemental to me.'

'Perhaps.'

'My marriage wasn't perfect either – well, you know that or I wouldn't be divorced. I met Alan in Bath when I was doing a season with the Bath Philharmonia. He worked at an IT firm there. Within six months we were married. He didn't object when I was offered the chance to tour with the London Symphony because he relished the prestige and the money.' Rosey sighed. 'But when I'd been away for a few weeks, it sunk in how big an impact my career would have on our marriage. We'd rented a little flat together in Bath, but I was rarely there and I suppose I never really did anything to make it a real home …' Rosey blinked back tears.

'Hey, it's okay.' Zach pulled them into the narrow alley that ran down by the side of the pub and wrapped his arms around her. For reassurance she buried her face into his soft red jumper and inhaled his now familiar clean, warm scent. 'What brought the two of you together in the first place?'

'It sounds needy but I think I was looking for security. That was unfair on us both. What about you and Laura?'

'She was never impressed by the whole Hollywood scene and maybe I saw that as a challenge?' In the dark shadows she sensed him blushing. 'It didn't hurt that she was beautiful and incredibly smart. Other people saw us as an unlikely couple but we were sure we could beat the odds.' His voice turned to gravel. 'For a while we did.'

'And me? Us?' *Whatever made me ask that?* she scolded herself silently.

'Oi, you pair! You're too old to snog in dark alleys,' Joe yelled in at them and Rosey spotted Beth hovering behind his shoulder.

'Who says?' Zach plopped a loud, wet kiss on Rosey's mouth. 'You can get the first round in for interrupting us.'

She joined in the fun but couldn't push from her mind the fact that he hadn't answered her question. The bigger question was how did she *want* him to respond?

'We'd better go and face the inquisition.' He sighed.

'It won't be that bad.'

'I'll need you to have my back.'

'Always.'

His eyes widened at her automatic response. Rosey thought it best not to say anything more and walked off, leaving him to catch up.

In the crowded pub they joined the rest of the pantomime group who'd crammed into their favourite corner near the fire. There was a shortage of chairs and, out of nowhere, Zach casually pulled her down to sit on his lap, clasping his arms around her waist. Plenty of sly glances and knowing smiles came their way but she made no attempt to move. *Let them think what they want to.* She and Zach knew the truth.

Didn't they?

Chapter Eleven

Zach helped Fred heft the last canvas roll of scenery on to the back of the older man's rusty old truck.

'Thanks, lad. Let's head on down to sort this out before the rehearsal gets underway. We don't want Anna getting her knickers in a twist about us making too much noise.' With a shifty glance around, he pulled a crumpled pack of cigarettes out of his pocket. 'Keep mum about this, all right? Wendy will have my guts for garters if she catches me.' He lit up and took a quick drag. 'Bloody doctor nagged me last time I had a check-up.'

'It's none of my business.'

Fred slid him a sideways look. 'You're a bit quiet tonight. You usually have plenty to say for yourself. Don't tell me Rosey's given you the heave?'

The delusion they'd been living under that no one apart from Anna, Joe and Beth knew about his and Rosey's relationship had been blown out of the water at the pub a few days ago, and he only had himself to blame. Zach had recklessly made their closeness clear and the gossip-loving pantomime group lapped it up. He'd been obsessively checking ever since for any pictures of them hitting the internet but so far hadn't spotted anything. He'd almost unburdened himself to Joe but couldn't put a damper on his friend's good spirits. He'd lied about having a stomach bug when he'd cancelled his date with Rosey on Friday and used the same excuse to avoid helping at Saturday's rehearsal.

'And me? Us?'

Rosey must have seen everything he said about Laura as applying to her too. Beautiful, incredibly smart and, on the face of it, they made an equally unlikely couple. It was no wonder she'd asked such a pointed question. Of course she didn't know the full story behind the deterioration of his marriage and the final stab Laura made to his heart after her death but, if he was completely honest, would she understand?

'Nah, but … it's nothing, Fred. Let's get on.'

'All right, boy. But if you need an ear, I'm not a bad listener and I won't try and tell 'ee what you should do either.'

Zach jumped into the truck without another word and kept his gaze focused out of the window. A big part of his acting success rested on his almost effortless ability to express emotion, but tonight he had no desire for the old man to see how much that offer had touched him.

Down at the hall they carried the scenery in through the back door, but when he heard the piano, he realised pretty quickly that it wasn't Rosey playing. The accompanist was adequate, but he or she didn't have her style and immaculate timing.

'Ah, there you are. I need your help.' Anna breezed over and her flowing bright orange dress billowed around her.

'Me?'

'Yes. I need a stand-in for the genie. Harry's home in bed with a streaming cold.'

'I couldn't—'

'Why? Aren't you over your tummy troubles by now? It was unfortunate you passed it on to Rosey.'

Zach's face heated. 'Is she sick?'

‘Apparently so.’ Anna’s jet-black pencilled eyebrows arched so high they disappeared under her exotic arrangement of pure white hair studded with orange silk flowers. ‘Ethel Trethurgy’s standing in tonight. The poor soul does her best but she’s got no … spark.’

‘I’m real sorry about Rosey, but there’s no way I can go on stage.’ He was acutely aware that everyone around them was stopping to listen. ‘I made that clear from day one. Sorry but I think I’m done here for tonight. Fred can manage the rest.’ Zach barrelled out past her, and out of the corner of his eye he spotted Joe frowning at him from the top of ladder where he was doing something with a coil of electric wire.

The sting of rain on his face as he stepped out of the door came as a welcome relief. Zach glanced back at the hall, unsure if he was pleased or relieved when no one came after him.

Rosey studied Albert Rundle’s disconcerting new addition to the shop’s Christmas display. Was she the only one who found the group of goggle-eyed plastic reindeer creepy rather than festive? Last night her mother insisted they drag out their own feeble box of decorations because she’d taken umbrage when the sewing group had a good-natured laugh at their un-Christmassy home. Now Anna was determined to prove she could do Christmas as well as the next person. Rosey hadn’t the heart to point out that their lame fluorescent pink tabletop tree with its mismatched collection of random ornaments, the single strand of coloured lights hanging in the front window, and sparse sprigs of artificial holly on the mantlepiece were hardly the last word in festive decor.

Half an hour ago, she'd been mired with guilt over missing that night's rehearsal and hurried to get showered and dressed. Her mother would be thrilled if she appeared at the hall and announced her recovery, but she'd lost her nerve now about coming face to face with Zach again. After they'd left the pub on Thursday evening, she'd got cold feet and begged off going back to the farm with him, claiming that she was tired and had a headache coming on. He didn't argue but she'd seen the disappointment in his eyes. Too many contradictory questions had filled her head by that point. The biggest reason behind her reticence was that she'd been scared of what Zach might say if he answered her frankly. It had been a long, lonely, miserable weekend. Saturday night's practise should have distracted her but that turned into a disaster. Samira uncharacteristically forgot her lines. The senior chorus all developed two left feet and stumbled their way through the Jewel Dance. Gerry and Joe messed up the lighting and Aladdin was almost crushed when the plywood cave toppled over. And then there was Zach … or rather there wasn't. It didn't take a brain surgeon to work out that his supposed sickness was as fictitious as her own.

The sound of footsteps pounding along the street made her turn. 'Oh! It's you!'

'Yeah … Hi.' Zach, red-faced and awkward, stumbled to a halt.

'I'd ask if you're feeling better, but—'

'I'm sorry I lied.' A fleeting smile lit up his mesmerising electric-blue eyes. 'But I suspect we're quits on that score.'

'How did you …?' Rosey heaved a sigh. 'Don't tell me. You've come from the rehearsal.'

'Yep. I didn't stay long because your stubborn mother tried to talk me into standing in for the genie who is genuinely sick. I wasn't having it.'

'I could apologise but we both know I've no control over her.'

'Yeah, I get it. I found your stand-in plugging away at the piano. As your mom said "The poor soul does her best but she's got no … spark."'

His attempt at imitating a Cornish accent was atrocious and she burst out laughing. 'Never do that again, please.'

'I almost told her you've got more spark than a Fourth of July fireworks display.' Emotion thickened his voice. 'I was a coward the other day. I should've given you an honest answer.'

'You did.'

'What'd you mean?'

'You answered me by not saying a word. We *are* an unlikely couple and there's no guarantee we'd beat the odds. We've both messed up at least once already.' She managed a tight smile. 'I don't know how many other skeletons are in your closet and I'm not sure I want to, but the real question is whether we're both willing to take another risk?'

'Don't you reckon we've done that already?' Zach seized her hands and his touch ignited a flame that whooshed through her whole body. '*I* have. You need to know that. You were the one who insisted we kept things casual after that first magical night we slept together, so I've tried my damnedest to play along with that. I can't do that any longer, Rosey.'

'I was scared of feeling too much for you when we both know you're not staying long.' She heaved a sigh.

'But it's been a dismal failure.' She watched his face fall. 'It seems my heart has a mind of its own.'

His expression changed again. 'There are still some really important things I should share with you before we go any further …'

'Could they wait a little longer?'

'I suppose.' He looked troubled.

Rosey almost pressed him but couldn't bear to spoil their tentative reconciliation.

'So … what are we goin' to do? We can go back to the rehearsal or wait in the pub? Of course, we'll end up playin' gooseberry to Joe and Beth while he works on luring her up to our den of iniquity.'

'Are they back on track?'

Zach flashed a grin. 'I reckon so, judging by the smile plastered all over his face when he was really late back from rehearsal the other night. Beth's full of ideas to make more money from the farm and she's offered to help with the interior design of the new cottage conversion we've been working on.'

'That's awesome. Perhaps she could take a look at your barn too? I mean, it's great, but it's very stark and masculine.'

'I guess that's why I like it. I always had to shift piles of cushions off every chair, sofa and bed in our house before I could sit or lie down.' His smile turned wistful. 'Laura was tough, athletic and at the top of her game in a traditionally male field, but still loved to stink up the place with scented candles. She even wore satin underwear when she was climbing.'

A disconcerting flare of jealousy surged through her. He'd dropped plenty of hints about his troubled marriage but moments like this reminded her – and surely him too –

that it hadn't been all bad. 'You're an actor and must've studied enough characters to know they're all nuanced. The tough guy soldier who turns to mush handling a new born kitten. The ultra-feminine, high-maintenance model who swigs pints of lager at the pub. I can cheerfully spend hours at the piano working on a single phrase in a Mozart concerto, but I also binge-watch *Love Island* and would choose a Cornish pasty over caviar any day. Tell me you don't have any contradictions and I'll call you a liar.'

'You're right.'

'Going back to our present dilemma, there could be third option.' Rosey slid her hands up under his leather jacket.

'I'm happy to go with that.'

A wave of frustration rolled through her. 'It'll have to be your place because I'm a useless thirty-eight-year-old who still lives with her mother. It's shitty.'

'It's temporary.'

'Really? I told myself that three years ago and I'm still bloody there. It's not a question of money because I could make it work, but Mum likes having someone else in the house. She'd die rather than admit it, but she *was* lonely. Does that sound crazy?'

'Nah, it's not crazy.' The flickering shadows from the streetlight brought out the hollows in his drawn face. 'The people who appear the most confident and outgoing are often the loneliest.'

'Oh, come on. You can hardly compare my mum to your situation.'

'Maybe. Maybe not. If she feels a fraction of the isolation I've experienced …' He shook his head. 'I'm verging into sorry-for-myself territory and I've no right to do that. A lot of folk would give anything to have my problems.'

'That's rubbish. It's like saying someone suffering from depression should buck up and think of all the other people who are worse off.' Rosey rested her head against his shoulder. 'Let's go. A brisk walk up to Warren Farm should get the blood flowing.'

'Mine's doin' that already in case you hadn't noticed.' He grinned and rocked against her hips to prove his point. 'I need to hire a car and quick so we can make out like teenagers in the back seat.'

'A car's not a bad idea for getting about the place but you can forget snogging in it. You're not so old you've forgotten how bloody uncomfortable that is, surely? There's a huge soft bed waiting for us at The Old Hay Barn so get walking, Zach Broussard, and stop being a wimp.'

'You shall have your soft bed and plenty of proof I'm no wimp.' He stroked a wisp of hair from her face. 'I've missed you, Rosey Teague. You've got into my blood.'

'I've missed you too.' A flash of light brightened the street and she glanced towards the hall where the door was open. 'Rehearsal's over and the avid drinkers will be heading this way any second now. I don't know about you but I'd prefer they didn't see us.'

'Spot on, Sherlock. Let's put our running shoes on.'

Chapter Twelve

Zach handed Joe a steaming mug of black coffee. He'd spotted his friend returning from working in the fields, his face grey with the cold, and invited him in to warm up. 'Did I see a certain dark-haired barmaid leaving your place on Tuesday morning?'

Joe glowered at the floor and didn't answer.

'I should've thought to ask before, but I hope you don't mind Rosey stayin' up here with me some nights?'

'Mind? No. Why should I?'

'I don't want to take advantage of our friendship. At the end of the day, I'm a paying guest and you might—'

'I'm not bothered. Okay? Good on you.' Joe grimaced. 'At least one of us is happy.' He held up a hand. 'And, no, I don't bloody want to talk about it.' He slammed the mug down and coffee slopped all over the granite counter. 'I'm off. I've got work to do. Some of us aren't lucky enough to be rolling in money and on a perpetual holiday.'

The bitterness suffusing his friend's voice tone stunned Zach into silence. Joe stormed out and slammed the door behind him hard enough to make the windows rattle. Zach absentmindedly picked up a cloth and cleaned up the mess then grabbed his own coffee and settled down by the range. The comfortable dark red leather chair he'd moved in from the main living space made a good place to sit and think.

Was that how people saw him? Spoiled and self-indulgent. He hadn't been without a proper job since he was fifteen and had spent the summer holidays cleaning sticky tables at a fast-food restaurant, but when he'd lost Laura his generous savings gave him the option to step away from life and take refuge in a torrent of grief and guilt. Perhaps it hadn't done him any favours? He hadn't been totally idle because he'd kept fit by taking up mountain biking and going on long solo rides as often as possible. Apart from working on an idea for a book that he'd had, sparked by his own childhood experience in discovering the joy of being onstage, Zach had also regularly volunteered with a local group supporting LA's large homeless population. It didn't matter who the face and hands belonged to behind an offered sandwich or fresh pair of socks, after all. But it still nagged at him that it wasn't enough and never really had been. He continued to miss acting and everything connected to it like a missing tooth. Rosey would give him an honest answer. They were supposed to be going out for dinner because Friday wasn't a rehearsal night, but this wasn't a conversation to have over a meal.

He trudged over to the sink and tossed away his undrunk coffee. Zach sent a quick text asking her to come to the farm when she was ready, then flopped back down in the chair to wait.

'Mum, don't forget there's a cottage pie in the oven for your tea. It'll be ready in about twenty minutes.' Rosey raced around the room, lifting up cushions and wriggling her hand down the sides of the chairs. 'Where have you put the car keys? Why can't you hang them on the hook by the front door like I always do?'

'For goodness sake, calm down!' Anna fished around in the tapestry bag sitting on the carpet by her feet. 'They're here. Exactly where I left them.'

She snatched the keys and struggled to hide her exasperation. 'Now I don't know what time I'll be back, but—'

'Oh go. Please. Don't keep the poor man waiting.' A gleam brightened her mother's eyes. 'That's a new top, isn't it? Turquoise suits you. You're still a very attractive woman, you know? When you make an effort.'

Talk about a backhanded compliment.

'Now don't forget to invite Zach here for dinner on Christmas Day.'

'Are you sure that's a good idea?' Her mum had thrown herself into being the living, breathing epitome of the festive spirit and every supposedly bright idea she came up with was more bizarre than the last. This was the absolute worst. Every other Christmas they'd been perfectly happy to eat a Marks & Spencer ready meal, but now Anna was convinced she only had to read a recipe book to rival Nigella in the kitchen. Poor Zach was going to be their guinea pig.

'Absolutely. Don't you dare come home without asking him.'

Outside she forced herself to slow down. Bright red cheeks were never a good look. After adjusting the seat for her shorter legs, she turned the key in the ignition and exhaled a relieved sigh when the motor started. She realised it was probably time to look for a replacement car before this one died on her. Soon enough she was at the farm, but she was disappointed not to see Zach looking out for her.

'I'm here.' She opened the old barn door and stepped inside to silence.

'Oh hiya, I didn't hear the car.' He strolled out from the kitchen looking pale and dishevelled in old grey sweats and a ragged mud-coloured jumper.

'Are you okay?'

'Yeah … no … not really.' Zach shoved his hands in his pockets and shuffled from one foot to the other. 'I need to ask you something.'

'Anything.'

'Let's sit.'

What was bad enough that she couldn't hear him say it standing up? In a futile delaying tactic, she shrugged off her black wool coat and draped it on the back of the sofa. Rosey had her pride so she decided she'd say what must be on Zach's mind before he did. 'I thought it would come to this.'

'What?'

'You've had second thoughts about us trying to make a go of things because … oh, how many reasons shall we go with?' She blinked away a rush of tears. 'We're totally unsuited. You're going back to acting and Hollywood. You're still grieving for Laura and don't think you'll ever—'

'No! That's not … come here.'

She allowed him to wrap his arms around her, and with her head burrowed into his solid chest could almost believe things were fine between them.

'Am I spoiled and self-indulgent?'

Rosey's head shot up. 'What on earth are you talking about?'

'Joe was here earlier and in a crappy mood – things aren't right between him and Beth – but he said some things that stung and I've been mulling them over in my head ever since.' His eyes glazed over. 'His exact words were that some of us aren't lucky enough to be rolling in money and on some kind of perpetual holiday.' Zach frowned. 'Is that what everyone's saying about me?'

'No! Of course not. Obviously I've heard a few negative things going around, but you know there're always people who get pleasure from dragging celebrities down and I'm only talking about idiots like Mike Blamey and his mates,' Rosey scoffed. 'Do you really care what they think?'

'No. But it *does* bother me if you and Joe – people whose opinions I respect – think that way.' He persisted. 'Surely if I can see some truth in what he said, you can too?' Because she didn't rush to reply, his face fell. 'Yeah. I thought so.'

'Don't you dare to assume you know what I was going to say. I ran back home when my marriage and my career fell apart so I can hardly condemn you for doing a similar thing, can I?'

'But you've worked. Earned a living. Become part of the community. The pantomime couldn't do without you. Then there's the bingo club that means so much to the older folk. I bet there are other things too. What've I done?' Exasperation rolled off him in waves. 'Joe's right. It's time I sorted myself out. There are other things too that we keep putting off talkin' about. I'm a mess, Rosey.'

'I could help if you'd let me.' She wanted to cry when the light left his eyes.

He would have preferred a hard punch to the stomach to watching the realisation sweep over her face that he wasn't going to budge. The bright light from the wrought iron chandelier hung high in the rafters brought her glorious hair to life and he fought against the memory of running his fingers through its tangled length in bed.

'Rosey, until I'm in a better place mentally … maybe I've got nothing more to offer you.'

'Don't you think that's up to me to decide?'

Her belligerent tone almost dragged a smile out of him.

'And don't you dare say we can still be friends! That's not enough.' A tear trickled from the corner of one eye and she angrily wiped it away. 'I was all set to ask you to spend Christmas Day with us too. Mum's got a bee in her bonnet about celebrating this year and we were going to cremate a turkey for you.' A hitching sob escaped her throat.

'Maybe we could find a compromise?'

'We're either in a relationship or we aren't.' She tossed him a scathing look. 'There is no middle ground. Remember what you said about me having your back? Well, this is what it means. You do need to find a new focus in life the same way I had to. At first, I was worried that teaching piano lessons and being in charge of the pantomime music wouldn't be enough of a challenge, but I've discovered I really enjoy sharing my talents that way. I'm sure you could do something similar with your acting skills if you think outside the box a little more. Please let me help.'

'I can't, Rosey. I do see what you're getting at … but I'm just not sure it's gonna work.' Zach pulled away and went to stare out of the large picture windows overlooking Joe's hay fields. All he could see in the dark was his own haunted reflection in the glass. 'Perhaps you should go.'

'Go? That's it?'

He turned around and immediately wished he hadn't. Face to face with her pain, he faltered.

'I'm sorry but I need to think this through on my own. What else can I say, Rosey? I'd do anythin' to make this hurt less for you.'

'No, you wouldn't.'

The hushed words stung like mosquito bites. She was right. *Again.*

'I'll go.' She slipped her coat back on and sighed. 'I suppose you want me to tell Mum you won't be back helping with the pantomime?'

'Do you mind?' *Of course she minded. Yet another dumbass thing to say.*

'Don't apologise again. Just don't!' Rosey's eyes blazed. 'I hope you work out what it is you want from life, Zach, I really do. I'd like to say I understand why you're so convinced you've got to do this on your own, but quite honestly I don't.'

Zach stood rooted to the spot. He didn't breathe again until after she'd stormed out and he'd heard her car drive away.

Chapter Thirteen

Rosey ducked to avoid hitting the low-hanging silver garland hitched up across the bottom of the stairs. Her mother never did anything by halves and must have bought every Christmas decoration on sale within a twenty-mile radius of Polcarne. She'd adorned every non-living thing in the house, and no doubt would have done the same to her daughter if she'd dared to stand still for too long. Her mother was decked out brighter than their Christmas tree in a gold jumpsuit, and Rosey waited for a scathing remark about her own un-festive black trousers and pearl-grey silk blouse. She'd been in such a down mood after last week's argument with Zach that her mother had decided to hold a party at their house tonight for the pantomime backstage crew under the delusion it might cheer her up.

'Do try to drag a smile up out of somewhere, Rosey love.' Her mother breezed in from the kitchen. 'I know you're down in the dumps but don't put a dark cloud over the evening.'

She couldn't be bothered to argue that she'd every right to be "down in the dumps", especially as she'd been the subject of a lot of whispered conversations and sly looks during the three excruciatingly long rehearsals. Joe was still helping with the lighting but he and Beth were pointedly avoiding each other. Clearly love's young dream wasn't working for them either. If her life was a pantomime script, they'd reached the end of the second act when the lead characters were failing to solve their problems and more obstacles were being thrown in their way all the time. The problem was, in her case, she didn't see an uplifting third act on the horizon.

Anna's face softened. 'Oh my love, I know you're miserable and, if he dares to come anywhere near me again, I'll swat that Zach Broussard from one end of Cornwall to the other for mucking you around.' She frowned. 'I shouldn't have encouraged you in the first place.'

'You didn't *make* me do anything. One day, when I'm old and grey, I'll look back on my fling with a Hollywood star and laugh about it.'

'Maybe you will. Not today though, my 'andsome.'

'No, Mum. Not today.' A wave of tiredness swept through her. 'I really can't handle this party tonight. I'm sorry.' The thought of spending the next several hours enduring sympathetic glances from the pantomime backstage crew was horrendous.

'Oh yes you will.' Anna's red Christmas ball earrings jangled. 'The Teague women are tough. Your father thought he'd found an agreeable wife who'd stay at home waiting with a hot dinner and a warm bed after he'd been out roaming like a tomcat but I soon put him right. I tossed him out on his ear. Good riddance to bad rubbish.' She smirked. 'Do you remember Princess Diana's revenge dress – the kickass black one? She showed them all and you can do the same.'

'I hate to burst your bubble but this little party won't make the front page of the national newspapers or be the headline grabber on the News at Ten. Zach's never going to know about it.'

'Don't be so negative.' A hint of smugness tugged at her bright orange glossy lips. 'Joe promised to come. He'll pass the word on.'

'But—'

‘I know you said they were out of sorts with each other, but that’s probably blown over by now. Men are like that,’ Anna persisted. ‘The others will talk too so Zach’s bound to hear it in the shop or the pub.’

Whether it was her mum’s fighting talk or the two glasses of sherry she’d knocked back while getting dressed, a surge of determination swept through her. She glanced down over herself and met her mother’s triumphant smile on the way up. ‘This won’t do, will it?’

‘You’ve got about ten minutes to do a Cinderella transformation before the early birds will be on the doorstep.’

‘But if I go too over-the-top, I’ll look out of place.’

‘Don’t you go worrying about that. The women will know what you’re doing and applaud you for it and the men will be too stunned to care. Trust me.’ She shoved Rosey towards the stairs. ‘Don’t hurry – and wait until you hear a good crowd before you make your entrance.’

In the bedroom she ripped off all her clothes and scrabbled around in the drawer for a red lace plunge bra and thong she’d bought in yet another desperate attempt to save her marriage. Only one dress would work tonight. Normally she avoided pinks and reds because of her hair, but the slinky red satin dress was a hangover from a production of *Moulin Rouge* when the orchestra had been ordered to jazz up their standard black and white outfits. The dress really needed towering red stilettoes, but she’d never been able to play the piano in high heels so it would have to be her low-heeled gold sandals. With dramatic smoky eye make-up and glossy scarlet lips, it certainly wasn’t tame.

Eat your heart out, Zach.

Rosey's nerves started back up and she hovered at the top of the stairs. The doorbell rang and no one else appeared to answer it so she headed down. An unfamiliar man stood on the step.

'I sure am sorry to barge in, ma'am, but can you tell me where to find Warren Farm? I've been drivin' around in circles and I'm no further along than I was ten minutes ago.'

American. Thin to the point of emaciation. Dressed all in black. Fashionably cut chestnut hair, razor short on the sides with the top flopping over his angular face, and square black-framed glasses. Definitely not one of their invited guests. Rosey flashed her brightest smile. 'It's not far and we'll be happy to help you get there, but why don't you come in and have a drink with us first? After all, it's nearly Christmas.'

'Thanks, and I'll be happy to take you up on the offer.' He aimed a brilliantly white, toothy smile her way.

You won't be when I wheedle out of you who you are and why you're here. If he wasn't connected with Zach, she'd do a song-and-dance number in the pantomime.

'Oh hiya, Joe … is everything all right?' Zach's mind raced. They hadn't spoken in a week so he couldn't imagine what the young man was doing on his doorstep.

'I'm okay but I found a mate of yours down in the village.'

In the glare of the security light fixed on the corner of the barn, he peered at the man Joe pushed forward. 'Cody? What the devil are you doin' here?'

'Hiya, Zach baby. Cool place this and the babe in red … wow.' An inane grin spread over his face.

'You won't get much sense out of him until he sobers up. Thanks to your girlfriend, or ex-girlfriend … whatever she is these days … he overindulged in Anna Teague's lethal punch.'

Nothing made sense. Cody should be in Los Angeles not Polcarne, and why had he been drinking with Rosey?

'Shift out of the way and I'll manoeuvre him inside for you.'

Zach stepped aside and Joe half-dragged and half-lifted Cody over the step then into the living room where he deposited him on the sofa like a sack of potatoes.

'I'll get his coat and boots off. You fetch a pillow and blanket.'

Five minutes later his agent was passed out cold and snoring fit to wake the dead.

'This is a first. I've never seen him drunk. He's uber health-conscious and rarely touches alcohol.'

'Well, he did tonight. And then some,' Joe scoffed.

'You fancy a coffee?' He expected the gesture to be thrown back in his face.

'I s'ppose.'

Zach headed for the kitchen, and by the time he'd turned on the kettle Joe had joined him. 'Look, I—' he began.

'I was a bloody idiot last week.' A flush crept across his friend's cheeks. 'I was pissed at Beth and took it out on you.'

'Things aren't goin' good with you two?'

'Nah.' He stared down at his hands. 'After she spent the night, she expected me to be romantic and stuff and I …'

'Blew it? Hey, it happens to us all.' Zach scooped instant coffee into a couple of dark blue pottery mugs, topped them with boiling water and stirred them before pushing one across to Joe. ‘Is there any chance a thoughtful Christmas present might get you back in her good books?’

Joe snorted. ‘Not unless it’s a bloody diamond ring.’

‘But you’ve only been back together a few weeks.’

‘Beth said she wasn’t going to waste another two years of her life only for me to toss her over again.’ He shrugged. ‘Her words not mine. I never tossed her over the first time. The break-up was mutual.’

No doubt his friend was telling the truth as far as he saw it, but he’d bet his bottom dollar if he asked Beth for her opinion the two would be worlds apart.

‘There was other stuff too but enough of that. You asked me about Sleeping Beauty out there.’

‘Yeah. I can find out why he’s here later, but how on earth did he come to meet Rosey?’

‘Anna held a party tonight for the backstage crew.’ Joe’s wry smile came back. ‘She’s going overboard with Christmas this year after the costume people teased her about being a proper old Scrooge. I didn’t want to go but—’

‘You wanted to see Beth.’

‘I s’ppose.’ Joe’s dour expression settled back in place. ‘For all the bleedin’ good it did. She was all over Gerry Tremayne like a rash, hanging on his every word and giggling like a schoolgirl.’

‘Trying to make you jealous, pal, that’s all.’

‘Mebbe. Anyway, your mate knocked on the door asking directions for this place. Poor bloke didn’t stand a chance when Rosey spotted him.’ He chuckled. ‘She was in a rare old mood. Dolled up to the nines she were, in a tight red dress and stuff.’ Joe cocked an eyebrow at Zach. ‘I reckon she and Beth were a good pair trying to make us both jealous. Rosey knew I'd come back blabbing it to you, I 'spect.'

A mixture of emotions engulfed him.

'She dragged it out of Cody that he'd come here to see you. He's your agent, right?'

'Yeah.' Zach clasped Joe's shoulder. 'Look I wanna say that you were right that I've been a self-indulgent wanker. See, I've even picked up some of your British insults.'

'I was harsh …'

'Maybe, but I needed a kick up the ass.' Weariness swept through him. 'How about a proper drink?'

'Why not? There's nothing to rush back to the house for.'

Zach fetched the whisky bottle and a couple of glasses.

'So … what're you going to do?'

'Bloody good question. I've been runnin' it over and over and I've got some ideas. Have you got any thoughts?'

'Me?' Joe threw his head back and roared with laughter. 'You're asking a farmer who's barely been out of Cornwall how a Hollywood superstar should reinvent his life?'

The whisky loosened Zach's natural reserve and he poured out everything he'd told Rosey. Zach still held back a couple of the most private things because he needed to share those with her first – if he ever gathered up the courage.

'Maybe you *were* right to call yourself a wanker.' Joe drained his glass and held it out for a refill. 'I bet Rosey told you the same, didn't she?'

'I guess.'

'Like she said, there are other places to act if you're done with Hollywood. One word to Anna and she'll stick you in gaudy satin trousers and put you in the chorus. I expect Cody might have some ideas too when he shakes off his brush with the Polcarne pantomime mafia.'

A trickle of hope snaked through him. Zach had forgotten the satisfaction that acting brought him in the first place when he'd started off in school productions and community theatre. That could be one avenue again. Perhaps it was time for Act Three to begin …

Chapter Fourteen

'We won't have any stage left if you kids don't stop thumping around like blooming elephants!' Anna's frustration rang around the room.

Rosey grimaced. The junior chorus wasn't the only thing thumping. Her sore head throbbed in time with the music. No one had made her drink too much of her mother's lethal punch, but she'd dragged poor Cody Tyler along too in her quest to find out what was going on with Zach. All she'd discovered, or all she could remember now, was that he was Zach's Hollywood agent and he'd come to surprise his most famous client in a last-ditch effort to persuade him back to work. According to her mum, Joe had given Cody a lift to the farm after whisking away the man's car keys for safe keeping. The sleek black rental wasn't outside the house any longer so somebody must have collected it today.

'Right, let's try one more time.' Her mother clapped her hands. 'Line up again.'

Obediently, she struck up the introduction and, by some miracle, things went better.

'I suppose that'll have to do.' By her tone Anna wasn't thrilled but clearly knew she'd cause a revolt if she pushed the little ones any harder. 'Remember, I expect every one of you here on Monday night.'

'But, Mrs Teague—'

'No excuses, Tina.' Her mother interrupted the spunky ten-year-old, the only child brave or foolish enough to argue. 'It's our last chance to practise until after Christmas, and don't forget rehearsals start again on Tuesday the twenty-seventh.'

There was the predictable grumble of discontent from a small group huddled in one corner centred around Mike Blamey, but first night *was* less than a month away and there was still a lot of work to do if they weren't to make fools of themselves.

Anna's smile softened as she spoke to the younger cast members. 'Zoe's got a few sweets for you all from me so run along and she'll pass them out. I know you're all trying your best and it's going to be lovely on the night. The rest of you,' she gazed around, 'I'm buying the first round at the pub.'

Rosey's stomach roiled.

'Are you coming?' Beth came to stand by the piano.

She shook her head then regretted it because that stirred up her lingering headache.

'Did someone have too good a time last night?'

Stupid to think she could hide a hangover from Beth. 'Good isn't really the right word.'

'Bit out of character for you.'

She was swept with a sudden longing to unburden herself.

'How about a quiet coffee at my place?'

'Yes, thanks. That would be good.'

'I've got a few bits to tidy away backstage but give me a couple of minutes and I'll be done.'

'No problem.' She collected up her music, then slipped her old black wool coat back on and wound a thick cream scarf around her neck. Joe was hovering in the doorway as if trying to pluck up the courage to come over.

'Are you ready? It's a bit of a hike to mine but at least it's not raining.' Beth returned, and over the young woman's shoulder she watched Joe turn and stalk off.

'I could do with the walk. It might help blow some of the cobwebs off me.'

'Me too. I spent all day stuck in that stuffy bar and then came straight here. Customers appreciate coming in out of the cold and warming up but it's bloody boiling when you're working.' Beth tugged the hood of her bright pink puffy anorak over her glossy, short, black hair. 'Come on.'

The chilly night breeze stung Rosey's face. 'That feels better already.'

'Let's cross the road.'

She couldn't blame Beth for avoiding walking past the pub because someone would be sure to spot them. They strode briskly through the village towards the main road.

'I'm down here. Miller's Lane.'

'Yes, I know. I sometimes go for a walk out this way so I've been past your cottage. It looks gorgeous from the outside.'

'It is pretty special.'

They turned on to a narrow unlit street and the ancient gnarled hedges looming over them gave Rosey the shivers. 'It's very remote though. Don't you mind being all the way out here on your own?'

Beth's smile grew in the dark. 'When you see inside, you'll know why I think it's worth it. You'll see.' She led them on around another corner. 'There. Welcome to Wisteria Cottage. Of course, in the middle of December you have to imagine the wisteria.'

Motion sensor lights came on illuminating a beautiful thatched cottage, a rarity in Cornwall, surrounded by a charming old-fashioned garden that she guessed would be a riot of beauty in the summer. 'It looks so cosy!' She'd overheard Mike Blamey making a snide remark to one of his mates the previous week at rehearsal about Joe being onto a good thing by courting Beth because she'd inherited this valuable property from a distant relative.

'I'm lucky.' Beth unlocked the bright green front door. 'Hang your coat up and I'll get the kettle on.' She turned the lights on and the cottage sprang to life. It was exactly what Rosey had pictured from the outside. Dark low beams, lovingly-polished antique furniture, uneven cream-painted walls dotted with traditional landscape prints and colourful woven rugs laid over wide oak floorboards worn to a shine by all of the footprints that had trodden them over the years. A Christmas tree decorated in old-fashioned glass ornaments and garlands of gold tinsel stood in the corner by the window with its top almost touching the ceiling. Rosey loved the fresh pine fragrance emanating from it which filled the room. The wood mantel over the fireplace twinkled with white lights woven through sprigs of holly that were heavy with bright red berries. 'I haven't changed much since I moved in.'

'Why would you want to?' Rosey entered the cosy country kitchen.

'Tea or coffee?'

'Black tea, please.'

'I did buy this.' Beth held up a modern stainless steel kettle jug. 'I'm pretty sure Great Aunt Edna's battered old kettle dated from the First World War.'

Soon they had their hot drinks and were sitting together at the tiny white wood table.

'Oh Rosey, what am I going to do? I thought donkeys were stubborn but Joe Warren beats them any day.' Beth suddenly burst into noisy, unflattering tears.

'I'm happy to listen and if I can do anything to help, I will.'

'Thanks.' Beth managed a watery smile. 'I need you to tell me if I'm being unreasonable.' She launched into a long rambling story, and the gist of it was that Joe was dragging his heels because he felt he had little to offer her. It was common knowledge that the farm was struggling and Joe had picked up on some nasty rumours that he'd only hooked back up with Beth for the financial advantages she brought to the relationship. 'I told Joe he was being stupid and that he needed to ignore the gossip. I tried to convince him we could make a real go of the farm with a bit of creative thinking, but he's got this idiotic macho idea that he's got to "provide" for me." She rolled her eyes. 'I mean, are we in the twenty-first century or back in Jane Austen's time, Rosey?'

'I'm a hundred per cent on your side. Joe needs to get his act together before he loses you for a second time.' Rosey puffed out a sigh. 'Do you want to hear about somebody who might just equal Joe's stubbornness?'

Zach pushed away the plate of unappetising grilled fish and steamed vegetables. 'So are you gonna tell me what's prised you out of Hollywood in the middle of party season?' They always joked that Cody never turned down a social invitation, although his agent swore it was only because all the real deals were made behind the scenes.

It had taken most of the day for his old friend to resemble a human being again. When Zach offered to make breakfast that morning all Cody had done was groan, swig a gallon of water and its equivalent in painkillers before dragging himself off to the guest bed. Much later, after a long sleep and a hot shower, Cody announced that he was starving. He'd raised his manicured eyebrows at the meagre offerings of leftover pizza and beer in the fridge. Zach dutifully trudged down to the village and scoured the limited selection at the shop for something resembling healthy food.

'I came to see you, of course,' Cody answered him, 'although why in God's name you've buried yourself in some place even the damn GPS couldn't find, I'll never understand.'

'It can't be that far off the beaten track if you managed to track me down.'

'Yeah, well, that's another story.' Cody's cheeks turned red on top of his year-round Californian tan. 'Maybe you aren't so dumb because the cute redhead who got me drunk last night was hot, hot, hot. She could give some of the LA girls a run for their money. That tight scarlet dress showed off a seriously fit body.'

Zach clenched his fists under the table. 'Rosey's attractive, but she's the exception rather than the rule here.'

Cody rubbed at his forehead. 'My memory is fuzzy but I could swear she said somethin' crazy about you helping out with some local show they're putting on. I probably got that part wrong because she kept refilling my glass with God knows what.'

'She's right. I was for a while but—'

'What the hell! Did you forget we've got a contract? I do the negotiations for you, remember? Yeah, I want you back acting but not in some two-bit part.'

'Cool it. Okay. Just listen for a minute.' Cody's incredulity grew as he heard the whole story, minus the part where he slept with Rosey and screwed things up. 'Fifteen per cent of nothing is nothing so you haven't missed out.'

'I've known you how long now? Sixteen years or so? There's more to it. Spill the beans.' He flashed a grin. 'Shit. It's the cute babe, isn't it? She got me trashed and milked me for info on you.'

'Did she?'

He leaned back and folded his arms. 'So you gonna start by telling me why you weren't at the party?'

'Leave that for a minute. I want to talk work with you first.'

His agent's face brightened. 'Sure. The sooner we get you back on track the better. Two years is a long time to be out of the loop, but I'm still getting offers for you every week so it won't be a problem. We could ease you in with—'

'Stop right there. We've got crossed wires. I'm not coming back to Hollywood.'

'I know Laura's death hit you hard but acting's your life. It's who you are. Look at Liam Neeson. He threw himself back in. You can too.' Cody angled him a long, hard stare. 'We both know your marriage wasn't in great shape. I know your secrets, Zach. Get real. It wouldn't have lasted much longer anyway.'

'I'm not arguing the toss on that now.' He couldn't win an argument anyway because it was the truth, although there was still one secret he hadn't shared with his agent. 'But you know acting was slowly killing me even before I lost Laura. You just didn't want to kill the goose that laid the golden egg.'

'That's fuckin' unfair!'

'You're right. I'm sorry.' At the end of the day theirs *was* a business arrangement and his agent had a living to make. They'd been through a lot together from the first night Cody saw Zach, fresh out of drama school, performing in an off-Broadway show where he had three lines and died in the first act. His agent stood by him when his world fell apart and swore to be patient enough to wait until Zach was ready to work again. They'd come to a fork in the road and it wasn't an option to take advantage of that goodwill any longer.

'So, what *are* your plans?' Cody's expression hardened. 'Or the plans you *think* you have. In case you've forgotten, there are still two years left on our present contract.'

'Is there any chance we could talk things through and renegotiate that? I couldn't live in Hollywood again or work there full-time, but I could maybe get into voiceover work for animated films. Stuff I can do in a studio from pretty much anywhere?'

'You're settling here?' Scepticism oozed out of Cody.

'I'm not sure, but maybe. I like it here. The peace. The remoteness. Most of the people take me at face value. Now the novelty's worn off, I can wander into the village shop and no one blinks an eye. It's rare that anyone whips a camera out or asks for an autograph, and if they do I oblige and that's it.'

'If you've got a yearning to be a hermit, buy a few thousand acres in Wyoming or one of those other places where all the land does is hold the rest of the country together. Nothing says you have to *live* in LA when you're not working.'

He didn't answer.

'You really think you'd be happy voicing some dumb children's cartoon character after the incredible parts you've had?'

'Do you think I'm happy now? I've been doin' a lot of thinking, particularly over the last week or so, and I realise

I still need a connection with acting but it's gotta be in a different way.' This was exactly what Rosey had tried to tell him but he'd needed to come around to it in his own time. 'I think I'd enjoy an involvement with community theatre, or maybe giving classes for kids who don't get any exposure to the stage. I've been trying my hand at writing too … I've almost finished a children's book. It only needs a few last tweaks, and I can see the possibility of turning it into a series. I might even have a go at a screenplay one day.'

'What brought that on? I've never heard you mention any interest in writing before.'

'I guess it's something I've always considered having a go at, and with plenty of time on my hands … it just sort of came to me one day.' He didn't know how to explain the way the story had got a hold on him, not loosening its grip until he'd written the first draft. 'It's about a boy who struggles to fit in at school until he discovers acting, which opens up a whole new world to him.'

'It sounds interesting. I'm happy to take a look if you want my opinion.'

'Thanks. I will when I'm ready.' He softened his tone. 'You know there's more to it as well. You met Rosey.'

'She's hot, yeah, but seriously? You're goin' to settle down with some honey whose be all and end all is this desolate place?' Cody shook his head.

Zach could defend himself. Defend Rosey. Explain to his old friend how special and unique she was. But those were all things he needed to tell her first after he'd sorted himself out. She might not be interested in giving him a second chance when he told her two crucial things. The first, the truth about his marriage, would probably arouse her sympathy … but the second? Kind-hearted Rosey would pity him, but the urge to walk away and find a man who could give her the one thing she clearly wanted might be too strong. 'Why don't we call it a night? We'll talk more tomorrow. I don't want to part on bad terms.'

'You're screwing yourself over here but you can't see it. I'm good with talkin' more in the morning but then I'm getting out of this god-forsaken place and back to civilisation.'

'Fair enough.' Zach glanced at the old black and white railway clock on the wall and calculated the time in Tennessee. He'd give his parents a ring to see if they fancied spending Christmas in Cornwall. More than anything he needed them to see he was doing well in his new life here. They deserved that much, and more, after all the worries he'd burdened them with over the last few years.

Chapter Fifteen

'Don't tell me. Let me guess. These have been in Perry's family since the Norman Conquest?' Rosey smoothed her finger over the teacup's delicate white lace pattern. 'I suppose they're worth more than my house?'

'You're teasing again. Stop it.' Amanda burst into giggles.

Her invitation to Sunday afternoon tea at the manor was wrapping up a very strange weekend, but was a welcome relief after Friday night's disastrous Christmas party, yesterday's hungover rehearsal and her heart-to-heart chat with Beth.

'When do the kids arrive?'

'They get out of school on Tuesday and Felicia's bringing them down from Exeter on Wednesday.' She grimaced. 'Perry offered to pick them up but Felicia enjoys being a martyr. That way she can complain about the traffic, turn on the waterworks at being separated from her babies over Christmas and generally upset everyone.' Amanda rolled her eyes. 'The fact she's flying to Barbados on Christmas Eve for a week's holiday at a wickedly expensive beach resort with her wealthy merchant banker boyfriend won't come up, of course.'

'Miaow!'

'That was bitchy but …' Amanda hesitated.

'I never met Felicia but she wasn't popular around the village and most people were glad to see the back of her. It still baffles me why your kind, sweet husband fell for her in the first place,' Rosey cut in reassuringly.

'He was twenty when they met and still thinking with a certain part of his anatomy that doesn't contain any brain cells. By the time the novelty wore off, he was stuck with her.' Amanda smirked. 'But that's more than enough about my nemesis. Tell me what's up with you. Did you and that cute American … you know …?'

'Absolutely not!' She shuddered. 'Please don't tell me everyone thinks I hooked up with Cody Tyler?' If Zach heard that rumour, she could say goodbye to any hope of them ever reconnecting. 'For a start, I wasn't drunk enough to totally lose my mind and for another, I—'

'Still love Zach Broussard? It's okay. If it's any consolation, he looked pretty miserable when I saw him.'

'When was that?'

'Fred Cann and I went over to the farm last week because Joe found an old granite feeding trough that'll be perfect for Wishee-Washee's laundry. It's super heavy but Fred's building a trolley so we can wheel it on and off the stage.'

Rosey couldn't help smiling.

'What's that grin for?'

'You. You're addicted to the pantomime already, aren't you?'

'It's fascinating.' Amanda's eyes danced. 'I'd no idea how much work went into putting it on and I'm enjoying every minute.'

'That's wonderful, and you getting involved was one of my better ideas if I say so myself. You're a huge asset so it's a win all around.'

'Thank you, and you were right – it's made a huge difference in the village. People are different with me now – in a good way.'

'You were saying about Zach?'

'All I know about Zach is when we were loading the trough into the back of Fred's truck, he hurried out from the barn and jumped in a shiny red Land Rover that I hadn't seen before and drove off without slowing down to say hello.'

'He's been promising to hire a car for weeks so I suppose he must've gone ahead and found one.'

'Joe's face was as stony as the granite trough, and when I asked if everything was okay all I got was a grunt.' She leaned in closer. 'Won't you have another try at getting through to Zach?'

'Absolutely not.' Rosey was adamant. 'He broke up with me and was very clear about his reasons. If there's any reaching out to be done, he'll have to do it.' She worked to change the subject. 'You go for lots of long walks around here, don't you?'

'I used to.' A smile lifted the edges of her mouth. 'I haven't had as much spare time recently though. Why?'

'Have you ever seen Beth Tregolls' gorgeous thatched cottage at the bottom of Miller's Lane?'

'Uh, yes. Wisteria Cottage. Seventeenth century and to die for. I'd love to see inside one day.'

'I'm one up on you for once.' Rosey laughed. 'Beth invited me over last night for coffee after the rehearsal because I was kind of down … and hungover.' She shared the story about Mike's snide comment on Joe's motive for chasing after Beth again. 'The sad thing is they've broken up over it.'

Amanda picked up a scone, dolloped on some jam and took her time spreading it around before adding a heaped spoon of clotted cream. 'I'm not sure how they'll find a way around the problem unless he can get over his stupid pride.'

'Agreed. She's utterly miserable and I'll bet you anything he is too.'

'What about you and Zach? Did Beth offer you any advice in return?'

When she didn't rush to answer, her friend smirked.

'I'm guessing you didn't like it.' A knowing look came Rosey's way. 'None of us appreciate having our judgment questioned. My mum tried to tell me a few home truths before I married Perry but I wouldn't listen. Oh, don't think for one second I regret marrying him but I could have saved myself a lot of grief if I'd been more objective. I floated around in this ridiculous bubble, convinced that love was enough to cope with it all.' Amanda lowered her voice. 'Zach's handsome and utterly charming, and he swept you off your feet, didn't he?'

That made her sound like an infatuated teenager. 'I suppose so. I knew he had problems but I didn't realise how hard they'd be to overcome.' She rubbed her hand over her face to disguise the tears stinging her eyes. 'I ought to get a move on. Mum's in a down mood too so this evening we're going to watch one of the old films she loves – she sees herself as a modern-day Lauren Bacall or Katharine Hepburn. We'll probably heat up a frozen pizza or something too.' Rosey managed a faint smile. 'We know how to live, don't we?'

'There's nothing wrong with that. I suppose Anna's fretting over the pantomime? She does seem to take it to heart so.'

'I know.'

'Anyway, I'll see you at rehearsal tomorrow.'

Rosey left far lighter in spirits than when she'd arrived. It was no consolation for losing Zach but she had gained two good friends in Amanda and Beth and was more grateful to them both than she'd ever be able to express.

'Are we good now?' Zach's breath caught in his throat. He needed Cody to be flexible and accept that his biggest client wasn't going to provide the retirement package of his dreams.

'I suppose so but I'm not happy.'

'I don't expect you to be but I appreciate it.'

Cody shrugged. 'I can't force you back on a film set. There are clauses in your contract about exceptional circumstances and protecting your physical and mental health. If I tried to crack the whip, you'd have me over a barrel with that little lot.'

'Always the pragmatist.'

'Gotta be in my game. You win some. You lose some. We had a decent run and at least I never had to rush you off to rehab or put a spin on your antics across social media.'

They'd had many chats about the trials of coping with some of the younger stars who thought they were entitled to exhibit appalling behaviour on the basis of one big movie role.

'I'll see what interest I can stir up in projects you might be interested in. What're you goin' to do in the meanwhile?' Cody winked. 'Romance the hot Rosey? Show the local yokels how acting's done?'

A shudder ran through Zach. The first option terrified him, and the second? He didn't need Mike Blamey and his entourage railroading him out of Polcarne for interfering with their precious pantomime.

'My folks are comin' over for Christmas.' He didn't try to hide his pleasure. 'I called them last night and talked them into it.' It hadn't taken much effort on his part. They weren't going to his sister's this year anyway because Paula and her family were travelling to Charlotte to spend the holidays with her husband Nick's family. His parents would arrive in London on Tuesday, spend the night there and take the train down the next day. Zach would have cheerfully paid for a chauffeur-driven car to pick them up and bring them down in comfort but wasn't dumb enough to make the offer. Money was a minefield where his family was concerned because they hated the idea that anyone could claim they took advantage of Zach. But what was the point of having money if he couldn't share it with the people he loved? There'd only been a few rare occasions when they'd allowed him to help out. Back in the spring his sister asked through gritted teeth if he could loan her some money. She and her husband were both underpaid teachers, and with four children money was tight. Their oldest, his nephew Ollie, was a talented artist and had the chance to attend a world-renowned summer school in Paris but he needed to raise the money for his travel to and from France. Zach could see an argument down the line when he refused to allow Paula to repay him.

'Maybe your folks will knock some sense into you.' Cody's hopeful dig made him laugh.

'You're not givin' up easy, are you?'

'Hey, a guy's got to try. I'm off to pack up my gear then I'm outta here.'

A short time later they stood outside in the cold, neither knowing quite what to say.

'Don't you let that cute babe get away.' Cody slung his small suitcase into the back seat of the rental car. 'Get your butt down there and turn on the famous Broussard charm. If you leave it too long someone else will snap her up.' He chuckled. 'I might even think of coming back and giving it a try sober.'

'Huh! Remember she'd be sober too so it'd be a waste of time. The woman's got taste.'

'She can't have that much if she fell for you! Anyway, you take care of yourself.' Cody leapt into his red sports car, fired up the engine and zoomed off out of the farm. If the Cornish equivalent of the California Highway Patrol were out in force today, they'd nab him for speeding before he reached the Devon border.

Zach spotted Joe outside his door gripping a colourful bouquet of flowers. 'You off to do some wooing?' His friend's face turned bright scarlet. 'You're braver than me.'

'Nothing ventured nothing gained, eh? I've been a right moron. I see that now.'

'Yeah. I'm pretty sure I have too.'

'Did you know Rosey usually gets to the hall early for rehearsals to run through the music on her own?'

He shrugged but didn't answer.

'Think about it.' Joe nodded towards the barn. 'Bloody lonely in there now, isn't it?'

There'd be no sleep for him tonight.

Chapter Sixteen

'*Cancelled*? I didn't cancel anything! What on earth are you talking about?' Her mum frantically beckoned Rosey into the kitchen whilst she talked on the phone. 'You should have checked to make sure the email came from me. This is your fault and it's your responsibility to put it right.'

Rosey helped herself to a mug of tea while she kept listening to try and guess who her mother was talking to.

'What do mean you've re-hired the costumes already?'

Her heart sunk. It must be the shop in Plymouth. They made most of their own costumes because they were so expensive to hire, but they'd splashed out and reserved two for Aladdin and Jasmine for the finale.

'What else do you have that might work for us?' Anna's pleading intensified. 'Nothing! What are we supposed to do now?' She glared at the phone. 'Well, thank you very much and we won't ever be doing business with you again.' One sharp jab with her red manicured nail ended the call. 'I think someone's got it in for us.' She swung around to face Rosey.

'Don't be silly, Mum. It must be a mix-up.'

'What about all the things we've had go missing? I suppose your explanation is that a Cornish piskie is responsible?'

Rosey was pretty sure if the mischievous spirits existed, they'd do something more exciting than steal a few pens and a paint brush. 'Now you're really being daft. Anyway, it wasn't much—'

'A couple more things have happened, but I didn't tell you about them because I knew you'd make light of it and laugh at me.' Her mum's chin tilted in defiance. 'Gerry swears that he put a new box of expensive light bulbs in his store cupboard but they weren't there on Monday when he needed one. Then there's what happened to the biscuits.'

'What biscuits?'

'I bought a new box for our tea breaks – nice chocolate ones that Albert had on sale at the shop – and I thought I'd open them yesterday for a treat but they'd already been ripped open and smashed to bits.' Anna wagged a finger in Rosey's face. 'You won't be laughing when I'm proved right. Somebody *definitely* has it in for us and the pantomime!'

This was getting crazier by the minute. She was sure there were logical explanations for all of these things, but when her mother was on a rant there was little to be done except ride it out. 'Okay. I suppose we'll have to wait and see. Anyway, what're we going to do about the costumes?'

'I'll pop around to see Zoe and hope she can rescue us.' She scrutinised Rosey. 'Are you going to do something to get that man of yours back, or just sit around with a vinegary face waiting for him to come to his senses?'

'What do you suggest?' The sarcastic question clearly went over her mother's head because a wide grin spread over Anna's face.

'A new hairstyle might help. Pep yourself up a bit. Demelza can work wonders.' She patted her own elaborate curls. 'Give her a ring and see if she can fit you in.'

'Yes, Mum.' Rosey didn't think for a moment that her mother's suggestion would do any good but sometimes it was easier to give in.

Rosey winced at her unrecognisable reflection in the shop window. She shouldn't have listened to her mother. Or

Beth. Or Amanda. As if a drastic change in her appearance would bolster her confidence enough to face Zach again. It'd been foolish to let Demelza loose on her hair with instructions to do whatever she wanted. Apparently, she now sported something called a "bixie" cut.

'It's fashionable this year, Rosey. Shorter than a bob but longer than a pixie. It'll look awesome on you.'

Awesome was *not* the word that sprang to mind. The only consolation was that it would grow back. Eventually. Crowds of bustling shoppers milled around her and all she wanted to do was escape the madness that was Truro city centre six days before Christmas.

A dark green velvet dress tucked away in the corner of a shop window caught her eye but her heart sank when she saw the price tag.

'Rosey?'

She turned at the sound of Samira Key's lilting voice and watched the other woman's jaw drop.

'Oh my God, your hair is awesome,' she squealed. 'I didn't think for a minute that Demelza would talk you into it. Zach's going to be bowled over when he sees you.'

'Is my love life or lack of it the talk of the village?'

The barrister smirked. 'I don't know about the *whole* village but definitely among the pantomime cast and crew.'

'I'm not sure which is worse,' Rosey groused. 'Are you trying to do your Christmas shopping?'

'I wish. I'm stuck at the Crown Court all day.' Samira gestured to her smart black suit, white blouse and high heels. 'That explains all this lot but I've got a break before my next case is up so I came out for some fresh air and to grab a coffee.' She gave a shy smile. 'Do you have time to join me?'

‘I’d like that. We could go to Annie’s?’ Rosey pointed to a small café on the other side of the road.

‘Perfect.’

They were lucky to find a table free and settled down with their hot drinks and the obligatory December treat of warm mince pies and clotted cream.

‘Feel free to tell me off if I’m being nosey,’ Rosey began, ‘but what made you buy a house in Polcarne? Isn’t it off the beaten track for getting to work?’ Her question made Samira smile.

‘Not really. It’s about halfway between here and Bodmin so it’s ideal for both courts. It suits me to be a world away from my work environment. I fell in love with Cornwall when my parents brought us here on holiday one summer, so when a job opportunity came up, I snatched at it.’ A touch of wry amusement crept into her dark brown eyes. ‘My family were not happy.’

‘Why not? Aren’t they proud of you?’

‘They’re conflicted. My father was about to go to university in Iraq when the first Gulf War broke out. His parents saw no future for them there so they came to England. My dad ended up working in the restaurant his father started to support them all, and I grew up in a cramped flat in a tower block in north London. Mum and Dad saved every spare penny to give me and my sister a good education so they’re happy I’m doing well in my career, but in their hearts they wish I was more like my sister. Marya went to Oxford too and got a First in International Relations but married a good Iraqi boy straight afterwards. She’s had three children in the last five years and is expecting her fourth in the spring.’ Sadness and frustration ran through her voice.

‘It’s unfair to compare the two of you.’

'Maybe, but it is what it is.' She shrugged. 'Every time I visit, my parents wheel out at least one "suitable" man who is prepared to marry their ancient daughter. At twenty-nine, I'm considered not just on the shelf but glued to it.' Her attempt to make a joke of the situation fell flat. 'I'm heading up to London on Thursday to spend the holidays with them all, but you can reassure Anna I will be back for rehearsal on the twenty-seventh. It gives me the perfect excuse not to stay longer.'

'Oh, don't worry. Mum would come up there and chase you back to Cornwall if she had to! We're happy you've made Polcarne your home and we're not the only ones.'

'Thank you. I wasn't sure how welcome I would be because small rural villages don't always have a reputation for being accepting of strangers … and there's definitely some of that in Polcarne.'

'Really? I'm sorry. Not in the panto, I hope?'

Samira gave a slight shrug and didn't quite meet Rosey's gaze as she continued speaking. 'Occasionally Mike Blamey and his little clique of equally ignorant friends think it's a big joke to make sly remarks about unwelcome immigrants and keeping Britain for the British when I'm around. Last week he threw out a backhanded compliment about how great it must be to have a deep tan in the middle of winter.'

'Oh, that's awful!'

She glanced at her watch. 'I'm sorry. I must go. I've got another case up at noon. That's enough of my troubles. Please forget I mentioned all this.'

'You can't seriously expect me to do that? It's awful! I'll tell Mum as soon as I get home. She'll soon put a stop to it.'

'Don't you dare say a word to her or anyone else!' Samira put a shaking hand to her throat. 'I grew up learning to deal with people like them. An Oxford degree or not, do you honestly think I don't face prejudice every day at work too?'

Rosey was clueless how to respond.

'If your mother says anything it will only make things worse for me. I know that from bitter experience.' She closed her eyes as if the memories were overwhelming. 'Promise me you will say nothing.'

She felt dreadful but reluctantly nodded.

'Now get back over to that shop and buy the gorgeous dress I saw you salivating over.' Samira's bright smile didn't quite reach her eyes.

Rosey nodded again and did her best to smile back.

Zach hadn't been this nervous at the Oscar ceremony. He'd been hanging around outside the hall for several minutes tossing up in his head whether to go in or walk away. If he didn't decide soon, Anna would catch him out and he didn't need her so-called help. Joe's success in talking Beth into going on another date with him had buoyed his own courage.

He pushed open the door and held his breath when it creaked. Rosey was playing and singing along to Aladdin and Jasmine's final duet. He found himself joining in because the lyrics Rosey created were hammered into his heart. They spoke of love overcoming all and being worth more than all the jewels in the world.

The music came to an abrupt halt but Zach continued to sing as he edged into the hall. Rosey sat motionless at the piano with her hands resting on the keys, and when she glanced over her shoulder the spotlight fixed over the piano picked up the fire in her hair.

He stopped suddenly. 'You cut it. It suits you.' The cropped style framed her face and allowed her striking features no place to hide.

'It's a bixie.'

'A what? That sounds like a rare African antelope.' It was hard not to laugh when she rattled off the hairdresser's description. 'Whatever you want to call it, I like it.'

'Really?' She sounded dubious.

'Yeah. It emphasises what a strong, beautiful woman you are.'

'Oh please.' Rosey snorted. 'Laying on the compliments with a trowel won't get me back in your bed. You made your feelings perfectly clear and nothing's changed.'

'Yeah, it has. Me.' Zach perched next to her on the piano stool and breathed in her unforgettable scent. 'I never meant to make you cry.'

'Oh yes you did.'

'Oh no I didn't.'

The snappy classic pantomime comebacks made them both laugh. She'd taught him a lot about the various traditions surrounding this most English of shows and he'd learned more by hanging about during rehearsals when he wasn't needed. Until recent years, the Principal Boy was always played by a woman and the dame by a man, but now some of the larger productions were deviating from the tradition. Not in Polcarne. Anna wasn't a fan of the changes and was experienced enough to realise her audience wouldn't be either. Zach understood about audience expectation. As a young actor, he'd played Mr Darcy in a modern stage version of *Pride and Prejudice* but it sunk without a trace after the first week because the script writer wrote his part as a sensitive, considerate man from the first scene. Jane Austen understood that without Darcy's transformation from arrogant and proud there was no story.

'So ... what exactly do you mean by—'

'There you are.' Anna swept in, trailing yards of emerald material in her wake. Her expression turned smug when she saw them together. 'Zach, my love, how are you? We've missed you terribly – haven't we, Rosey? Does this mean you've forgotten all that silliness about not wanting to be part of our lovely little show? I know we have.'

'Well, if you still need backstage help, I'm happy to lend you these.' Zach did his muscle-flexing thing again which made them laugh.

'You should know I'm determined to get you back on the stage, but I can be patient.'

Behind her mother's back, Rosey lifted her eyebrows.

Other people started to trickle in so he muttered something about going to find Fred and Amanda then made his escape. His reappearance would cause gossip – both the positive and the negative sort. Although he'd cultivated a thick skin after his first acting reviews described him as wooden and reedy-voiced, he'd prefer to imagine what was being said rather than hear it spelled out.

The next couple of hours crept at a snail's pace because Rosey was the only thing on his mind. Fred had to ask Zach three times to get Aladdin's cave ready to be shifted into place at the scene change and chuckled merrily when he finally paid attention. Amanda made unsubtle, pointed comments about Rosey's new haircut and even Joe joined in.

Finally, Anna strode out on the stage and clapped her hands for quiet. 'That wasn't too bad.'

He interpreted that as "good" in normal person speak. Directors were renowned for never praising their actors too highly in case it made them complacent.

'That's our last rehearsal until next week, and I'll expect everyone here on Tuesday at seven o'clock ready to work hard.' Her scrutinising glance swept around the room. 'We still have the hall booked for the usual nights and I'll be here this Thursday if anyone feels they could do with some one-on-one rehearsal time.' She nodded at Rosey. 'We'll have music if anyone wants to run though a song, won't we, my love?'

'I'm not sure yet what my plans are so don't rely on me being here.'

Good one, Rosey.

'Oh. I see.' Anna's gaze encompassed Zach now and there was a far less welcoming expression than he'd received earlier on her face. The blame for Rosey's intransigence was laid firmly at his feet. Fine by him. 'I hope you all have a Happy Christmas and I'm sure I'll see a lot of you at the Christmas Eve service over in St Merryn, but tonight I think The Trelawny needs our custom.'

The group broke up and he made sure Fred didn't need his help with anything else before he zeroed back in on Rosey.

'We can go to the pub if you want or—'

'I'll take or, please.' Her smile dimmed. 'We need to talk.'

'My place or yours?'

'Mine.' The corners of her mouth twitched. 'It's safer. Mum won't stay long at the pub because she's super tired, although she'd die rather than admit it.'

'Whatever you want. Let's go and work out how Act Three might go for us.'

Chapter Seventeen

Rosey switched the Christmas tree lights on and drew the curtains. 'I know pink flamingo lights aren't traditional but we both know my mother doesn't do ordinary. I suppose your family sticks to red, green and gold, or maybe silver? Or do they do a monochromatic theme with everything the same colour?'

'Oh Lord, the Christmas decorations were always an ongoing battle back home until my folks came to a compromise.' Zach's rumbling laugh filled the room. 'Now Mama gets to decorate the entrance hall and living room as she wants – we're talkin' tasteful and traditional – and Papa gets free rein on the rest of the house. His efforts are colourful to say the least. He totally goes back to his Cajun roots so everything is decked out in purple and gold for LSU – Louisiana State University. The Broussards are die-hard fans.' Zach shook his head. 'It about killed him when I went to college at Juilliard in New York. He was torn because he knew how prestigious a school it is and how few kids get in, but deep down he felt I'd betrayed my culture.'

She couldn't believe she'd forgotten the power of Zach's charismatic smile in the ten or so days since they'd broken up. Despite her best intentions, she melted. 'Wasn't he born and brought up in Tennessee the same as you?'

'Yeah, but that's irrelevant. According to him, if your heritage is Cajun, you'll never be anythin' else. The only saving grace was that I didn't choose my mom's alma mater, the University of Tennessee. See, the two schools are longstanding college football rivals and UT players tremble when the schedule sets them up to play at Death Valley – that's the nickname for the LSU stadium in Baton Rouge.'

This was the most animated she'd seen him talking about anything that wasn't connected with acting.

'If you reckon I'm spinning a yarn, you can get the truth straight from the horse's mouth tomorrow, or you might have to wait until Wednesday if they're too jet-lagged.' A touch of wariness crept into his eyes. 'I hadn't got around to telling you yet that my folks are flyin' over for Christmas.'

'That's great.' Rosey heard the false enthusiasm in her voice and guessed he hadn't missed it either. An Oscar-winning actress she wasn't. 'That's a bit of a surprise, isn't it? You never mentioned it before when we talked about the holidays.'

Zach reached for her hands, heating her skin with his stroking fingers. 'When I came to my senses a few days ago, one of the first things I did was call them up. My mom's been worried about me and I guess my dad has too but he doesn't say much. I thought they needed to see I'm doin' better.' He cocked his head. 'Am I rushing things to ask you to meet them?'

'That depends, doesn't it?'

He shifted a motley collection of Christmas-themed stuffed animals out of the way, including a geeky looking Rudolph with big red glasses, so they could use the sofa. 'I understand you met Cody, my agent?'

'Not one of my finest hours.' She covered her hot face with her hands. 'Oh God, did he tell you … and I suppose Joe …?'

'Yeah, they did. But it gave me hope.'

'Why?'

'I reckoned if you were plying a stranger with drink to find out what was goin' on, it meant you still had feelings for me. Once Cody sobered up, we talked a whole lot.' He laid out every detail. 'I can't say he was happy in the end, but he's a decent guy. So you reckon I'm on the right track?'

'It all sounds great.'

'So … I'm right to think you still care for me?'

Rosey fought to hold onto a shred of common sense. 'Caring is all very well, Zach. I *care* for Amanda. I *care* for friends like Fred Cann and Beth. But you …' Her nerve faltered.

'Will it help if I tell you I love you?' The words tumbled out of Zach's mouth, and for a few paralysing seconds he couldn't breathe as she stared at him, wide-eyed and pale.

'Well, isn't that a lucky coincidence? Because I love you too.' Her Cornish accent turned stronger and throbbed with emotion. 'Aren't you going to kiss me? I rather hoped you would.' Rosey's flirtatious manner would have amused and aroused him if he hadn't been burdened by the secrets he hadn't had the courage to share with her yet.

'There's something I've got to tell you.' It was like dimming a light switch and her eyes turned wary. 'It's not about us. You've got to know the full truth about my marriage.'

'I know you were at odds with each other when she died, but you were also having a child together and—'

'No … we weren't.' Zach couldn't swallow the lump in his throat. 'It wasn't my baby.'

'Laura was unfaithful to you?' She sounded so incredibly disbelieving it broke his heart.

'Yeah. It happens.' The effort to convey indifference didn't quite come off.

'But there was surely still a chance it *was* yours? You can't be certain.'

Rosey was handing him the chance to get things straight with her on a plate. All he had to do was tell her the truth. But something about her desperate need to be kind, to say whatever it took to make him feel better about a lousy situation made Zach lose his nerve, again. 'We hadn't slept together for almost a year before Laura died so unless my maths is lousier than I thought, it definitely wasn't my baby.' That was the absolute truth. 'Cody helped me to hush it up. My folks know but I managed to keep the truth from Laura's. They were torn apart by her death and the knowledge they'd lost a grandchild too … I couldn't make it any worse for them.'

'But didn't the other man—'

'Trust me, he didn't want it getting out either. He's a fine, upstanding, hardcore right-wing conservative politician with a doting wife and clutch of adoring children.' Zach could feel his mouth twist into a grimace. 'Getting a famous married woman pregnant and having it splashed all over the news was the last thing he wanted.'

'Oh Zach, that's just awful.'

He couldn't do this to her any longer. 'There's something else … and it's kind of a biggie.'

Rosey rested a finger against his lips. 'Would you mind saving it? I'd like to enjoy the whole being in love with each other bit a little longer before any more reality intrudes.'

Her beguiling smile rendered him helpless. 'Well, aren't I the dumb one?' Zach wrapped his arms around her and buried his face in her silky hair, smelling her familiar lilac shampoo. 'Do you really think your mom's coming home soon?'

'Let's chance it.' Rosey draped her hands around his neck and drew him into a deep, satisfying kiss.

The tension running through his body unknotted. 'So you're up for meetin' my folks? They'll ask a whole bunch of questions and I'm not sure we're—'

'Shush.' She gave him an indulgent smile. 'They won't expect you to announce wedding plans, and if they do then *I'll* soon put them right if *you* don't. We're a long way off anything like that.'

Zach found her pragmatism a little unsettling.

'Don't give me that look like a disappointed little boy on Christmas morning when he doesn't get the train set he asked Father Christmas for.' Rosey caressed his face. 'Do you think there isn't a part of me that's swept away by all of this? By you? But I've got one unsatisfying marriage under my belt and I don't plan on having another.'

'You're right.' Zach tweaked a lock of her hair. 'Typical. I should've learned my lesson with Laura. I talked her into marrying me after only three months and it was a disaster.'

'It's getting late. You *should* probably go now.' Rosey sounded as desolate as he felt. 'Give me a ring when your parents are up for a visit.'

'Has your mom bought the turkey you were threatening me with yet?'

'No. I'm taking her to Asda first thing tomorrow morning to do our big Christmas shop. She'll probably get the bright idea of inviting your parents as well now and it'll be awful because neither of us have ever cooked one before.'

'Why don't I save us from food poisoning and y'all come up to the barn and eat with us?'

'We couldn't possibly intrude.'

Zach planted his hands on her shoulders. 'Intrude? You're the woman I love, remember? I want my folks to get to know you and your mom, so where's the problem?'

'But you can't expect your poor mother to rustle up a full Christmas dinner in a strange kitchen.'

'Here was me thinking you're a liberated woman who believed in equality between the sexes.' He gave an exaggerated head shake. 'Sad.'

'Of course I do, but what's that to do with it?'

'I'll cook.' Heat prickled the back of his neck. 'I'm not just a pretty face I happen to be a damn good cook too, if I say so myself.'

'Well, excuse me.' Rosey giggled. 'Mr Hunky Chef extraordinaire.'

'Apology accepted. What do y'all usually have to eat for Christmas? I know everyone's got different traditions.' He chuckled. 'We end up with a ton of food because we've got to appease Mama's southern roots and Papa's Cajun heritage. It won't be a problem to add in whatever is typical here too.'

'You don't need to go to any trouble for us. I'll be relieved not to have to endure Mum's efforts at trying to emulate Nigella – she's a sexy famous chef, by the way. I'm sure she'll be absolutely thrilled with your invitation.' Rosey grimaced. 'I'm warning you now, we might have more trouble with *her* asking awkward questions, especially if you ply her with too much wine.'

He couldn't help laughing. 'Can you believe I was almost stupid enough then to ask whether you could have a quiet word with her first and warn her? Then I remembered – no offence – this is Anna we're talking about.'

'What little conspiracy are you two love birds up to now?'

He almost toppled off the sofa when Rosey's mother materialised in the doorway like the genie appearing from Aladdin's magic lamp.

'I assume you've stopped messing my daughter around and she's accepted your apology?'

'Mum!' Rosey's face matched her hair.

'It's okay, sweetheart. That's a fair question.'

'It most certainly is not.'

'Well, *he* thinks it is.' Anna smirked. 'So I assume I'll get an answer sometime this week.'

'You sure will.' He snaked his arm around Rosey's shoulder and drew her close. 'I've had the sense to realise that I love Rosey and amazingly she loves me back. Before you ask, we're not rushing into anything more than that for now.' Zach swiftly shared their idea for Christmas Day and was amused to see Anna lost for words.

'We could bring something to help out,' Rosey said. 'Perhaps some champagne and a few traditional English bits like mince pies and Christmas pudding. Don't worry, we'll buy them from the shop. Neither Mum or I are bakers.'

'You might not be but people are still talking about the miniature lemon meringue pies I made for the pantomime bake sale.' Anna bristled.

'Oh come on, Mum, we know that's because you misread the recipe and put double the amount of cornflour in the lemon curd. Your victims were picking gluey bits out of their teeth for days.' She sprang up off the sofa and hugged her mother. 'You know I love you to death but cooking is not your forte or mine. However, it appears to be Zach's so let's make the most of it and accept his gracious invitation.' She lowered her voice. 'Can you honestly resist the opportunity to meet his parents?'

'But what on earth am I going to wear?' Anna put a hand to her mouth.

Whatever she chose, Zach suspected it would send his mother's eyebrows sky high and make his father smile. Pierre Broussard would be decked out in a gaudy purple Christmas jumper with the letters LSU picked out in gold bells that jangled when he moved and a Santa face that played the football team song when you pressed its nose, no doubt.

'I'm sure you've got something tucked away that's suitable.' He admired Rosey's ability to keep a straight face. So far he'd never seen her mother in the same outfit twice.

'I'll find something, I suppose.' Anna's smugness returned. 'I'm off to bed and I'll leave you young things to say goodnight.' She winked and sashayed out of the room.

'You've done it now.' Rosey rolled her eyes. 'Don't say I didn't warn you. As for having nothing to wear, Mum owns so many clothes she filled up her own wardrobe ages ago and has taken over the guest bedroom wardrobe too. If she buys much more, I can see her spilling up into the attic.'

'Duly noted, ma'am.' Zach trailed his hand down her neck and toyed with the deep vee of her fluffy black jumper.

'We really shouldn't. Not here.'

'Is that a yes or a no?'

She picked up the Rudolph cushion from the floor and turned it face down. 'We don't want to shock the poor thing.' Rosey lifted her arms and peeled off her top then laid back on the sofa with a playful smile.

Making love on an average-sized sofa was a challenge for anyone, let alone a man of his height, but Zach wasn't about to turn down the offer. If his knees were sore tomorrow, so be it. Rosey loved him. Nothing else mattered. At least that's what he hoped.

Chapter Eighteen

'So who's the lady we've got to thank?' Zach's mother nabbed him the minute his father disappeared upstairs with their suitcases. 'I haven't seen you this happy in ages and we both know it's not just because we're here.'

'Can't hide anything from you, can I?'

'You've tried hard enough over the last couple of years but we saw right through you. Your poor father's been worried sick, although being a hard-headed Broussard man he'd never say so.' Her pale blue eyes turned misty. 'You've inherited his stubbornness.'

Zach wasn't dumb enough to argue that no one matched Marie Broussard when it came to determination; she simply covered hers with a veneer of southern good manners.

'Go fix us some decent coffee and I'll drag Pierre back down here so you won't have to tell the whole story twice.'

He left his mother checking out the view from the spectacular panel of floor-to-ceiling windows along one wall which showed off Joe's land. Zach laid a tray and added a plate of Cornish gingerbreads; spicy and crunchy, they were his new obsession – next to Rosey. He carried their coffee tray back in and set it down on the gnarled oak table Joe had made himself from wood reclaimed from another of his old farm buildings.

'See, I told you so he's grinning like a loon.' Marie tugged her husband down to sit by her on the black leather L-shaped sofa that dominated the living space.

'I saw it too but I figured he'd tell us the reason in his own time.'

His mother snorted. 'I'm not waiting any longer.' Zach got the full force of her stern gaze. 'Pour the coffee then get busy talking.'

'Yes, Mama.' Being a worldwide heartthrob made no difference. He was a regular guy who loved his mother, so when she ordered him to jump, he jumped. Once he fixed everyone up, he took a gulp of his own coffee, scalding his mouth in the process. 'Her name is Rosey. Rosey Teague.' His heart raced. 'And I … well, I love her. I know it sounds crazy when I haven't been here long, and after the funk I've been in the past couple of years, but—'

'No disrespect to Laura but you never sounded this way talking about her. You know I had my reservations when you married but I kept my mouth shut because your papa warned me not to interfere.'

Brave man.

'I want to hear every last thing about Rosey and then you'd better get her up here to meet us.'

By the time he finished, his mother was wiping away happy tears but his stoic father hadn't said a word. Zach noticed his coffee sat untouched though: something which never happened. It was a longstanding family joke that Pierre would be better off hooking himself up to a coffee IV first thing in the morning and be done with it. Back home he favoured the strong coffee and chicory mix popular in New Orleans, but would usually knock back anything on offer.

'You'd better get on the phone to her quick, son.' Pierre bit a chunk out of his gingerbread. 'Decent cookies, these.'

'Hang on.' His mother's smile dimmed. 'You know I'm happy for you, but have you told her about—'

'No.' Zach cut her off. 'Not yet.' He stared at his feet. 'I will soon. Promise.'

'She needs to know before you two get tangled up any closer.'

'Yeah. I get that, okay?' A resigned sigh slipped out of him. 'I'll … um, step outside a minute. Sometimes the reception isn't great in the house.' The brisk easterly wind cut in across the farmyard and cooled him down in a heartbeat. They were as inland here as anywhere in Cornwall got, only about eleven miles or so as the crow flies, but the weather was still affected by both coasts.

'Everything all right?' Joe ambled across from the house carrying a pot of paint in one hand and a wide, fat brush in the other.

'Yeah. My folks want to meet Rosey sooner rather than later so I thought I'd better give her a quiet heads up. Are you and Beth good?'

'Yep. Couldn't be better. She made me see I was being an idiot.' Joe gave a wry smile. 'Beth used the words annoying, stubborn and old-fashioned, then said I should be grateful that she loved me enough to take on the challenge of straightening me out.' He held up the paint tin. 'She picked this colour. It's for the outside of the buttery walls. Beth said it matched the name and I didn't argue.'

'Smart guy.' Zach chuckled. 'By the way, what're you two doin' on Christmas Day?'

'I'm not sure yet. Beth's got the day off but she won't be seeing her family in Dorset until they come down for the panto.' A flutter of panic skittered across his face. 'Bloody hell, I need to get her a present. I hadn't given it a thought and there's only four days left to shop.' He groaned. 'I hate shopping at the best of times, but for Beth? That's a minefield. Too personal and that'll be wrong, but not enough and I'm back to being a thoughtless idiot again.'

'We're in the same boat then. I'll ask my mom to give us some clues.'

'Cheers.' Joe looked sheepish. 'You're going to say I'm mad but … I'm tossing up whether to go ahead and buy a ring and propose over the holidays. I mean why not? We love each other and we've wasted enough time already.'

'You're not mad at all, and if you're ready then go for it and more power to you.' He clapped his friend's shoulder. 'While we're throwing supposedly crazy ideas around, there's somethin' I want to ask you. I was goin' to wait until after the holidays to bring it up but hear me out a minute. Would you consider selling me one of your hay fields so I can build a house?' Joe's jaw dropped. 'I've fallen in love with Cornwall as well as Rosey … I've decided I want to settle here.'

'Well, I'll be buggered!' Joe chuckled. 'Of all the things I thought you might be going to say that wouldn't have crossed my mind.' His forehead wrinkled in a frown. 'I always swore that I'd never sell any of my family's land, but maybe it wouldn't be the end of the world. I can't deny the cash would be useful.'

'Think about it. Talk it over with Beth. I don't want to push you for a decision, but if your answer is yes, it would be kind of cool to surprise Rosey with the news over Christmas.'

'I won't make you wait. Promise. Anyway, you'd better get on and make your phone call.' Joe turned to walk away then stopped. 'Were you asking about Christmas Day for any particular reason?'

'I'm cookin' for my folks, Rosey and Anna. Why don't you and Beth come along too?'

'No way. You don't need us butting in.'

'Oh yes I do.' Zach grinned. 'Look on it as helpin' me out. It'll take the heat off us so we won't have all three parents interrogating us over the roast turkey.'

'In that case, we'll be happy to come along.' Joe winced. 'Oh hell, will I never learn?'

'I get it. What you *really* meant to say was: "that sounds great but I'll have to check with Beth first then get back to you."'

They burst out laughing.

'You'd better get on with your painting.' Zach shooed him away. 'Don't be surprised if my dad wanders over to see what you're doing. He'll have a brush in his hand before you know where you are.'

'Bit of a handyman, is he?'

'Plumber by trade but can do just about anything.' He grimaced. 'Unlike me. Pretending to do stuff is all I'm good for.'

Joe angled him a hard stare. 'Don't put yourself down. The buttery wouldn't be as far on as it is without your help.'

'I only followed instructions.'

'Yep, but you did it well and took your time to get it right.' He kicked a stone away with the toe of his rubber boot. 'Funny, isn't it?'

'What?'

'Here you are with probably millions in the bank and jealous of your old man because he can fix a leaky toilet. I bet he'd say you were an idiot if he heard you now.'

'Maybe.' Zach shrugged. 'I'll see you later.' Before his mum came to see why he was taking so long, he got Rosey on the phone. 'Hey, sweetheart. We've got a date with destiny tonight.'

'Stop playing with your hair.' Anna swiped Rosey's comb away. 'You're the one who stupidly got all chopped off. It won't grow any longer by you tugging on it.'

'You were the one who suggested I had it done in the first place!'

Her hair had been a sensitive topic since she'd revealed the drastic new style. Anna's first reaction was that the only good thing about it was that Rosey was tucked away behind the piano. It would have been a different story if she was one of the pantomime leading lights.

'I know that but I didn't expect you to get it quite that short. Anyway, you look lovely and if Zach's parents think any different, that's their problem. Zach will stand up for you unlike your useless worm of a father.'

The first time her mum met Brian and Leonora Teague, they'd made it clear she wasn't good enough for their precious son and the only reason they weren't objecting to the marriage was because Anna had got herself pregnant – as though Will had nothing to do with that.

'Off you go.'

'Will you be okay on your own?'

'Oh my love, you've got to stop this.'

'What?'

'Worrying about me.' Anna's frown deepened. 'I've got a nice bottle of wine in the fridge and a big bag of salt and vinegar crisps. There's an old Cary Grant film on the telly so I'm going to wallow in a bit of old-fashioned romance.'

'Good.'

Once she was in the car, she took a few calming breaths and practised her smile before setting off up the road. Rosey turned into the farm and immediately slammed on the brakes. A car belonging to the out of hours doctor service stood in front of the barn and a few people were milling around. She spotted Joe, left the car parked where it was and jumped out.

'What's going on? Where's Zach?'

'He's fine. It's his dad.'

'Oh God, is he—'

'I'm fine, ma'am.' A stocky, grey-haired man pushed away the smart bottle-blonde woman holding onto his arm. 'At least I would be if everyone would stop makin' a fuss about nothin'. You must be Zach's girl.'

Before she could reply, Zach appeared.

'I'm sorry about all this, honey. My dumb Papa fell off a ladder he wasn't supposed to be on – bumped his head and did something to his ankle.' He cracked a smile. 'Shame it doesn't seem to have knocked any sense into him.'

'I need you to come inside now so I can check you over or I'll call the ambulance to take you to hospital.' A thin Indian lady with fierce, dark eyes squared up to Zach's father. 'Which is it to be? The Christmas silly season has started and A&E at Treliske will be overrun with drunks. You'll be stuck there for hours.'

Rosey noticed the lady she assumed to be Zach's mother whispering in
her husband's ear. The fight drained out of his stubborn expression and he let himself be led away.

'I expect Mama threatened to cancel his LSU Tigers season tickets. She knows her man.' Zach chuckled. 'I'll explain later.' He hitched an arm around her shoulder. 'Let's go inside before we freeze to death.'

'What was your father doing up a ladder in the first place?'

‘He was bored already and insisted on helping Joe paint the old buttery.’

Everyone congregated in the barn and Rosey stayed back out of the way. She felt a tiny bit grateful for the minor emergency that had smoothed over this first meeting. The doctor announced Zach’s father had no sign of any concussion but should be kept a firm eye on overnight. She gave strict instructions for him to rest, elevate his sprained ankle and treat it with ice, then she left.

‘Any chance of an old guy gettin’ a drink around here?’ Pierre boomed.

‘That would be a no,’ Marie snapped. ‘You’re on painkillers.’

‘I haven’t taken any yet, have I?’

‘But you’re going to. Zach, fetch your papa a glass of water.’ She waved around a bottle of tablets. ‘Otherwise, Rosey will think you don’t have the sense you were born with, won’t you, honey?’

‘Uh …’

‘Mama, don’t bring her into this,’ Zach warned. ‘You might as well give in now, Papa. I’d prefer Rosey to get a good impression of you both so she won’t turn and run as fast as she can in the opposite direction.’

‘I won’t do that. Promise.’

‘Good. Now let’s get on with dinner before you pair crash out.’ He nodded at his parents. ‘I can’t believe jet lag hasn’t slayed you yet.’

‘The Broussards are made of tough stuff, boy. You should know that.’ Pierre’s brag was ruined by a loud, gaping yawn.

Rosey’s optimism blossomed. Act Three traditionally threw a new spanner in the works of true love but the star-crossed lovers triumphed in the end. She crossed her fingers that she and Zach wouldn't prove the exception to the golden rule.

Chapter Nineteen

Zach manoeuvred Joe's old Land Rover into one of the last free parking spaces outside the supermarket. His friend had suggested they use it instead of Zach's pristine rental so he wouldn't be held responsible if it was scratched or worse. Joe had warned him that Asda would be a battleground.

'It's only three days until Christmas so you'll experience us Brits at our worst. Doesn't matter if you're there when they first open the doors, it'll still be a zoo. It's every man for himself, especially when it comes to parking. Anyone would think we're stocking up for the apocalypse instead of a stupid turkey dinner.'

His father was still gingerly hopping around on his dodgy ankle so they'd left him at home this morning to rest. Not that Pierre was given a choice. Marie had insisted he'd get in everyone's way and that they were perfectly capable of buying the right ingredients. Zach had done his best to smooth things over and hoped the Cornish shops sold what they needed or there'd be trouble.

'So are you gonna tell me yours and Rosey's plans now? The pair of you were mighty cagey the other night.'

He should have expected her to ask a lot of awkward, pointed questions.

'No, because we don't have any yet.' That brought an annoyed look to her face. 'At least nothing definite. Don't push.'

'I'm not!' Her face turned bright red. 'If you had kids, you'd understand how hard it is to see them miserable and not being able to do a damn thing about it.' Tears welled up in her eyes. 'Oh my love, I'm sorry—'

'Yeah, I know. Forget it please, Mama. It is what it is.' He stared out of the window in a struggle to regain control of his emotions.

'Oh sweetie, I'm sorry for bein' an interfering old thing, but—'

'You're not old, Mama.'

She broke into a peal of rich, throaty laughter. 'But interfering is a yes?'

He mimicked zipping his mouth shut. 'We need to hurry up. The vultures are stripping the shelves bare while we're sitting here.' Hordes of determined shoppers swarmed through the car park, wrangling overflowing trolleys with little regard for the parked cars. 'There is something I do need your help with though. Another Christmas present idea for Rosey. I've got one underway already, but it's a work in progress and might not come off. I'll share it with you when the time's right.'

'We'll battle the grocery store first then chat about it on the way home.'

An hour later they staggered out, exhausted but triumphant. The Cornish shoppers hadn't stood a chance. His determined mother beat one woman to the last tin of pineapple slices, essential for his father's glazed ham, and sweet talked a gullible man into letting her have a bag of frozen peas he'd swiped from under another shopper's nose. Zach wrangled the mountain of bags into the car. 'You were brutal back there.'

'Sometimes you have to fight for what you want. You know that.'

'Yeah. I do.' He joined the queue of cars inching back onto the main road. The roundabout was blocked with bumper-to-bumper traffic. 'So Rosey's present?' Zach heaved a sigh. 'Oh. I forgot to mention that I need ideas for Joe too.'

'Joe? I've only met him briefly and haven't seen his girlfriend, so how am I—'

'You'll do it, Mama. I've got faith in you.' He brushed a kiss on her cheek.

'You can't get around me that way.' The half-hearted protest didn't fool him. She loved nothing better than being needed.

'Oh yeah, I can.' Zach put his foot down and edged into a narrow gap between two cars.

'Just for an hour? Please.'

Rosey steeled herself against her mother's wheedling tone.

'You'll be through by eight o'clock at the latest.'

'All right. But I don't care how many you have turn up. An hour is my limit.' She might have known she'd give in. 'I'm going to change and I'll text Zach so he knows to pick me up from the hall.'

'You're an angel. I won't forget this.'

There would be a million other similar pleas before this year's pantomime was one for the record books. In her bedroom she stripped off the old jeans and baggy sweatshirt she'd worn all day and replaced them with dark grey trousers and an emerald-green cashmere jumper she'd picked up on sale last week. She sprayed mousse in her hand and ran it through her shorter hair with her fingers.

'Come on, lovey! People will be waiting to get in and it's a rough old night,' Anna yelled up the stairs. 'We'll need our macs.'

It was rare for Cornwall to enjoy the cold, crisp white Christmases beloved of all the holiday films and glitter-laden Christmas cards. This week's miserable weather was far more normal. Howling wind. Lashing rain. A damp cold that seeped into people's bones.

They trudged along the street but, despite her mum's dire predictions, no one else had beaten them to it. Rosey tinkered on the piano, running through a few ideas for new songs while Anna bustled around backstage. By a quarter to eight it was clear no one was coming. It was hard to stomach her mother's disappointment.

'You might as well ask Zach to pick you up early.' Anna heaved a sigh.

Rosey's conscience pricked. She felt mean leaving her mum to walk home to an empty house. 'Why don't you come with me and Zach for a drink?'

'Don't be daft, you don't want me there being a gooseberry.'

She pulled out her mobile. 'I'll suggest he brings his parents along and we can introduce them to the delights of British pub life.' Zach's swift reply came in the form of emojis – a sequence of exclamation points, question marks, a sad face and eventually the thumbs up she'd known would eventually come. 'They're coming. We'll go ahead and grab a table, Mum.'

'Zach's a good man.'

Rosey wouldn't argue with that.

The first person she recognised in the crowded pub was Mike Blamey surrounded by a group of his like-minded friends. By their loud voices and raucous laughter, she guessed they'd been drinking for a while. Of course, the only free table was right next to them.

'Hiya Red, come and join us. We could do with some female company, couldn't we, lads?'

She hated his nickname for her because it smacked of a familiarity she'd never encouraged. Out of the corner of her eye, she spotted Zach and his parents coming through the door and lifted her hand to wave.

'Oi, watch out everyone, the Yanks are here. Lock up your daughters,' Mike jeered. 'Your mothers too.' He ogled Anna. 'I hear they ain't too fussy.'

'You need to watch your mouth, pal.' Pierre hobbled towards them. 'If it wasn't for brave men like my father, y'all would be speaking German.' His face mottled with anger.

'Didn't fucking turn up 'til the last minute as usual though, did they, old man?' Mike swayed on his feet and he stumbled towards Zach. 'Aren't you going to introduce me to our so-called saviours?'

'Sure.' Zach's icy tone made her cringe. 'Mama. Papa.' He turned to his parents. 'I'd like you to meet Mike Blamey. When he's not one of the stars of the pantomime, he's an ill-mannered lout. But don't worry, he's not typical – all the other Cornish people I've met are decent folk.'

'Mind your mouth, pretty boy.' Mike made a half-hearted swing at Zach. 'Who'd you think you are anyway, coming over here with your fancy Hollywood ways, taking over our show and every other bloody thing?'

'That's enough, Blamey.' Jock Stewart barrelled out from behind the bar and grabbed Mike's arm. 'I've warned you before. Out.'

'You can stick your crappy pub where the sun don't shine. I'll spend my money somewhere else.' Mike smirked at Zach. 'Enjoy your little redhead. I hear it's natural all the way if you know what I mean. I s'ppose you've got women offering it to you on a plate everywhere you go. Big film star. Money up to your eyeballs. No inconvenient wife to make a fuss if you spread it around.' He leered at Rosey. 'It's all working out well for you, isn't it? You came running back home with your tail between your legs when your career went down the toilet and now you've hooked up with a multi-millionaire. I'd say you hit the jackpot.'

She felt the colour draining from her face, and out of the corner of her eye she caught a couple of Mike's friends sniggering.

Zach grabbed Mike by his shirt collar. 'You'd better damn well apologise to Rosey and my parents right now.'

'Or what? You going to make me?' Mike wriggled away and raised his fists in front of his thick chest. 'Here or outside?' When Zach didn't rush to answer, his coarse laughter filled the room. 'Not so flaming big now, are you? Bloody Americans. All the same. Lily-livered cowards, the lot of you.'

In slow motion she watched Mike throw a punch at the exact same moment as Pierre stepped in front of his son. It caught Zach's father on the nose and bright red blood spurted everywhere. The force sent Pierre stumbling back against Jock, who had the presence of mind to stop him falling to the ground.

'You bas—'

'Zach.' Rosey kept a tight grip on his arm. 'Don't make things worse.' People were taking pictures with their phones and she could visualise the unwelcome publicity already.

Pierre straightened his shoulders, dabbed at his nose with a tissue and flashed a broad grin. 'Well, I sure didn't expect to be getting' in a bar brawl at my age.' He glowered at Mike. 'Don't think I couldn't have taken you down either, punk, if I'd seen that punch coming. I was an All-State high school wrestling champ back in the day.'

‘I still haven’t heard that apology.’ Zach’s voice throbbed with anger. ‘We’re waiting.’

‘You heard the man.’ Jock prodded Mike’s arm.

‘Yeah, yeah. I’m sorry. Spoke out of turn, didn’t I? It was the drink talking.’ He gave Zach’s father a shamefaced look. ‘I never meant to hit you. You okay?’

‘Yeah. I’ll live.’ Pierre cautiously touched the tissue to his nose again. ‘It’s stopped bleeding.’

Marie glared at Mike. ‘If you can’t hold your drink, you need to steer well clear of it. Now get off with you and leave decent people to enjoy themselves.’

Mike’s bleary gaze swept around the room as though he expected someone to stand up for him but there was dead silence. Jock tightened his grip on Mike’s arm and frogmarched him over to the door.

‘And you can stay out. You’re banned.’

‘But it’s bloody Christmas!’

‘You should’ve thought about that before you ran your mouth.’ Jock glared back at Mike’s companions. ‘And if you lot cause any trouble, you can join him.’ Nobody moved. One shove and he was out of sight.

‘Well, y’all promised us an entertaining evening but I sure didn’t expect it to be this interesting.’ Pierre chuckled.

‘C’mon Papa, sit down.’ Zach manoeuvred his father over to their table and pulled out a chair. ‘How about you say hi now to Rosey’s mother, Anna? It’s not quite how I expected y’all to meet but this is Cornwall.’

She’d been too caught up in all the fuss to remember about introductions.

‘Are you all right, my ‘andsome?’ Anna fussed over Pierre. ‘I’m afraid Mike’s a bit of a hot-head but you should see him in a fancy silk dress, colourful wig, high heels and fake boobs.’

Rosey choked back a laugh. 'Mum, you need to explain.'

'Oops! Silly me. Mike is the dame in the pantomime so every year he dresses up as a rather over-the-top woman.'

'Sure sounds crazy.' Pierre smiled at his wife. 'I reckon we should stop on long enough to see this mad show.'

Her heart sunk. She already liked Zach's parents a lot but there still was almost a month to go before the pantomime.

'We'll talk about it later, dear.' Marie nodded at Zach. 'Off you go and fetch us some drinks.'

'Make mine a scotch. Double.' Pierre patted Anna's hand. 'This poor lady needs a good stiff drink too after all that palaver.'

They'd clue him in later on the fact that her mother thrived on drama.

'You're not havin' any scotch,' Marie intervened. 'You're on—'

'I know, honey, but this is medicinal.'

'I give up.'

'That's rare.' Zach leaned in to whisper in Rosey's ear. 'He'll pay for this later.'

'I can imagine. There's a lot I can learn from your smart mother.'

'Oh Lord, that I don't need.' He mockingly cringed. 'So much for our quiet drink tonight. This is all your fault.'

'I'd apologise but, quite frankly, I think your dad's rather enjoying the whole thing.' She laughed. 'You're certainly discovering that Christmas in Cornwall is unique no matter which way you look at it.'

Zach kissed her cheek. 'I'm lookin' at the most unique thing in the whole county right now, and wishing we could—'

‘Me too. But it’s not an option tonight. We need our own secret garden to meet in like Aladdin and Jasmine.’

‘Might be a bit cold and damp.’

‘And you complain about me being practical.’ Rosey shook her head. ‘Buy me a large G&T and we’ll put our heads together. Surely we can come up with a better solution than a chilly garden or Mum’s tiny sofa?’

Chapter Twenty

'So what's the plan for today?' Marie nibbled a slice of toast. 'I'm guessin' Christmas Eve in Cornwall isn't that different to back home. Does everyone go to the village church for Midnight Mass?'

'I'm afraid not. It closed years ago according to Rosey.' Zach flipped his father's fried egg and let it cook for another minute before he slid it on the plate. 'She said most people drive down the road to St Merryn instead. It's about five miles away and the only service is at seven o'clock.' He finished cremating his mother's egg the way she preferred and added it to the bacon, sausage and tomato already on her plate. 'I'll be leaving around eleven this morning to take Rosey out for the first part of her Christmas present. You did good to wangle out of her that she's been longing to go to a new posh hotel in Newquay where they serve a fancy afternoon tea. I'd never have thought of anythin' like that in a million years.'

'It was easy. I just picked her brain for ideas of things me and your papa could do while we're here and that's one of the places she mentioned.'

'We're goin' in time for a light lunch then we can take a walk around the grounds before we stuff ourselves with tea and crumpets or whatever's on the menu.'

He hoped his mother wouldn't ask for any details. Even telling her this half-truth face to face taxed his acting talents. 'My other plan has come together pretty darn good too so I'm happy.' The previous evening Joe had told him that he was happy to sell him the land he wanted, with Beth's approval too, and they would settle the details after

Christmas. His friend also confided that he'd bought an engagement ring for Beth but hadn't yet decided when to pop the question.

'Good. You deserve to be. That Joe sure is a sweet man too.' Her voice softened. 'He came in yesterday to show me the watch he's bought Beth. It's one of those fancy hi-tech ones. You get the credit for getting me thinking on those lines when you said she's always fretting about being on time. The gift that'll touch her most though is the antique silver picture frame he's filled with candid shots of them as teenagers and more recent photos. It'll get her here.' Marie tapped over her heart. 'I reckon it won't be long before he's ring shopping.'

It was on the tip of his tongue to say that Joe was one step ahead on that score already, but he held back.

'Don't worry, I didn't try to interfere. I'd never do that!' she exclaimed.

Zach and his dad exchanged wry smiles.

'So what're we going to do today while this one's out gadding about?' She turned to his father.

'I've got cooking to do. You might've sloughed off your part of the Christmas feast to the boy but I'm not trusting him with mine.'

'Fine by me.'

She wouldn't be happy unless she had something to keep her busy and he wracked his brains for a solution. 'Mama, I'm pretty sure Anna could do with an extra pair of hands down at the old church hall. During the year she runs a bingo club there, and on Christmas Eve they put on a lunch for all the regulars. Other folk do the cooking because that's apparently not one of Anna's talents, and Rosey's usually there to help but I negotiated permission for her to miss it this year so you can stand in for her.'

‘Give me Anna’s phone number and I’ll find out what time she wants me.’

Zach kept a poker face when his dad gave a thumbs up sign behind his wife’s back. The plan had the added benefit of getting her out from under her husband’s feet. The two of them together in the kitchen were a combustible combination because both thought they knew best and didn’t hesitate to say so. ‘I’ll send it to you.’ As soon as it popped onto his mother’s phone, she rang up Anna and a brief animated conversation ensued.

‘I’m goin’ to get dressed.’ She sprang up from the table after she’d ended the call. ‘I’ll wear the red sweater with the appliqued poinsettias and black jeans. It’s festive but sensible for working in.’ She frowned. ‘What should I take?’

‘Take? Yourself?’

Marie threw him a withering look. ‘No one would think I’d raised you right. No southerner goes to an event without taking a dish or a gift – usually both.’

‘But you’re goin’ to the lunch to work. You’re not an invited guest.’

She rolled her eyes. ‘You’ve lived in California too long and everyone knows they’re a mannerless lot.’

‘Forget I said anythin’,’ he muttered.

‘I sure will.’ Her attention switched back to his poor father. ‘You made a whack of bread rolls yesterday, didn’t you?’

‘Well yes, but—’

‘I’ll take them. You’ve plenty of time to make another batch today. Wrap them up for me while I get dressed.’ His mother breezed out of the kitchen without waiting for a response.

‘You should’ve seen that coming.’

'Damn woman still catches me out after all these years.' Pierre shook his head.

'It's one reason why you love her. She keeps you on your toes so you don't get bored.'

'You nailed it. She's a keeper, that's for sure. I love every bone in her stubborn body and can't imagine life without her.'

The emotion misting his father's eyes forced him to stare at his uneaten breakfast. He played with a rasher of bacon while he reined his emotions back under control. 'Do you need any help from me before I go out? I've a couple of hours free. I know you've a bunch planned to do and I'm concerned too much standing will aggravate your ankle.'

'Don't be an idiot, son. I'm not in my coffin yet. Nothing's gonna stop me makin' the gumbo and everythin' else we need.'

He wouldn't waste breath pointing out that they'd hardly be short of food.

'You could chop up some of the vegetables and dig out all the utensils I'm gonna need. Then run your mother down to the village and scarper for a bit of afternoon delight with your honey.'

'Papa, I never said—'

'You didn't need to, son.' A far-off look filled his eyes. 'I remember one time we dumped you with your grandparents for a few hours, and I whisked your mother off—'

'Okay Papa, that's enough. I don't need details.'

'Good because you're not gonna get them.' He laughed some more. 'We'd better look busy when your Mama comes down or she'll want to know why and I'm sure not tellin' her!'

‘Wasn’t it kind of Zach’s mum to offer to help out today? She’s a nice woman.’ Anna carried on packing Christmas paper plates and serviettes into a cardboard box. She’d wheedled them out of Albert Rundle at the shop – few people could say no to her mother. ‘Please tell me you’re not carrying that clunky black tote bag with your pretty new dress? My small grey leather one would look so much smarter.’

‘Thanks, but that’s okay.’ She couldn’t explain that she needed room for a clean pair of knickers, make-up and a few other items not to be shared with her mother. ‘I don’t have time to swap it over now anyway. Zach will be here in a few minutes to drop Marie off and pick me up. You’re sure you don’t mind giving her a lift back to the farm later?’

‘Of course not, but aren’t you and Zach a bit early? What time does the hotel start serving lunch?’

‘We thought we’d leave in good time in case the traffic is bad.’ Heat prickled her neck. Other things would be top of the priority list when they checked into the Pirate’s Bay Hotel. Lunch could wait. Zach’s smile zoomed off the charts when he told her this part of her Christmas present was as much for his benefit as hers – a few precious hours on their own with no family or commitments. ‘If we’re too early, we can wander around the shops first.’

‘In Newquay? There’s nothing but surf shops and tourist junk these days, and have you seen the weather?’ Anna gestured out of the window. ‘It’ll be blowing a gale on the north coast.’

She was desperate to change the subject. ‘If you like we could drop you at the hall with all this stuff before we run off?’

'You don't need to bother. I wouldn't want to make you late. Marie and I can manage.'

Rosey spotted Zach's red Land Rover pull up outside and yanked on her black raincoat.

'Hiya.' Zach soon knocked and walked straight in.

These days it struck her as perfectly normal to see the man she'd once swooned over at the cinema and on the cover of all the celebrity magazines strolling into their kitchen, totally at home.

'One assistant as promised.'

Marie engulfed Rosey in a warm hug. 'You're looking mighty pretty. You'd better be off. You don't want to be late for … "lunch".' Her exaggerated wink turned Rosey's face hot enough to roast chestnuts on.

A peal of Anna's raucous laughter followed them out.

'Oh Marie, you wonder about them sometimes, don't you? My girl must think I was born yesterday.'

She wished she could disappear in a puff of smoke like the pantomime genie.

'They forget we were young once too. I remember—'

Zach closed the door behind them. 'We've heard enough. I've had more of the same from my dad already, and even without the full details, it was more than I needed to know.' A brilliant smile lit up his bright blue eyes. It struck her as manifestly unfair that women's laughter lines got dismissed as crow's feet, but Zach's were described in the media as "crinkling appealingly". 'Come on. Let's not waste time.' He hooked an arm around her shoulder and they ran towards his car together, dodging the rain.

A chill ran through her and she shivered. He was talking about their hotel interlude today, but she kept dwelling on the future and wondered if they realistically had one together. Rosey couldn't stop thinking about the mysterious secret Zach kept hinting at. The last time he'd tried to bring up the subject she'd put him off, but she'd tortured herself ever since by imagining what it might be.

'Getting cold feet?' Zach pointed to her strappy sandals. 'Should've worn your fur-lined boots.'

'And how sexy would that've been?' Rosey faked a smile. She wrapped her arms around his neck and drew him down for a kiss. 'I'm relying on you to keep me warm.'

'Ready, willing and able.' His husky laugh brought her back to simply wanting him. For today that would be enough. 'Hop in and let's go enjoy the delights of the Peter Pan Suite.'

'Please tell me you haven't got a twee green outfit with a pointed hat lined up?'

Zach waggled his dark eyebrows. 'I've always fantasised about Tinkerbell tempting me with fairy dust.'

'I suspect the hotel room won't be big enough for aerobatics.' She poked his arm. 'Are we going or not? You're wasting valuable lunch, walk and afternoon tea time, or whatever nonsense we dreamed up to try to pull the wool over our parents' eyes … in vain.' Rosey heaved a sigh. 'Wouldn't it be lovely not to have anyone else to consider and actually have a private life?'

'Private is one thing. Lonely quite another. Problem is they often go together.' A faraway sadness shaded his gaze. 'Give me a loving, nosey family any day. I've largely shut mine out over the last couple of years and regret every minute I've missed with them.' He opened the car door to let her jump in then slid into the driver's seat. 'Don't let's spoil our Christmas treat.'

'Agreed.' Rosey walked her fingers up his firm thigh. 'Come on, Peter Pan. Time to show Tinkerbell what you're made of.'

There was no harm in forgetting the rest of the world for a few hours, she reasoned.

Zach squeezed Rosey's hand tight as cameras flashed in her face. He'd spotted a small crowd of people gathered outside the small hotel but hadn't paid them any attention until they'd climbed out of the car and the swarm moved their way. They were trapped between their parked car and the hotel's front door. No matter how hard he tried, he seemed unable to outrun his celebrity status.

'Hey Zach, do you want to give your side of the story on the pictures we've got of a pub brawl you and your father were involved in? And who's your pretty lady friend? Are we going to hear wedding bells soon? Is she helping you get over your wife's death?'

'Don't answer them,' he whispered. It didn't take long for him to discover the more he gave journalists, the more they thought they were entitled to. A few minutes ago, Rosey had been gloriously happy but now her sunny smile had been replaced by a worried frown. Compassion filled her dark, sultry eyes when she gazed at him, and it tore him up to see she was more concerned about him than herself.

'We've nothing to say except to wish you all a Merry Christmas.' Zach held onto Rosey and used his free hand to push past the media who were still yelling questions after them.

'I'm terribly sorry about this, Mr Broussard.' A harassed-looking, white-faced man held open the glass door and waved them on in. 'I can assure you when I find out who's responsible for gossiping to the press, they'll be severely reprimanded.'

He didn't bother to point out that was equivalent to shutting the stable door after the horse had bolted. Their

Christmas Eve was ruined. No matter what he did or said, nothing would make up for this. Zach wouldn't blame Rosey for having second thoughts about their relationship now she'd been forced face-to-face with the downside of his fame. If she did, he'd be broken all over again.

Chapter Twenty-One

'Don't you dare apologise.' Rosey held up a warning hand to Zach. She thought the hotel manager would never leave them alone. The poor man had said sorry at least a hundred times, insisted on personally showing them to their room and ordered a goggle-eyed maid to bring up a complimentary bottle of champagne. 'None of this was your fault.'

'But—'

'But nothing.'

'It's spoiled our—'

'Only if we let it.' The determined response brought back a trace of Zach's smile. 'We can't do anything about the idiot who made a quick few pounds blabbing about you to those journalists, but we *can* choose how we react.' She waved her watch in his face. 'We've only got five hours before we're due back in Polcarne in time to go to the Christmas Eve service. Personally, I can think of better ways to spend the time than moaning over something we can't change.'

'Like what?' His deep voice turned raspy.

'Oh, come on, Peter Pan. Use your imagination.' Rosey linked her hands behind his neck and tugged him closer. 'Do I need to sprinkle you with fairy dust or will this do the trick?' One roll of her hips and a growl escaped the back of his throat. 'Gosh, I'm terribly hot in this dress.' Zach's eye gleamed. That was a blatant lie, considering the miniscule amount of fabric making up the silver sheath dress she'd tracked down in a vintage shop in Truro.

‘I guess we’d better do somethin’ to help you out.’ His hand reached around her back and worked her zipper down inch by inch to reveal bare skin. A flash of heat ran through her when he used his teeth to drag down the thin shoulder straps, never taking his eyes off her. With the dress pushed down out of his way, it pooled around her feet. ‘Step out of it.’ She obeyed and caught his dark gaze sweeping over her. ‘Well, who would’ve thought Rosey was such a wicked girl?’

Leaving off her underwear had been a brave move for her, but with Zach everything was different.

‘I would’ve pulled the car over to … touch you … and more if I’d known.’ His voice turned to gravel.

‘Ah, but I knew.’ She stroked the front of his shirt and felt a shudder run through him. ‘So are you going to catch up with Tinkerbell?’

‘Oh yeah.’

The sight of his big hands shaking and fumbling with his buttons then struggling to undo his belt boosted her confidence. He almost fell over in his haste to take the rest of his clothes off. Zach dragged them into a deep kiss, moulded his hard body to hers, and his breath heated her skin as he whispered slow, excruciating details of everything he intended to do with her for the next few hours.

‘Talk is cheap.’ Rosey slipped her hand between them and her caress made him groan.

‘I reckon it’s time we stopped talkin’.’ He scooped her off her feet and deposited her in the middle of the four-poster bed before crawling in over her. Zach’s hands pressed deep into the mattress, making his arm muscles bulge. Rosey gasped as he lowered himself, inch by inch, eyes blazing. 'I'm done being Peter Pan. All that never growin' up stuff doesn't appeal. I'd miss this too much.'

'I'm finding the fairy wings a nuisance too. They get in the way. Let's just be us.'

As they came together, Rosey's last conscious thought was that "us" sounded pretty good to her.

Zach nibbled a cucumber sandwich left over from their room service feast and watched Rosey sleep. He'd been determined to give her no cause for complaint about being deprived of lunch or the fancy afternoon tea, not that she would have done, so he'd arranged for a trolley full of food and drink to be delivered.

'Seriously? You're eating again?' Rosey's eyes fluttered open.

'I'm a growing boy. I've got to keep my strength up.'

'What for?' The flirtatious question made his body stir and he smiled as her gaze travelled south. 'Wow, you do have stamina. All those hours you spent in the gym are still paying dividends.'

When they weren't making love, they'd fitted in time to talk, and one of the things that seemed to surprise her most was the disciplined life he'd led when at the top of his career. Actors who over-indulged in the party scene, drink and drugs rarely lasted long. Even when he wasn't filming, Zach's days were structured down to the last minute between the nutritionist who created a focused diet plan, the personal trainer who led him through a gruelling workout every single day, and meetings with his agent, manager and publicist.

He tossed the remains of the sandwich back on the plate then whipped the duvet off Rosey. 'If you want proof, you can have it.'

'I suppose we might have time.'

'Only suppose?'

'Depends how fast you can be. Remember we both need to shower and turn back into something resembling respectable people again.'

'You're talkin' to a man used to performing on a tight schedule. One Take-Zach they used to call me. Directors loved me because I didn't hang around and got on with the job.' He put a palm to her breast and she arched into his touch.

'I wouldn't want to be the one to destroy your reputation so we'd better get on with it.'

'Yes, ma'am.' He settled over her with a satisfied groan. 'Yeah, that's better. Look at me, Rosey.' Her velvety eyes, soft and glazed with desire, were all the incentive he needed.

Afterwards, he cradled her in his arms and knew in his gut he never wanted to let her go. *Ever*.

'Do you think the press will have given up and gone home?'

'Yeah.' He smoothed a stray strand of hair away from her face. 'For a start, the manager knows I'll have his balls on a plate if they're still hangin' around.' Zach regretted being so blunt. 'Sorry, honey. I didn't mean—'

'I know. It's just …' A sigh slipped out of her. 'Nothing's ever straightforward, is it?'

'Doesn't mean we can't push through it and come out the other side okay.'

'You really think so?'

Zach's heart thumped. 'Yeah. Yeah, I do. Let's get through Christmas and the pantomime, then we'll talk. Really talk.' A flicker of worry ran through him. He'd been a coward and avoided a certain subject which might end up being a deal-breaker, but he couldn't put it off much longer. 'If that's all right with you? I don't mean to take you for granted. Ever. It's what I did with Laura … or at least she thought so.'

'Well, trust me. I know what being taken for granted feels like and you've never done that with me, but if you want to tell me more, I'm happy to listen.'

He needed to unburden himself. 'We'd been married about two years when I asked Laura to join me in Australia for three months while I was filming because I didn't want us to be apart so long.'

'That was a loving gesture … but I'm guessing she didn't see it that way?'

He couldn't let her see Laura as the baddie in all this. 'I'd forgotten the dates were right in the middle of when she was leading a team to Mount Khuiten in Mongolia. When she pointed it out, I made the biggest mistake ever and casually suggested that, as she was in charge, she could consider changing the dates.'

'I'm taking a guess that wouldn't have worked?'

'No. In very sarcastic terms, she told me they'd calculated the most suitable time frame for the weather to achieve optimum success.' Zach shrugged. 'Then Laura stuck in a barb that perhaps I could suggest the director altered the filming dates. That couldn't happen either, of course. I admitted I'd been thoughtless and urged her to forget it, but it put a barrier between us which never quite went away.'

'That's a shame, but there's got to be give and take in every relationship. She should've given you a break.' Her smile blossomed again. 'I think we need to hurry up and try out the fancy shower.'

'We?'

'Oh yes, absolutely.' She batted her eyelashes in fun. 'You don't want me to get scared in there on my own, do you?'

'I sure don't.' Zach flexed his muscles. 'One protector at your service.'

Rosey was out of breath when they reached the church. 'I must be the same colour as my name after rushing around like that.'

'And whose fault is it we're late?' Zach whispered.

'You played your part.' Her arch response made him chuckle. After the shower that turned into a whole lot more, they broke every speed limit on the drive back from Newquay to make it here on time. She hoped the candlelight would be forgiving of her damp hair and sketchy make-up job. 'Come on. They've saved us seats.' She dragged him in through the ancient stone doorway, framed with large boughs of holly bursting with fat red berries and threaded through with white lights. Rosey scanned the packed church for their group.

'You're never going to spot your mom in all this crowd.'

'There she is.' The light from the flickering candles, set in wooden frames stretched between the elegant stone pillars, picked up her mother's distinctive outfit. 'I'm fairly certain no one else is wearing a fluffy white fake-fur hat and matching floor-length coat. It's Doctor Zhivago and the snowy Russian winter tonight.'

'I sure love your mom.'

'I do too … at least most of the time.' People stared and pointed as Zach followed her down the side aisle but she studiously ignored them. 'Can we sneak past you please, Mr Rundle?' The shopkeeper tucked his legs under his chair. Every year the villagers made a point of getting to the church early and reserving enough seats for the group from Polcarne to sit together. It helped to make up for not having their own service.

'I'm some sorry your treat today got spoiled.' Anna whipped out her phone and shoved it in Rosey's face. 'Crying shame, it is. Why they can't mind their own business is beyond me.'

She stared at the candid pictures of Zach glaring at the journalists then pushing past with a grim expression on his face. Rosey looked like a scared rabbit. She collapsed in the seat next to her mother in a daze.

'Pierre doesn't seem bothered at his fame by proxy but Marie's not best pleased, I can tell you.'

'I can imagine.'

Thankfully, it was now that the vicar appeared to announce the first hymn so the conversation stopped. They stood up and Zach draped his arm around her shoulder. The warmth seeping through from his body pressed up against hers and the hint of hotel soap in the air let her blot out everything except for being here with him. They sang the familiar carols together and his melodious tenor voice made more than a few people around them turn and look. The most touching moment came when half a dozen young children dressed as angels, in the usual white bedsheets, tinsel crowns and glittery cardboard wings, sang 'Away in a Manger'. That made all the rushing around to get here worthwhile.

'That sure was a pretty service,' Marie declared when they filed out at the end. 'According to your mom, it's traditional to eat some of those funny mince pie things y'all like and drink sherry now. Of course my man's insisting we make room for some of his food too so you'd better have a good appetite.'

Thankfully, it was a crisp, dry night for a change so they stood around outside talking for a while before making the short drive back to the farm. Rosey sniffed the air as they entered the barn.

'What's that delicious smell?'

'That's my gumbo.' Pierre boasted. 'C'mere and I'll show you.' He dragged her away from Zach into the kitchen where a huge pot simmered on the range. 'Back home we always host a Christmas Eve open house for our friends. It's my way of honouring the New Orleans tradition of having watch parties to see the bonfires lit up all along the levees.'

'Zach told me about that. It must be an amazing sight.'

'It sure is and it's been too long since we did it as a family.' His eyes twinkled. 'Maybe next year we can all go?'

'Maybe.' Rosey left it there.

'Come on you lot,' he shouted out to Marie and Anna, who were still talking nineteen to the dozen in the living room. 'We're havin' the chicken and andouille sausage gumbo and fresh homemade rolls tonight, and I'll cook the rest of our special foods for tomorrow.'

'No one makes gumbo like my papa.' Zach joined them. 'It's equivalent to your Cornish pasties in that every family has their own recipe and they all think theirs is the best.'

Pierre put a scoop of plain rice in the bottom of the bowl then ladled over a generous helping of the steaming soup and passed it to her with a spoon. 'Here you go.'

The tempting aroma reminded Rosey she hadn't eaten anything today apart from a few delicate afternoon tea treats earlier. She dived in.

'Beware, he goes heavy on the cayenne.' The words had barely left Zach's mouth before the first burst of spice hit the back of her throat and she almost choked.

'Wow, that's powerful.' She grabbed the glass of water he passed over and gulped it down.

'Should we warn your mom?'

'Not at all. She'll love it.' Rosey laughed. 'She's passionate about spicy foods and makes a mean Vindaloo curry I won't touch with a bargepole. One of the few things she *can* cook.'

Zach lowered his voice. 'I'll let you into a little secret. I add an extra dollop of rice to mine to tone it down.'

'I'll remember next time.'

'There'll be plenty of those.' His face heated. 'At least I hope so.'

'Me too.'

'C'mon you two, stop drooling over each other and stick your coats back on.' Marie broke them apart. 'Your papa's got a surprise.'

Rosey raised an eyebrow at Zach.

'Don't ask me. They're a law unto themselves.' He took her bowl and set it down on the counter with his. 'Come on. Let's go see what he's dreamed up.'

Everyone got wrapped up and headed out to the farmyard where Pierre led the way up to the first field and stopped at the gate.

'Y'all stop here and keep looking up the hill.' He tramped off on his own.

Zach settled Rosey in front of him and wrapped his arms around her. 'Wow! I'll be darned.'

‘Oh my.’ Rosey stared at the huge bonfire blazing in front of them; it must have been visible for miles.

‘Trust Papa.’ He checked his watch. ‘Bang on midnight.’ Zach drew her around to face him. ‘Merry Christmas.’

‘Merry Christmas.’ They kissed, and over his shoulder she caught everyone watching them. For good measure, she kissed him again.

Chapter Twenty-Two

Zach closed the oven door on the turkey, poured a mug of strong coffee and took it outside. Despite not getting to bed until almost two o'clock, he wasn't in the least bit tired. This place suited Christmas. It was the timelessness of the land spread out around him, brown and dormant, waiting for spring to bring it back to life. He found it easy to imagine previous generations of Joe's family celebrating the season in a similar way to themselves. No doubt they too had good food, natural decorations taken from the hedges and trees, and lights to banish the darkness of winter.

'You're lookin' mighty sad, son. Cheer up. It's Christmas.' His father came to join him.

'I'm not sad, Papa, just thoughtful.'

'You love that girl, don't you?'

'Yeah. Yeah, I do.'

'And this place?'

Zach nodded. 'I could make a life here. A good one. But that doesn't mean I'm goin' to cut myself off from you and Mama again.'

'I know that,' Pierre scoffed. 'You've got that nonsense out of your head at last and we're damn glad of it. I could've cheerfully strung you up for putting your mother through the wringer that way. Didn't do me a pile of good either.' He angled Zach a questioning look. 'You can't escape your past though. The run-in with those journalists at the hotel proved that.'

'Yeah, I know, but Rosey took it in her stride so helped me do the same. Eventually they'll lose interest.'

'But giving up your career for good? Are you sure about that?' Deep frown lines creased his father's face. 'You come to life when you're acting.' Pierre spread out his hands. 'These get itchy if they're not kept busy. You don't think you'll be the same? I know you said about voiceovers and the like, but I'm not convinced it'll be enough.'

He tossed up in his head how much to say. It wasn't that he wanted to keep secrets from his mother, but she tended to take over and dole out unasked for advice. His father was a good listener. A man of few words but meaningful ones. 'I haven't sat around on my backside the last two years, Papa. Amongst a few other things, I've written the first draft of a children's book and have ideas to turn it into a series.'

'You sly devil.' His father chuckled. 'Reckon it's any good?'

'Perhaps.' Zach shrugged.

'You shown it to anyone else?'

'Nah, haven't had the nerve yet.'

'What's your next move then?'

Zach grinned. 'Get off my ass and knock the book into shape. Then take the plunge, I guess.'

'You could make it your New Year's resolution if you go in for all that nonsense?'

He sensed his father wanting to say more. 'What's on your mind?'

'I guess maybe I should keep my mouth shut … but did you see Rosey's face at church last night when those little kiddies dressed up as angels were singing? She needs to know about—'

'Am I missing something?' His mother bustled out. 'I found this little girl wonderin' where you'd disappeared to.'

Over Marie's shoulder he spied Rosey and knew she'd overheard something – how much he couldn't be sure, but her smile didn't reach her dark violet eyes and the tightness around her mouth spoke volumes. Zach doubted they'd be lucky enough to seize a minute alone in the chaos of Christmas Day, so for now he'd have to do a good enough acting job that she wouldn't realise he'd rumbled her.

A quiver of disquiet stirred in Rosey's stomach. Zach and his dad looked like naughty children caught out in mischief. He surely wasn't planning to do something as stupid as proposing in front of everyone today after they'd agreed to take things slowly?

'Hi honey, you look gorgeous. Love the dress.' The appreciation in his eyes momentarily pushed away her fears. 'That dark green is awesome on you.'

'You can thank Samira because she saw me gazing longingly at it in the shop window and convinced me to buy it.' Remembering the rest of her conversation with the pantomime's princess brought another trickle of unease.

'What's wrong?'

'I'm trying not to think about next month's credit card bill.' This wasn't the time to broach the subject of Samira's problems.

'Oh, it'll work out, my lover.' Her ever-optimistic mother joined in. 'Things do. Let's bring our stuff in from the car and get Christmas started.'

'I'll give y'all a hand.' Zach's offer was interrupted by a knock on the door.

The arrival of Joe and Beth, loaded down with presents and more food, put a definite end to any serious conversation and she allowed herself to be swept into the general goodwill.

Hours later, they all sprawled around the living room swearing they'd never eat again. The buffet table had groaned under the weight of Zach's roast turkey with all the trimmings along with his father's generous contributions. Apparently, a giant ham baked with Coke, brown sugar and pineapple, oyster stuffing, cauliflower cheese, and what Pierre informed them were petits pois – French style peas cooked down in a roux – along with mouth-watering bread rolls with lashings of butter, were an essential part of the Cajun tradition. No wonder her mother was shouted down when she suggested getting the puddings out.

'So presents or a long walk?' Anna was still chirpy. 'Which is it to be first?'

'I vote for a walk before I turn into a blob of lard,' Beth groaned.

'Can't have that, can we?' Joe wrestled her onto his lap. 'Bloody hell, the woman's right.' He squeezed her hips. 'It's happening as we speak.'

Rosey applauded the well-deserved smack he received.

'A walk it is then.' Her mother lumbered to her feet.

'I'm gonna pass. My ankle's still dodgy.'

Zach scoffed at his father's excuse and whispered in Rosey's ear, 'Funny how it didn't bother him when he and Joe built that bonfire, or while standing up to cook all the food he stuffed us with.'

Anna turned to Marie. 'How about we have a stroll together and leave the young ones to do their own thing?'

Amid the bustle of everyone getting wrapped up to go outside, Zach tugged Rosey away.

'Don't argue when I tell Joe and Beth we want to go off on our own.'

'Why would I?'

'Because you might think I was being rude or somethin'. There's a good reason. Promise.'

Rosey's churning stomach had nothing to do with the amount of food she'd consumed. She'd spell things out clearly once they were away from everyone else. Instead of being the best Christmas in years, it could turn out to be memorable for completely the wrong reasons.

'What? No, that's not what this is …' Zach bit back a laugh. He'd no clue why Rosey had jumped to such a bizarre conclusion, but he realised, if he wasn't careful, whatever he said now would be taken the wrong way.

They'd tramped over Joe's fields hand in hand until they reached the far boundary of the farm. If it wasn't for this awkwardness hanging between them, it would be perfect. Blue skies. The right amount of crispness in the air to make them grateful for their thick coats without shivering. An occasional squawking seagull swooped in from the coast to peck at something in the ground before taking off again. Not another person in sight.

'I swear I didn't engineer this to propose to you. Not today.' Zach hoped that left the door cracked open the right amount. 'Joe confided in me that he's bought an engagement ring for Beth, and yesterday he swore me to secrecy and told me he'd decided to ask her to marry him out here today where his dad proposed to his mom. He also asked me help keep everyone else away so he didn't have an audience.'

'Oh God, I'm sorry.' Tears welled in her eyes. 'I've made a complete idiot of myself. I know we agreed we weren't going to rush into anything but I thought … when I saw you and your dad whispering together and then … Joe dragging Beth off …' Rosey's face couldn't have grown any redder if she'd been dropped in a vat of boiling oil.

'It's okay.' Zach dipped his head to kiss her. 'I do have a gift for us both – at least I hope it's what you'll want – but it's not an engagement ring. I was goin' to tell you about it when we swap presents later but maybe it's best now, so—'

'I don't say more stupid stuff and make a fool of us both in public?' A resigned smile tugged at her mouth. 'At least out here it's only the birds and worms who might eavesdrop.' Rosey peered at him. 'Come on then, where are you hiding this present?'

'It's not hidden anywhere. You're looking at it already. Give me your hand.' He bent down and scooped up a handful of the rich brown soil. 'Here you go.'

She stared at the dirt he'd dropped in her hand then back at him. 'You've completely lost me.'

'I'm gonna buy this field from Joe, plus a strip of land running down the south side of Joe's property for an access road. I'll obviously need planning permission for that and a house but he doesn't think it'll be an issue.' Rosey looked stunned. 'I was dubious about asking Joe but he's thrilled. It gives him much-needed cash as a breathing space while he works out his and Beth's next move, but he still holds onto most of his family's land. We haven't signed anything yet but we can still tell everyone today, if you're good with that?' Zach gave her a cautious smile.

'Is this your way of saying you're putting down roots here?'

'Yeah.' His heart raced. 'I thought it's what you wanted … what we wanted—'

'It is, you darling man.'

'My hope is that you'll help me with the design and maybe one day you'll think about sharing the house with me?' Zach hadn't planned to say that last part yet but was so swept away by her obvious pleasure he couldn't resist.

Rosey blushed. 'They both sound like pretty good ideas to me.'

'Me too.' He should be over the moon but it was tempered by worry over the secret he was holding back. 'Is it the weirdest present you've ever received?'

'Definitely. My mum's going to be so pleased.' Rosey flung her arms around his neck and kissed him. 'If I'm getting dirt on you, you've only got yourself to blame.'

'Doesn't bother me. I'm ready for a fresh start all around. Personally and professionally. You've shown me the way on both. There's still one thing I—'

'Hey mate, she said yes!'

Joe's loud yell cut him off and he tamped down his irritation at the badly timed interruption. He spotted his friend heading towards them with Beth in tow.

'I've no idea *why* I agreed to marry him, but I did.' Beth thrust out her left hand to show off a glittering diamond ring.

'Oh my God, it's beautiful.' Rosey squealed. 'When's the big day?'

'We're not sure yet. Maybe the spring?' The adoration with which she stared at the young farmer made Zach's eyes sting. It'd been a good day's work when he convinced Joe to try for a second chance with Beth. 'Neither of us want a big fuss so there's no reason to wait.' She giggled at Rosey. 'This way I'm making sure you'll have his help with the pantomime lighting again next year.'

'Oh stop it, you're as bad as my mum.' Rosey giggled too.

‘Are you coming back down with us so we can tell everyone our good news?’ Joe’s goofy smile was a million miles from his old dour expression.

‘Sure.’ Zach kept his voice upbeat but Rosey slipped her arm through his and angled a sympathetic smile his way. She knew something was up with him. She always did.

When the four of them walked back into the barn, his parents and Anna all looked up with expectant smiles.

‘Don’t keep us in suspense.’ Anna’s glee was off the charts. ‘Do we need to go out and buy wedding hats?’ She winked at Marie. ‘It’s traditional here, you know?’

Beth’s smile dropped away. ‘I’m not sure *our* exciting news is what you were hoping for.’ This time she held out her left hand less confidently.

Zach felt terrible, and by Rosey’s distraught look they were on the same page. ‘You sure do need to go shopping because we don’t want to let Joe and Beth down.’ He smiled at Beth. ‘I’m assuming we’re invited?’

‘Of course! There wouldn’t be a wedding if you hadn’t intervened.’

‘Thank goodness we’ve got champagne!’

‘Well, ain’t that something. Well done, lad.’ Pierre slapped Joe’s shoulder. ‘You’re marryin’ out of your league but the luckiest of us do.’

‘I certainly am.’ Joe’s smile lit up the room. ‘My plan is to get her down the aisle fast before she changes her mind.’

‘Rosey and I do have some other news, although it won’t be a surprise to Joe because he’s in on this secret in a big way so I suspect Beth knows too.’ He explained about the land he was in the process of buying and squeezed Rosey’s hand. ‘If there’s no hitch with planning permission, I'm hoping to build a house there that'll be ours together one day.'

'Well, aren't you a dark horse?' Pierre's grin widened. 'Not done shaking us up, are you? Never know what's comin' next.'

'Well, I'm thrilled.' Anna beamed at them both. 'We've got a lot to celebrate. Hurry up with the champagne.'

'You comin' to help me get the drinks?' He steered Rosey into the kitchen and made sure to close the door behind them.

'Whatever made my mum say that about us and weddings?' Her voice turned shrill. 'I swear I never gave her any hint—'

'I know that.' The champagne could wait. Reassuring the woman he loved that nothing her outspoken mother said could put him off was far more important. Zach brushed a strand of red hair away from her face and traced a finger over her pale, freckled skin.

'Don't worry, I'll put her straight later.'

He imagined Rosey metaphorically pinning her mother to the wall and threatening Anna with what would happen if she embarrassed them that way again. But Zach was a realist. It was Anna's habit to speak first and think afterwards, so they'd no doubt go through the same sort of problem again sooner rather than later. 'Let's get the champagne before someone comes to see what's up.'

'We should probably wash the dirt off our hands too.'

Their gazes locked in silent agreement.

Chapter Twenty-Three

Rosey stifled a yawn and shuffled through her music for the second act chorus song her mother intended to practise first. Now she understood why people were reluctant to start rehearsing again so soon after the holidays. The last forty-eight hours had worn her out. Two days of non-stop Christmas festivities would be challenging enough without throwing in the joy of Joe and Beth's engagement. For surprises though, she had to give Zach credit. She heard his distinctive tread on the old wooden floorboards behind her.

'How's my favourite pianist today?' He swooped in for a kiss.

'Tired.' She leaned against his shoulder. 'What're your parents doing tonight?'

'Takin' it easy. Eating leftovers.' Zach nuzzled a kiss on her neck. 'Any chance we can sneak away after practise?'

'Why don't we have a drink in the pub with everyone else then slip back to my place?' She shrugged. 'It's the best we can do.'

'Yeah, and I'm sorry to say it won't get better anytime soon.' He looked sheepish. 'My folks are definitely staying for the pantomime. You can partly blame your mom because she's talked up the show so much, they're completely reeled in.'

Rosey checked around them and lowered her voice. 'We might have to pay the Pirate's Bay Hotel another visit.'

'There's no "might" about it.' Zach's grumble was good-natured but she felt his pain.

'Any chance of you doing some work or are you too busy chatting up our Rosey?' Fred Cann ambled across to join them and winked at her.

'You can have him.' She shooed the men away and went back to tinkering on the piano as they disappeared backstage.

'Right, everyone listen up.'

The room fell silent and her mother launched into a warning spiel about there being no slacking from now on because their first performance was in a little over a fortnight.

'You're not gonna talk to Samira or anyone else that way.' Zach's angry voice suddenly boomed out, and Rosey's jaw dropped when he reappeared dragging Mike Blamey by his shirt sleeve. Samira, red-faced and silent, trailed along behind them. 'Anna, I caught this idiot makin' vile racist remarks to Samira.' Zach pushed Mike forward. 'It's not the first time either – right?' Samira said nothing and stared down at the ground.

'Mike, please tell me this is a misunderstanding.'

'Yeah, of course it is.' His fleshy mouth curled in a sneer. 'Some people can't take a joke, that's all. Tell the bloody Yank it's none of his business and let's get on with the rehearsal.'

Producing the pantomime was an exercise in diplomacy, and the last thing her mother needed with opening night looming was a bust-up between two of her main actors. Rosey's guilt blossomed. Everyone knew Mike was a bigoted loudmouth when he had a few drinks in him but some things couldn't be swept under the carpet. When she'd first heard about the problem, she should have told her mother.

'It *is* his business, Mike.' Rosey spoke up. 'No one should be made to feel less than part of the group, and everyone should be welcome on equal terms. I'm sorry, Samira, I know this is difficult but everyone deserves to hear what you've been putting up with.'

'I told you my feelings the other day and you promised not to interfere. Let us drop this. Please,' Samira begged.

Out of the corner of her eye, she caught Zach frown. 'We can't do that.' Rosey shook her head. 'You spend your working life defending people who've been wronged, so don't you deserve justice too?'

'That's different,' Samira murmured.

'No, it's not.' Zach backed her up. 'Nobody here is going to tolerate it. Are we?'

A couple of people glanced away when his gaze swept around the room but a groundswell of agreement came from the majority.

'So, Mum, what're you going to do?'

'We'll have a ten-minute break while I find out more about what's been happening under my nose and then we'll carry on with the rehearsal.' She hitched up her sparkly red skirt and beckoned to Mike and Samira. 'Come with me.' A nod came Rosey and Zach's way. 'You two as well.'

She hoped they could resolve this swiftly and peacefully, but Mike's bullish expression wasn't encouraging.

Zach managed to calm down and trailed along behind the others. Rosey kept throwing him wary looks, and although he respected the promise she'd made Samira, he still wished she'd felt able to talk it over with him. They all squeezed into the office and he settled with his back to the door.

'Samira, love, I need you to tell me how long this has been going on?' Anna's voice softened.

'I would prefer us to talk alone.'

'No way.' Mike growled like a pit bull. 'I've a right to hear what lies she spouts about me. I don't know what she's doing in our village show anyway. We don't need foreigners sticking their nose in.' His antagonism reverberated around the confined space. 'That goes for you too.' He scowled at Zach.

'Your mother would turn in her grave hearing you talk that way.' Anna glared at Mike. 'Eileen never had a bad word to say about everyone.'

Mike shuffled his feet and didn't respond.

'Samira is a wonderful woman and an incredible Princess Jasmine and I'm eternally grateful she wanted to join us. It wouldn't have mattered if I had a queue of locals a mile long beating down the doors at the auditions, I would've given her the part anyway. As for your nonsense about this nastiness you've been spreading being a joke, there's nothing funny about it.' Her Cornish accent thickened when she was angry and Zach struggled to understand her. She turned to Samira. 'Do you have to put up with a lot of this sort of horrible stuff even these days?'

'Yes, I'm afraid so, but I have learned to grow a thick skin.' Samira's voice strengthened. 'Even if it is a dark one.' Mike turned puce. 'I fight the battle every day at work, and it is tiring if I have to do the same in my private life. Perhaps it's best if I step aside.'

'No!' Anna shook her head. 'If you do that, what happens when the next person doesn't fit Mike's narrow-minded idea of how things should be in our village? I suspect he's not the only one who's been unwelcoming to you, but I won't press for names.' She straightened to her full impressive height. 'I'm going back out there now to make it clear this sort of behaviour won't be tolerated. As for you.' Her fierce glare bored into Mike. 'You can change your ways or get out … that's assuming Samira is even willing to keep working with you.'

Samira's eyes flared in horror. 'Oh please, do not—'

'I've had enough of this crap,' Mike scoffed. 'I'll bugger off to keep the PC brigade happy and I won't be the only one. You wait and see. Your precious pantomime will fall apart when the word gets around.' He hitched up his jeans over his drooping belly. 'You've got things your way, Yankee boy, you happy now?' He swaggered out of the room and slammed the door hard enough to make the thin walls shake.

What on earth had he set in motion? He'd seen red when he'd overheard Mike spouting vile innuendos at Samira, but perhaps he should have dealt with the incident in a less public fashion? It might have been wise to take Anna to one side for a private conversation but it was too late now. They might all wish he'd kept his big mouth shut.

She sympathised with her mother's dilemma but Zach had absolutely done the right thing. Apart from herself, no one else whole-heartedly backed him up. 'Mum, don't you think you should thank Zach?'

'I don't need thanks,' he muttered.

'Rosey is right.' Samira managed a forced smile. 'I've been a coward. She was spot on when she said I spend my days championing other people's rights and should've had the guts to stand up for myself here.' Her dark eyes flashed with anger. 'If I didn't want to do it for myself, I should still have spoken up for everyone else who's experiencing a similar thing.' Her voice strengthened. 'I need things to be better if I have a son or daughter one day.'

'Mum, do you remember you had a go at Tony Cooper's mum because he called me Carrot Top in school and made me cry? Knowing you'd stood up for me made all the difference.'

Anna's heavy nod spoke volumes. 'I'm some sorry, Samira.'

'It's all right. I—'

'No, it isn't.' The flush on her mother's cheeks deepened. 'My girl's right and so's this good man here.' She squeezed Zach's arm. 'I'm going out there now. Anyone who isn't a hundred per cent behind me can leave. I don't want them associated with the show.' Anna marched out of the room.

'We should join her.' Zach's quiet suggestion made Rosey squirm. Why did he have to keep pointing out the right thing to do?

They lingered together at the back of the hall, and Rosey saw her mum have a word with one of the junior chorus mums who herded the children backstage out of earshot. Anna started to speak, and by the time she finished the majority of people were giving Samira shocked and sympathetic looks. A few predictable ones were grumbling.

'We're not spending any more time on this now. If your conscience won't let you stay then leave now. Rehearsal starts in five minutes. Everyone who's supposed to be on stage for the start of the second act needs to get in place.'

A huddle of Mike Blamey's closest friends were having a heated discussion in one corner. Jago Walker, a long-time member of the senior chorus, broke free from the group and slouched out of the hall. No one else followed immediately but Rosey held her breath as Rob Wilkins was harangued by another of Mike's supporters. The thin, balding man played the lead Spirit of the Cave but was also the dame's understudy. Rob shook him off and strode through the crowd over to Samira.

'C'mon love, we'd better get a move on or Anna will have our guts for garters.'

Rob's courage and kindness brought tears to her eyes.

'It's gonna be okay.' Zach slipped an arm around her shoulders. 'Sometimes people live up to our best expectations of them instead of the worst.'

'Like me?' she whispered. 'I wobbled for a bit there.'

'I knew you'd come through.' His bright blue eyes bored into her. 'I wish you could've told me about Samira but I get why you felt you couldn't.'

'I wish I had too.' Her heartfelt response made him smile.

'We're all a work in progress.' Zach ruffled her hair. 'Now get your butt over to that piano before your mother strings me up for delaying you yet again.'

'We both know you'd never do that!' Rosey laughed and strutted off.

Chapter Twenty-Four

Zach was determined to make the most of the last few hours before his parents returned this afternoon to see in the New Year together. After they'd recovered from the Christmas festivities, his mother had dragged her long-suffering husband away from Polcarne for some sightseeing. The weather had been kind to them and the last he heard they'd made it around three stately homes, an Iron Age village, a china clay museum, Land's End and the Eden Project. For him the biggest bonus was the three blissful nights it'd given him with Rosey. She'd be with him now but Rob had begged for an extra practise on his own. It'd be polite to call his first performance as the dame at Thursday's rehearsal a shambles. As a "reward" for stirring things up at the pantomime, Anna had assigned Zach to stand in for the Cave Spirit who'd been promoted to Rob's old lead role. The uncompromising stare she'd given him left him no room for argument. On Monday evening, he'd step on a stage for the first time in almost three years and the thought was daunting.

He tugged a sweatshirt over his T-shirt, fixed a second mug of coffee and took his laptop out on the patio. After he did a last read through of his book, he'd send it to Cody tomorrow. The agent had a long-time friend in the publishing industry, and between them they'd be sure to give him an honest opinion. Zach opened up the file and gave in to a satisfied smile.

'Boo!'

He jerked around to see Rosey standing with her hands on her hips, grinning at him.

'What are you so engrossed in that you didn't hear me coming?' She gave an exaggerated sigh. 'I suppose after three consecutive nights together the novelty's worn off.' She peered over his shoulder. '*The Reinvention of Harry Browne*. What's this?'

Zach closed the lid and pushed the computer away. 'C'mere.' He pulled her down on his lap. 'You smell wonderful. It's been far too long since I kissed you.'

'Yes, and it'll be even longer if you don't answer the question.'

A dark red taxi crunched in over the gravel and parked on the other side of the patio fence.

'That must be Mom and Dad back early.' He nodded at the laptop. 'This is no big deal and I'll tell you all about it later. Promise. I'd better go help with the luggage. If I know Mom, she's bought up half of Cornwall while they've been away.' Reluctantly he shifted so he could stand up and Rosey followed him out the gate. 'Hiya, have you had a good time?' Behind his mother's back his dad raised his eyes to the heavens.

'Oh my God, it was incredible. Cornwall sure is beautiful.' Marie threw open her arms. 'Rosey! Come over here.'

Zach smiled as she succumbed to his mother's smothering hug.

'This girl did an awesome job tellin' us everywhere we should go, didn't she, Pierre?'

'Yes, dear.' His father's arms were loaded with packages. 'Zach, pay the driver, will you? I'll put it right with you later.'

'Yeah, of course.'

'How about a cup of tea?' Rosey's offer made his mother yelp with pleasure.

'It's a yes from me. I'm addicted to y'all's tea now.'

'If you don't mind, I'd prefer a decent cup of coffee.' Pierre grimaced. 'I'm about swimming in tea. No offence.'

'None taken. I'll go and make it while you sit down.'

Zach gathered up the luggage and hauled it off to the guest bedroom. By the time he returned, Rosey had brought the hot drinks in.

'C'mon son, sit down and tell us what you've been up to while we've been gone.' His father flopped on the sofa.

'Not all of it, please.' Marie's suggestive laughter rang around the room. 'Just the decent bits.'

'Did you get your manuscript ready?' Pierre nudged him. 'It's New Year's Day tomorrow, you know?'

'Manuscript?' Rosey sounded confused.

'Yeah, the boy's been working on a children's book. Isn't that something?'

'I don't suppose it's called *The Reinvention of Harry Browne* by any chance?' Her dark eyes pinned Zach down.

He nodded, desperately wanting to give her a proper explanation, but on their own and not with an audience.

'Drink up your coffee, honey, and let's go take a nap.' Marie set down her empty tea cup. 'I'm plum wore out after all that gallivanting around and I don't want to miss seeing in the New Year tonight.' She turned to Rosey. 'Is your mother comin' up here with us?'

'Yes. We had to dissuade her from turning it into a costume party. Joe and Beth would've come too but she's working. We thought we'd have dinner around eight then maybe play a few board games.'

'Oh, you'll have to watch out for our boy. Talk about competitive. He's a demon at Scrabble.' She prodded his poor father's arm. 'Get your butt moving or you'll fall asleep in the soup tonight.'

Once they were gone, Zach wondered where to start.

'Writing hardly falls in the same category as, say, a gambling addiction so why hide it?' She tried to keep her voice calm and rational. Only the other day, they'd idly talked about what they might like to do in life and she'd shared her ideas about composing the music for other pantomimes, which he'd thought was great. He'd even come up with a suggestion that she might consider organising small concerts at Lanhay Hall – putting together Rosey's enthusiasm for the acoustics at the beautiful house with Perry and Amanda's financial struggle with the upkeep of the old building. Zach had never once mentioned writing a book.

'Because I'm dumb.'

'Don't do that.'

'What?'

'The damn eyelash thing.' Like most women who swooned over him on the big screen, she melted when he glanced at her from under the shadow of his illegally thick, dark lashes. It was one trick he'd employed to turn Jean Laffite, a notorious and brutal Louisiana pirate, into a modern-day heartthrob in one of his films.

'Sorry.' The wide streak of mischief running through his thick drawl said the exact opposite. 'The only reason Papa found out is because he dragged it out of me on Christmas morning. Lots of people write stuff and it never sees the light of day.' He shrugged. 'That'll probably be the fate for Harry Browne. I've always had stories goin' around my head, and when I was at a loose end, I put some of them down. The Harry Browne one stuck, I guess.' The floodgates opened and he spilled out the whole plot and his plans for a series of books.

Rosey swallowed a rush of emotion as he talked about Harry Browne as if they were old friends. The pale, thin, shy boy was hopeless at sports and friendless in school but blossomed when he stepped on the stage for the first time. She stroked her fingers against the stubble he hadn't shaved off that day and lowered her forehead to rest against his.

'I wish I could take you to bed right now.'

'So do I.'

'Hey kids, I've had an idea.' Marie burst back into the room. 'After we've had dinner and you've trounced Rosey at Scrabble, why don't we see in the New Year at the pub? We can keep Joe company while Beth's busy pulling pints.' She grinned. 'Don't worry, my man won't get us into any brawls tonight.'

'That's what she thinks.' Pierre ambled in and snaked his arms around his wife's waist.

'Sounds perfect.' She smiled to herself. Later on, Zach would discover something he didn't know yet about her talent at a certain board game.

'Okay, that's it. I concede defeat.' Zach swept into a low, dramatic bow in front of Rosey. 'I declare you the official Scrabble whiz. Queen Rosey of the Scrabble board.' In the Broussard family he was considered unbeatable, but even taking the spelling differences into account – they'd agreed that either British or American spellings were allowed – Rosey trumped him with ease.

'I might teach you a few of my tricks if you're good.'

'Oh, I can be very good.' His ribald laugh made her blush. Fair pay back for his humiliation. 'If y'all want to get your coats we ought to make our way down to the pub. It'll be a bit of a squeeze in my Land Rover but we don't want the hassle of two cars, do we?'

'That's a smart idea.' Anna took off her reading glasses and gathered up her handbag. 'We can walk home afterwards and pick up our car tomorrow, can't we, Rosey?'

His mother rolled her eyes. 'You can go home. He needs to bring the girl back here. We've got earplugs.'

Zach felt for Rosey, whose face now resembled a traffic light. His mother was right. He shouldn't be such a coward about inviting her to spend the night here with him whenever she wanted to. Parents or no parents.

'Right, that's settled. Let's go.'

He noticed Anna pull her daughter to one side for a brief whispered conversation. He took the laughter and long, warm hug as a good sign.

'C'mon, sweetheart.' He grabbed his coat and Rosey's then whisked her outside while their parents got organised. 'Are you okay? I've been an idiot, haven't I?'

'No, *we've* been idiots.' She snuggled into him. 'We'll make them glad of the ear plugs later!'

They were still kissing when his mother's wicked laughter interrupted them.

'Children. Who'd have them!'

The breath caught in Zach's throat and he saw Rosey's speculative look. He said nothing and turned to unlock the car.

'We're lucky the rain's stopped.' Anna wedged into the back between his parents and Rosey jumped in next to him. 'I bet the pub will be heaving with people.'

She was proved to be right as they wended their way through the noisy crowd and found Joe propping up the bar.

'There's a small table back by the toilets with our name on it.' Joe chuckled. 'Not a prime spot but the best I could do.'

'You did good to nab anythin' in this mad house. I'll find them all a seat then be back to get in a round of drinks.'

'That's music to my ears. I'll be relieved when Beth chucks this all in.'

'Is that the plan?'

'Yep. She's almost talked me around to her idea of opening up a small restaurant at the farm, either in the old buttery or your barn. It all sounds a bit mad to me but she's convinced we can make it work. Beth's an awesome cook and she's worked in the pub long enough to know what's what.' Joe's face turned ruddy. 'You know I'm only scraping by, and we want to start a family so we'll need steady income coming in. She's going to turn her cottage into a holiday rental so that'll help too.'

'You'll be a good team. I predict a whole football team of little Warrens runnin' around in a few years.'

'Dunno about lots, but two or three, I hope. What about you and Rosey? Not too late, is it?'

Zach fell silent. He couldn't answer Joe honestly without talking to Rosey first. 'Bit early to think about anythin' like that.'

The noise level rose along with the heat from too many bodies crammed into the small space, and it was only a marginal help when Jock opened the door. Shortly before midnight the volume on the television behind the bar was turned up so they'd be able to hear the chimes of Big Ben ringing in the new year.

'Everyone got a drink?' Zach topped up glasses with champagne and everyone stood up to join in the countdown. Last New Year's Eve he was alone in his dreary rented flat in LA without a whole lot of optimism that the upcoming year would bring any improvement.

'Happy New Year!' Rosey's warm lips crushed his and his eyes misted over when she mouthed that she loved him.

'Love you too, sweetheart.'

Chapter Twenty-Five

'Oh my God, what's happened to the piano?' Rosey dabbed her finger in the dark, sticky goo oozing all over the keys and took a sniff. 'Black treacle!'

'I'll set the police on him for this. The old devil.'

'On who, Mum?'

'Mike Blamey, of course.' Anna snorted. 'This is his revenge for being thrown out.'

'You can't know that.'

'Don't be daft. Who else could it be?'

'But what about the other weird things we've had happen? You were convinced all of those items going missing and the costume rentals getting cancelled were down to someone with a grudge against the panto. Mike wouldn't have had any reason to do all of that, and we can't have two people out to get us? That's ridiculous.'

'I don't know about the rest of it, but this is different. Much nastier.'

Rosey lifted the piano lid and peered inside. 'It's all in here too.' She could have cried. 'Maybe we can clean it up?' She didn't believe that for a moment, but her mother's volatile emotions see-sawed more than usual close to opening night and she couldn't handle her going off the deep end now. This was the worst possible way to kick off the first rehearsal of the new year.

'What's all the fuss about? Have we run out of tea bags or …?' Zach's voice trailed away. 'What the hell happened?'

'Mum suspects that Mike did it but we don't have any proof.'

'Are you goin' to call the cops?'

'Not yet.' Anna sighed. 'I want to see him myself first.'

'The three of us could go around to his place after the rehearsal for a quiet word maybe?'

'That's all very well but what do we do now?' Her mother wailed. 'We can't practise without the music.'

Zach pulled out his phone and tapped a couple of buttons. The strains of the opening chorus filled the room. 'I recorded our last full run through for my own benefit.' He flushed. 'I reckoned if I was goin' to be roped into performing, I needed to nail the show in my own mind. Can you make this work for tonight? We can get something better in place before Thursday.' He offered Rosey the phone.

'Oh, you lovely creature.' Anna enveloped him in a tight hug and when she let go her eyes were glassy with tears. 'You won't stop us, Mike Blamey!' With a swirl of her bright blue and red caftan, she swanned off backstage.

'I know she's jumping to conclusions but it gives her somewhere to put her anger for now.' His smile was tight and forced. 'I'd better go. Some of us have to get ready to perform.'

Rosey dragged her mind away from the vandalised piano. 'Are you sure you'll be okay?'

'I guess we'll find out.'

The door swung open and people started to trickle in, starting with Rob Wilkins. The ex-Royal Navy man was always first because he stuck to the old adage that navy time was five minutes before time. Of course, the rambunctious Dunn twins and their harassed mother would roll in last with another improbable excuse. It didn't take long for someone to spot the damaged piano and pass the word around. The hall soon hummed with speculation about who might have done such a thing and how they'd manage to rehearse and put on a show without a functioning piano.

'We're going to start in five minutes as scheduled.' Her mother put a determined stop to the gossip.

Rosey stood at the ready with Zach's phone. She'd done some odd performances in her time but this topped all of them.

Zach rubbed his sweaty palms together and managed the semblance of a smile when Harry Webb, the genie, asked if he was okay.

'Hope you aren't coming down with something, mate. You're a bit wished looking.' Harry's green eyes twinkled. 'That's an old Cornish expression for pale and lifeless.'

'I'll have to remember that one.'

'Had a few too many to see in the New Year, did 'ee? You aren't the only one. You'll be all right.' Harry ambled off.

Better to let the other man think he was hungover rather than scared witless. All he had to do was follow the other spirits on stage to gather around the lead spirit and listen to their orders for guarding the jewels in Aladdin's cave. A few nods and grunts and they trooped off again. Zach slipped off into a quiet corner in the wings and took a few moments to breathe and focus his mind on his character. His first drama teacher had drummed something into him that he'd never forgotten.

It doesn't matter if you're the third footman in the back row of Cinderella's ballroom scene and out of sight of ninety per cent of the audience – be the best footman there. The ten per cent of people who can see you deserve a hundred per cent of your performance.

'Spirits of the cave, take your places.' Anna's voice boomed out from the hall.

The music struck up and Zach found his spot at the rear. He was petrified his feet wouldn't move when the man in front of him stepped forward, but somehow they did. The stage lights bathed his face and the magic happened all over again, exactly as it had done over thirty years ago in his first performance. Zach Broussard ceased to exist and he became Hassan – the name he'd given his character rather than the anonymous "one of the spirits" mentioned in the script.

Five minutes later, he exited the stage with his heart thumping and punched his arm in the air. A couple of the other men gave him odd looks but didn't say a word. They probably thought it was some strange Hollywood gesture. He wished he could run out and sweep Rosey up in his arms but he'd have to wait until later.

The second time the spirits went on stage was easier, and by the time they joined in with the finale Zach was enjoying himself.

'Someone deserves a drink.' Rosey sidled up to him and brushed a soft kiss on his cheek. 'You were awesome.'

'Yeah, no one shuffles onto the stage, manages a few nods and grunts and shuffles off again quite like me!'

'We both know that's not all there was to it.' Her dark eyes filled with love and he fought to rein his emotions back in.

'Aren't we goin' to tackle Mike first?'

'Oh God, I can't believe I forgot. It might be better rather than waiting until Mum has a couple of glasses of wine inside her. Let's help clear up then get it over with.'

Zach stopped by the piano and touched the tacky syrup.

'What's going through your brain now?'

'Are there any piano shops nearby?'

'There's one in Truro. I buy music there sometimes. Why?'

'If you're free in the morning, we could go check it out. See if they've got a suitable replacement.'

'But we can't afford—'

'Don't fret about that.' Zach hugged her. 'Let's round up your mom. I suppose y'all know where he lives?'

'Yes, he rents a ramshackle old cottage behind our place. We stand a good chance of catching him at home, seeing as he's still barred from the pub.' She waved at her mother. 'Are you ready to go to Mike's?'

'I suppose so. Let's get it over with.' Anna flung one end of her blue wool shawl over one shoulder and raised a fist in the air. 'I shall channel Boadicea.'

Zach avoided looking at Rosey or they'd both burst out laughing. 'I'll make sure all the windows and exits are locked. We don't want any other nasty surprises.' He didn't spot anything out of place until he reached the fire exit at the back of the building. A blob of something dark was stuck to the door knob and Zach touched his thumb to it to confirm it was congealed treacle. Their culprit must have left this way. He thought hard about what that might mean and re-joined Anna and Rosey. 'Ready, ladies?' He offered them both an arm. 'We'll re-enact the Three Musketeers.'

Rosey tried not to be intimidated by Mike's belligerence. 'Please don't think we're accusing you, but—'

'Bloody sounds like it to me.'

She turned her head to avoid his stale breath. They'd found him slumped in a chair swigging beer from a can with a collection of abandoned empties laying on the floor around him and a box of half-eaten pizza balanced on his lap.

'Do you have a key to the hall?' Zach asked.

'No. Why should I?' Mike's bleary eyes struggled to focus. 'There's plenty of others do, so why don't you go ask them about it instead of picking on me?'

'We will.'

'Bugger off the lot of 'ee.' He belched and popped open another can of beer.

There didn't seem to be much choice, and back outside Rosey gulped in a few breaths of fresh air.

'I don't know about you two but I could do with that drink now.' Her mother sounded defeated.

'We'll walk along with you but I think we'll give it a miss tonight.' Luckily as they reached the pub, Rob was on his way in so Anna joined him.

'So Miss Teague, do you have something in mind for me tonight?' Zach wrapped his arms around her and nuzzled kisses on her neck.

'Yes, but you're not going to like it.' She wriggled out of his grasp. 'We're going to my house. To talk.' This time she mustn't lose her nerve at the last minute when it came to hearing what he had to say.

'Can't we do that at the farm?'

'No, because I'd give in to my baser instincts.'

'And that's a problem because …?'

'Don't you dare do the flirty eyelash thing when I'm trying to be serious.' Rosey forced herself not to give in. 'Come with me now or go home on your own.'

Zach took hold of her hand. 'You're right and I'm an idiot. We both know there won't be any proper talking done if you're distracting me with awesome sex.'

'Awesome, is it?'

'Don't you think so?' A twinkle sneaked back into his eyes.

'Behave.'

It was a silent walk and at the house she dived straight into the kitchen to turn the kettle on. 'Sit at the table.'

'Yes, ma'am.' Zach dragged out a chair.

Rosey started with a softly-softly approach. 'I was so proud of you tonight. It took guts to go back on stage but no one else portrayed a spirit of the cave better.'

A tinge of heat flushed his cheeks. 'Yeah, well, it wasn't easy but thanks to you—'

'I'm not taking any credit. It was all down to you. I encouraged you a bit, that's all.'

Zach tilted her a heart-melting smile. 'If that's what you want to believe, darlin'.'

Rosey struggled to focus on more serious matters than when they'd kiss again. 'Back before Christmas you told me that the baby Laura was expecting wasn't yours … but you really wanted to tell me something else. I put you off but I've been regretting it ever since. It's driven me mad, imagining all sorts of terrible things.' While she waited for him to speak, a deep pit of dread formed in her stomach.

Zach shifted his hands down out of sight so she wouldn't see them shaking. 'I never meant to make you worry, but there's somethin' I should've told you when we started to get serious.' He heaved a sigh. 'Back in my junior year in college, I contracted mumps and, well … it's affected my fertility. It's highly unlikely I'll be able to father children.'

'Oh Zach. I don't know what to say.' She turned white. 'That's … awful. I thought mumps wasn't around much these days? Weren't you vaccinated?'

'Yeah, I was, but with fewer people getting the vaccine the disease still happens and living in close living quarters at school didn't help. I was unlucky.'

'There must be new medical research going on all the time though. Isn't it possible they'll come up with a cure?'

He couldn't blame her for clutching at straws because he'd done the same thing for years. 'They might.' Zach could hardly bear to say the words she wouldn't want to hear but he'd been a coward for long enough. 'It was wrong of me to lead you on. I should never have let you believe that a future with me could include us having kids.'

Rosey came over to kneel down by his chair and reached for his hands. Her gentle, warm touch almost wrecked him. 'I agree you should've told me earlier, but it doesn't change anything.'

'Of course it does!'

'That's rubbish. You still love me, right?'

'Well yeah, but—'

'But nothing.' She touched his cheek. 'There's far more to our love than this one thing. Who else knows?'

'Only my folks, and they've been hassling me to tell you since they arrived. I'm pretty sure it wouldn't go down well with my female fans to find out I'm shooting blanks.'

'I don't think you give people enough credit.'

A rush of anger shot through him. 'I don't need their pity or yours. It is what it is and plenty of people have far worse to deal with.' He waited for her to speak, sensing her hesitation. 'Come on. Say it. Whatever it is.'

'Did you tell Laura before you got married?'

'Of course I did! What sort of man do you think I am?'

'Sorry. Perhaps I shouldn't have asked … but I needed to be clear in my own mind.'

He wasn't being fair. 'Yeah, I get that. When we got together, Laura claimed it wasn't a big deal because her career meant everything to her and she'd never been that bothered about having kids.' A hard knot formed in his gut. 'We both know that was a lie.'

'Perhaps she got pregnant by accident? Don't get me wrong, it's terrible that she was unfaithful but …'

'I'll never know, will I?' The darkness that never left a corner of his mind took over again. 'That's what eats at me, Rosey. I'm well aware we had other problems in our marriage but I can't help wondering if this tipped the scales in the end? Did she change her mind and want a baby badly enough to sleep with another man?'

'Don't make excuses for her. If she did start to feel differently, she should've talked to you about it. You can't torment yourself with what-ifs.'

'Can't I?'

'No. I won't let you.' She rested her hand against his cheek and the drift of her soft floral perfume performed insidious tricks on his resolve. 'It's time to set the burden down, Zach.'

The loving words broke him. Heaving sobs wrenched through his body and, despite his misery, Zach was aware of her strong arms cradling him. After what seemed like an eternity, he regained some measure of control and had the strength to ease away.

'You're not thinking straight, Rosey. You obviously love kids. You told me you're envious of your friends who've got children and I saw how teary you were at the carol service when the little group of angels sang "Away in a Manger". It's obvious that one of your favourite parts of the pantomime is working with the junior chorus. If anyone should be a mother, it's you.' His voice cracked. 'I love you far too much to end that dream.'

'Oh Zach.' Rosey shook her head. 'Unless they're made of stone, everyone in the church had a lump in their throat on Christmas Eve. And, yes, the panto kids are adorable but it doesn't mean I want to take them all home with me.' Her smile held an edge of sadness. 'Let's get real here. I'm thirty-eight, Zach. Even if you were a super stud, my chances of getting pregnant are diminishing by the day. Before I ever met you, I'd already accepted it probably wouldn't happen now.'

His heart pounded.

'There are other ways for us to make a family together. What about all the children waiting to be fostered or adopted? Is that something you'd consider, because I certainly would?'

'I guess so. I hadn't given it much thought.'

'A wise person said it takes a village to raise a child. Everyone plays a part in raising the next generation in one way or another. You know cute little Maisie Evans in the panto? The lively five-year-old with blonde curls and a smile that lights up the room? Her father was sent to prison last year and things aren't easy for her at home. Forgetting all of that for a few hours makes a difference. And what about Tim Watson? I watched you take him to one side the other day and help him when he was struggling to get the steps of the finale dance.'

'Yeah. He's a good kid.'

'I know for a fact Tim's been bullied at school, but the other day his mum told me that he idolises you and wants to be an actor. You boosted his confidence so he can see a future that doesn't include mean classmates.' Rosey rubbed at her eyes. 'There are plenty of kids who need a helping hand, Zach. They need mentors. People who'll be there for them.'

'Are you certain that's enough for you? Because I can't go through …' Words failed him but he knew she'd finish the sentence in her own head.

'*You* are all I need, but maybe …' A flood of emotion swept over her face.

'You can't stop there.'

'Maybe *I'm* not enough for *you.*'

'Oh darlin', you're everything I've dreamed about and never thought I'd find. I reckon we need to go up to the farm. We need my big bed.'

'Whatever for?' Rosey's smile blossomed.

'Well, if you can't guess, I'll have to show you.'

Chapter Twenty-Six

'Mum, we've got some amazing news.' Rosey rushed into the house. 'Where are you?' She poked her head into the empty kitchen then heard a faint sound from the living room and raced in there. 'Zach's bought us a new piano. I know I shouldn't have let him but … Oh my God what's happened?' Her mother was standing in the middle of the room sobbing.

'Someone broke into Zoe's house and did this.' Anna's voice and hands shook. She held out the dress she was clutching onto and Rosey could barely recognise what was left of Princess Jasmine's exotic red and gold ballgown. The elaborate costume that had taken weeks to sew had been slashed into ribbons. 'They did the same thing to Aladdin's finale costume that Zoe made to replace the cancelled one from the hire shop. Luckily, she came home and disturbed them before they could do any further damage.'

'Did she catch the culprit?'

'No. They must've heard her car and run out the back door.'

'You really should call the police this time,' Zach cut in.

'I suppose so. We've only got a week before opening night and Zoe can't possibly make new costumes before then.' Anna did her best to smile. 'Did you say Zach's been our fairy godfather?'

'Yes.' Rosey managed a faint smile despite the circumstances. 'Harmony Pianos in Truro are delivering one tomorrow morning.'

‘I hope no one sees it as interfering. That’s not what I—’

‘Interfere as much as you like, dear boy,’ Anna proclaimed. ‘You’re a godsend and anyone who says different will have me to deal with.’

‘Do you still reckon all this trouble is down to Mike?’ Zach asked. ‘I can’t picture him thinkin’ up something like this or the treacle on the piano. He’s more likely to throw a few punches when he’s drunk and regret it in the morning. This is sly. Devious.’

That made sense to Rosey but she wasn’t sure her mum would agree.

‘I suppose you could be right. I can’t be dealing with any of that right now. The priority is to ring around the costume shops to see if they’ve got anything that’ll work and I need to do that before one o’clock because I’ve got a rehearsal with the kiddies then. They’re back at school tomorrow so I thought it’d be nice if they didn’t have to come tonight.’ She looked awkward. ‘I’d forgotten to mention it to you, Rosey dear. Are you free?’

‘Of course, but why don’t you concentrate on the costumes and I’ll practise with the little ones?’ She threw Zach an apologetic look. ‘Do you mind helping?’

‘No problem. My folks are off to see Falmouth today. For once, Mama let my long-suffering father choose the destination and he picked the Maritime Museum.’

‘Aren’t you supposed to be working on the children’s book Rosey told me about?’ Her mother chimed in.

‘I sent it off to my agent a few days ago. There’s nothing else I can do ‘til I hear back.’

‘In that case, I’ll let the two of you whip the junior chorus into shape.’ Anna chuckled. ‘Not literally though or their parents won’t be happy!’ She grabbed a thick emerald wool cape off the back of the sofa and wrapped it around her. 'I'll pop over to see Zoe and we'll put our heads together. You can scrape up something for lunch out of what's in the fridge.'

After she breezed out of the house, they smiled at each other.

'Scraping up something for lunch doesn't sound very appetising,' Zach said. 'Why don't we get something at the pub?'

'Or …' Rosey let her gaze drift towards the stairs.

'You insatiable creature.' Large, strong arms wrapped around her waist and she was lifted off her feet with Zach's wicked laugh rumbling in her ear. 'Not that I'm complainin'.'

After they'd made love in her childhood bed – something that still seemed vaguely naughty – Zach gathered her up in his arms. 'Why're you looking so thoughtful?'

'When you were acting, did all this have to be trimmed and spray tanned and stuff?' Rosey stroked his broad, warm, hair-roughened chest.

'Sometimes. Depended on the role.' His white, toothy smile broke free. 'The natural look was fine for Jean Lafitte because pirates are supposed to be rough and manly, but the suave Winston Grainger the Third, my snobbish Virginian with a pedigree tracing back to the Mayflower, was definitely a manscaping job. At least I can be myself all the time now.'

A loud pounding started on the front door.

'Who on earth is that?'

'I'd offer to go peek out the window but it might be a tad awkward if I'm spotted.'

Rosey threw back the covers and dragged on enough clothes to be decent. 'I'll go down. You might want to get dressed.'

'Really?' He arched an eyebrow. 'That wouldn't have occurred to me.'

She stuck out her tongue.

'If the wind changes your mouth will stay that way, at least that's what my Mamaw Alice used to say.'

Without dignifying that with a response, she hurried out of the bedroom and ran to open the door. 'What's the—'

'I found your culprit.' Jago Walker hovered on the doorstep and shot her an uncertain look. This was the first time they'd seen each other since he'd stormed out of rehearsal in support of Mike.

'What on earth are you talking about?'

'I heard about the troubles you've had at the pantomime with the piano and stuff. It's this old bugger's fault.' He dragged Roland Stephens forward. The former music director looked grey and drawn.

'What's goin' on?' Zach came to stand behind her.

'I'm not quite sure yet.'

'Would it be better talked about inside?'

'Probably.' She was grateful for the suggestion because her own brain wasn't firing on all cylinders. 'Jago, you can let go of poor Roland now.'

'You won't be so charitable when you hear what he's been up to.'

'Maybe not.' Rosey steered the older man inside and settled him in one of the wingback chairs by the fireplace. She plonked herself down in the other chair and left Jago to slump on the sofa alongside Zach. 'Now, Roland, can you explain why Jago's blaming you for those incidents? I'm sure it's a misunderstanding of some sort.'

'No. He's absolutely right.' The man's flat voice betrayed no emotion. 'I damaged the piano and the costumes. I'd held onto my key to the hall, you see, so it wasn't hard to make a few bits and pieces go missing too. I'm not sorry.' Roland threw her a venomous look, leaving her too stunned to respond.

'Mr Stephens, we haven't met but I'm—'

'Oh, I know who *you* are.' The old man turned his disgust on Zach. 'The whole village knows the pantomime's been hijacked by a has-been Hollywood superstar and a failed concert pianist. It deserves to be a disaster.'

'The sad old geezer didn't even have the sense to get rid of the evidence,' Jago scoffed. 'I spotted him shoving a bundle of old clothes in the rubbish bin outside the shop. Covered in black treacle, they were. I challenged him and he admitted he done it all so I hauled 'ee over here.'

'But why?' Rosey couldn't get her head around it all. 'I don't understand.'

'I'm not saying another word.'

'He's jealous of you, Rosey.' Zach's quiet assertion stunned her. 'I'm takin' a guess it's been eating away at him since you took over. He can see how talented you are and it galls him. Roland, do you have any other tricks planned?'

'Maybe. Maybe not.' His thin lip curled at one corner. 'You'll have to wait and find out.' Roland sat upright in the chair.

'Aren't you going to call the police on him?' Jago jumped into the conversation again. 'For a start, the pantomime lot have the right to know who mucked them around.'

Rosey picked her words carefully. 'Please don't take this the wrong way, but you chose not to be a part of the group any longer. I think this is as far as you need to be involved.'

'Well … I might've been a bit hasty that day I walked out.'

She threw Zach a pleading look, at a loss how to respond.

Talk about being stuck between a rock and a hard place. He'd been the driving force behind exposing Mike's treatment of Samira, which in turn led to Jago leaving the show.

'Rosey can correct me if I'm wrong, but I'm pretty sure that, although you're missed, it's difficult to see a way back in for you now.'

'But I never said none of those things like Mike. I never would.'

'Yeah, but you didn't challenge him and you walked out. That implies you agreed with his racist remarks.'

'That's true,' Rosey added.

'I told Mike last week that I don't want no more to do with 'ee and his mates. If I talk to Miss Key and apologise, do you think that might …?' Jago sighed and hunched in on himself. 'I don't 'spose that'll do any good. Poor maid didn't deserve the way Mike spoke to her.'

'What you *really* need to get is that it's not just Samira we're talking about.' Zach's tone became more emphatic. 'Yeah, this time it was about her but what if someone else joins the pantomime who isn't born and bred here in

Polcarne and they're different in another way? Are they goin' to get hassled too and made to feel unwelcome?'

'Not by me, they won't. I've learned my lesson. Honest.'

'It's not up to me.' He'd done his part. This was on Rosey now.

'I'll have to talk to Mum and see what she thinks. When I've done that, I'll give you a ring and we'll have another chat.'

'Can't say fairer than that. Thanks.' Jago stood up. 'I'll see myself out.'

'I'm off too.' Roland sneered and levered himself out of the chair. 'If you want to set the police on me, you know where I live.'

By Rosey's sad expression, he could see the old man's lack of remorse struck hard. When they were alone again, he struggled to know what to say. 'That was … unexpected.'

'Unexpected? I suppose that's a word for it.'

'Should we go track down your mom and give her an update?'

'Not right now.' Rosey frowned. 'She's got enough on her plate for the minute. Let's leave it until tonight. I suppose we'd better eat lunch then face up to corralling a dozen little monsters who've spent the last couple of weeks going to bed far too late and are on a sugar high from all the sweets they've consumed.'

'Sounds like fun.' Zach grinned. 'Scrounging in the fridge or the pub?'

'If you don't mind too much, let's just go with whatever we can find here. Jago might be in the pub.'

‘He won’t blab about Roland Stephens, will he?’ They didn’t need that piece of news spreading around the village until they’d told Anna.

‘Let’s hope not.’

It didn’t take long to discover the pub would have been a wiser option from a food standpoint, but Zach didn’t dare to complain about the plate of cold sausage rolls, shrivelled up tomatoes and stale crisps Rosey put together.

‘It’s almost one o’clock. We’d better go,’ she said once they’d nearly finished.

Fast forward an hour and they were ready to tear their hair out. Rosey had nailed the mood of the junior chorus to a tee earlier. Wrangling cats would have been easier. Anna had begged them to work on the dance for the first act set in Wishee-Washee’s laundry. They’d practised it over and over with no noticeable sign of improvement. ‘Tell them to take a five-minute break before we get tempted to kill them,’ he whispered in Rosey’s ear. ‘I’ve got an idea you might or might not like.’

‘I’ll consider anything. This is a disaster.’

When she returned to the stage and had sent the children off to have a run around, their exuberant reaction was akin to prisoners serving a life sentence granted an early release.

‘I’m wary of interfering—’

‘But I want you to.’ Rosey pleaded. ‘This is what you do for a living. I know our little production doesn’t compare to a Hollywood film set, but there must be certain similarities.’

‘Well, yeah.’ He cautiously explained his plan and was rewarded with a kiss. ‘It might not work.’

‘Nothing else we’ve tried has done the trick so let’s give it a go.’

They rounded up the junior chorus again and split them into two groups. Zach took his section backstage to work with while Rosey stayed with hers in the hall. He'd come up with his plan after remembering a musical in high school that he'd been part of. They'd had a similar problem and the director solved it in a unique way by turning it into a competition to see which group could nail the tricky musical number first.

Today he had a slight advantage over Rosey because the kids, and their accompanying parents, were still intrigued by him and a little in awe. At the end of the allotted half hour, he chivvied them back out. 'C'mon, let's go show them what you can do.' Everyone trotted out behind him to meet Rosey and her charges onstage.

They turned it into a game by pretending they were entrants in a singing and dancing reality television contest. At the end, he and Rosey were the judges and, after pretending to confer, they declared it a draw.

'Now we'll perform together as a team again.' Rosey's challenge drew a few anxious looks. 'I'm sure it'll be great.' She pointed to Zach. 'Someone is going to film it on his phone so I can show it to my mum later.' The children perked up then. They all loved Anna.

With everyone in place, she sat down at the new piano and struck up the first chords. His throat tightened at the sight of the children's fierce concentration. They made it to the end of the song with no mistakes and there was a burst of loud cheers and a few high-fives. Their joy was contagious. This was what he'd missed out on for too many years now, burdened with the expectations that came along with multi-million-dollar leading roles. He'd rediscovered more than one kind of love in Cornwall. Finding Rosey was the most important, but the satisfaction he'd gained today helping young people to discover the wonder of performing on stage burned almost as bright.

'That was incredible.' Rosey flung her arms around him. 'You're incredible.'

Zach could argue the toss on that statement but her wide, infectious smile left him unmanned. He simply kissed and hugged her right back.

Chapter Twenty-Seven

'You've made a proper fool of me, young lady.' Anna stormed into the kitchen, eyes blazing.

'What on earth are you talking about?'

'I've just been to the shop, and soon as I walked in the door Albert pounced on me to ask what I thought about Roland Stephens being behind all our trouble at the panto. I didn't have the foggiest idea what he was talking about, did I? Apparently, that blabbermouth Jago spread it all over the pub last night at the karaoke.' She planted her hands on the kitchen table and scowled at Rosey. 'What were you thinking? Too busy with your hot and heavy romance, I suppose, to think about me.'

'That's not fair!'

'Fair?' Anna snorted. 'Your mobile didn't die, did it?'

Her cheeks flamed. 'No. I honestly intended to tell you when you got home, but you were late and I was tired, so I thought it'd wait until today. I'm sorry. Okay?' Some of the puff went out of her mother. 'You were so down about the costumes, I couldn't face piling on more bad news.' By the time she finished retelling the whole sad story, her mother looked grey and weary. 'How do you want to handle it? Do you want to go back and see him together?'

'I suppose so.'

'How did you get on with the costumes? I haven't had a chance to ask.'

'Not too bad.' Anna managed a tentative smile. 'None of the hire shops had anything suitable but Zoe has come up trumps again. She happens to be friends with the wardrobe person for the Penryn Players and they're happy to lend us any dresses from previous shows that they aren't using this year. Zoe's going down there this morning to pick out two or three of the best ones. Luckily Samira's a standard sort of size so it won't take too much to alter them to fit her.'

'What about Aladdin's finale costume?'

'Zoe has some material left over and she swears she's got time to make it up again. We're bloody lucky to have her. How did you get on with the rehearsal anyway?'

'Look at this.' Rosey pulled out her phone and found Zach's video. She pressed play and held her breath while her mum watched with widening eyes. 'Well?'

'Oh my Lord, it's 'andsome. They're proper little troopers. How on earth did you do it?'

She couldn't take all the credit and explained Zach's bright idea that had worked wonders.

'Well, all I can say is that boy's a miracle worker.'

Rosey wouldn't argue with that.

'I'll get dressed and we'll go to see Roland.' Anna patted her bare face. 'I might need a bit more war paint on though before facing him.' She managed a weak smile and disappeared back upstairs.

Rosey pushed away her uneaten plate of toast and was deep in thought when her mother returned. 'Does Roland have any family?'

'Family? What makes you ask that?'

'I just wondered.'

'No, my 'andsome. He's a crusty old bachelor through and through.' Anna shook her head. 'I've always felt a bit sorry for him. He had one brother over in Australia but he died a few years ago. Apart from teaching violin to private pupils and in the schools, the pantomime was his life.'

And I took that away from him. 'I feel partly responsible, Mum. I didn't give any thought to Roland's feelings when I stepped into his shoes as music director.'

'But you're so much better for the job and the pantomime needs the best person. That's always been our priority when we're casting the parts, so how is this different?'

Something about Anna's bluster didn't ring true. Rosey wasn't the only one feeling guilty.

'Put your coat on and let's get this over with.'

They strolled along the street arm in arm and slowed down for a moment outside the shop to chuckle at the bedraggled Christmas display in the window. Every year Albert Rundle clung onto it as long as possible.

'He'll replace it with Easter eggs soon,' Rosey mused.

'Then it'll be buckets and spades for the beach as if we need that here!'

They turned onto Moor Lane and stopped about halfway along at the broken gate leading to Roland's cottage. The weather-beaten blue paint, scattering of missing roof tiles and overgrown tangle of a garden all spoke of creeping neglect.

'It weren't like this last time I were here. Poor old soul can't manage to keep it all up any longer, I s'ppose.'

Rosey bit back the uncharitable remark that sprang to her lips along the lines of him having the strength to dream up mean ways to sabotage the pantomime.

'Oh, it's you. What do you want, as if I can't guess?' Roland opened at their first knock and peered behind them down the path. 'Thought you'd have brought the police with you.' He glared at her mother.

'Aren't you going to invite us in? We can talk about this mess over a cup of tea.'

'I told her yesterday that I'm not sorry.' He scowled at Rosey. 'I never meant to make things rough on you though, Anna.' A sudden flush rose in his gaunt cheeks.

'Well, you certainly did and we need to sort it out once and for all.' Her mother's firm tone made Roland wince.

'I know. I know.' He nodded sadly.

She didn't say a word, and before long they were ushered into Roland's cramped living room, stuffed with toppling piles of books and an excess of dusty, worn furniture. Rosey instinctively touched the old mahogany upright piano as she walked past and sensed the smooth beeswax polish under her fingers. No neglect there. It seemed wise to make herself scarce so she tracked down the cluttered, and not particularly clean, kitchen to make a tray of tea. Through the half-open door, she was surprised to hear her mother and Roland reminiscing about long-ago pantomimes. They stopped talking as she walked back into the room and the old man sunk back into his chair. Rosey passed around the mugs of tea and took one of the dining chairs for herself.

'I really don't want to prosecute you, Roland. We've been friends too long.' Her mother's calm announcement didn't come as a complete surprise, although Rosey had mixed feelings about the charitable act. 'But there's one condition—'

'I knew there'd be one of those.' He sighed.

'You've got to promise you won't do anything else to spoil the pantomime. If nothing else, think of all the kiddies looking forward to it.'

'That American chap was right. I *was* jealous.' He heaved another sigh. 'I only ever intended to be a bit of a nuisance … it all just got a little bit out of hand, Anna.'

'It happens to the best of us.'

Rosey took the opportunity to chip in. 'I still think what you did was dreadful and mean, Roland, but I should have considered your feelings more when I took over.'

'That's kind of you to say so, my dear, but I see now that I've behaved like a spoiled child.' The old man looked wretched. 'I've heard nothing but good stuff about the panto this last couple of years and everyone always praises the music.'

'Thank you.' An idea popped into her head but she knew this wasn't the time to mention it. When all this fuss had quietened down, she might have a word with Roland and ask him to come back to help her out with the pantomime music.

Worry flickered in his pale eyes. 'Will you allow me to apologise to everyone at your next rehearsal?'

'Come to the hall tomorrow night. Seven o'clock sharp.' Her mother's tone was brisk. 'You can have a quick word before we start.' The softening started with Anna's faint smile. 'Then, if you're up to it, you could stay to watch the rehearsal and join us for a drink at the pub after.'

'I'll be there at seven, then we'll see about the rest.' Roland smiled at Rosey. 'You're a very generous woman. You've got a good heart.'

'I learned from the best.' She couldn't look at her mum or they'd do something uncharacteristic like cry and hug each other.

Zach gaped at the phone. 'Seriously? You're kidding me.'

'Would I get up at this ungodly hour to prank you?' Cody sounded peeved.

No doubt he'd expected profuse thanks but the stunning news had taken him aback. Cody's friend Patricia had shown the book to a top agent she knew who was apparently interested in representing Zach. Simone Ravell was so enamoured by *The Reinvention of Harry Browne* that she predicted a bidding war when publishers heard about it.

Alarm bells jangled in his head.

'It's a great story, plus it comes with your name attached, so why wouldn't Simone be interested?' Cody breezed on without giving him the chance to respond. 'Don't get on your high horse about the name recognition thing either. You know it's part of the business. Contacts matter. She isn't stupid, Zach. She's worked hard for her reputation and wouldn't throw it away if you'd written a piece of trash.'

'Yeah, I get that.'

'But?'

The last thing he wanted was to come across as dumb and ungrateful. After all, he'd approached Cody, not the other way around.

'You're freaked about what it'll do to your desire for a quiet life, aren't you?' His agent laughed. 'It's not *War and Peace*, Zach, it's a kid's book about a wannabe actor. Even if it became a successful movie franchise—'

'Movie?'

'Cool it. Simone mentioned she could see it on the big screen, but you and I know there's a lot of hoops to jump through before that's even a remote possibility. And you'd only be the writer of the book it's based on; that's usually low down the totem pole when it comes to movie fame.' Cody kept on 'You might get winkled out of your rural idyll for a few book signings or interviews but that's about it. Promise.'

'I overreacted. Sorry. I'm appreciative, really I am.'

‘Good. You can expect a call from Simone later today. If you two hit it off, she’s anxious to lock you into a contract before anyone else gets a whiff of the book. Patricia swears she’s the best in the business, but it’s important you get a gut feeling that you’ll work well together.’ His tone softened. ‘We had that in spades, which is why we’ve put up with each other for so long.’

‘Yeah, you’re right about that.’ They’d been together longer than most Hollywood marriages. ‘I’ll talk to Simone and we’ll go from there. Thanks again. You’re a good friend.’

‘I’ve tried to be.’ Cody cleared his throat and Zach took a guess he wasn’t the only one struggling against giving in to his emotions. ‘Are you still painting scenery or whatever to keep Ms Rosey happy?’

‘Something like that.’ He almost admitted he was performing again – albeit as a lowly spirit of the cave with no lines and a garish yellow and red costume – but didn’t want to turn it into a big deal. ‘I’ll let you get back to bed.’

‘Hey, I’m up now. Places to be. People to see.’

‘Yeah, me too.’

They ended the call but he didn’t rush to move from the chair. After two years of existing, he was ready for full on make-the-most-of-it living again. *About time too.* A wave of sadness swept through him remembering Laura. Although they’d drifted apart by the end, it still seemed impossible to believe that someone so alive and vital wasn’t in the world any longer. Perhaps they would have moved past the bitterness and her betrayal and become good friends again, but he couldn’t be certain. But Zach *was* certain of Rosey and it was time he told her so. Properly.

Chapter Twenty-Eight

'Why the frown?' Zach's supple fingers stroked her forehead. 'I hope you aren't regretting coming home with me last night?' His free hand caressed her hip until she eased away. 'Did I do somethin' wrong?'

'No. It's not you—'

'Not that line. Please.' He sat up. 'Come up with something more original.'

'Fine.' She felt at a disadvantage huddled under the covers with Zach looming over her. 'I'm thrilled for you about the book. It's awesome.'

'But?'

Her smile returned. 'I'm not laughing *at* you, not really. But I'm afraid your fierce, intense stare reminded me of Winston Grainger in *Emeralds are Forever*. Remember when he corners that poor maid in the library and she shoots him?' For a fleeting second, she thought she'd blown it until the crinkly thing happened with his eyes and the corners of his mouth twitched with amusement. He smirked, lifted the covers and peered underneath, then swept a hand over his forehead with a loud sigh.

'No gun. You had me worried there for a moment.' The smile faded. 'Something's up though. Spit it out.'

'It's great you're getting it all together—'

'But you think I'll tire of you?' He waved a hand towards the window. 'Of all this? Go rushing back to Hollywood and you won't see me for dust?' Pain filled his eyes. 'I love you, Rosey, and I thought you loved me?'

'I do!' Tears trickled down her face and she clutched the crumpled sheet in front of her. 'I wish I was bringing more to this relationship, that's all.'

'You'd better not be talking about money. Surely you know that's way down the list when it comes to things that make a worthwhile life?'

'Of course, but you heard what Mike said about me at the pub the night he ended up hitting your poor father.'

'Yeah, but it's garbage and you know it. I can't believe you're takin' anything that idiot or any of his moronic friends say seriously.'

'I've tried not to but it's not always easy to ignore nasty gossip. You know that.' She dredged up a weak smile. 'Anyway, maybe you're *not* a multi-millionaire. For all I know, you've frittered it away on drink, drugs and wild women.'

'Nah. Only the occasional beer. A couple of ibuprofen for a headache.' His eyes turned dark and brooding. 'There is one semi-wild woman I'd like to spoil occasionally. She's incredibly talented. Smart. Funny. Compassionate.' Zach shrugged. 'Of course none of that matters because her bank account's on the empty side and she still lives with her mother.'

'Now who's making fun of who?'

'As they say, if the cap fits …' Zach gathered her up in his arms. 'If I haven't made myself clear enough, I love you. I love Cornwall and *most* of the Cornish people.' His warm laughter filled the room. 'The jury's still out on Mike Blamey but nowhere is perfect.'

It was as though the sun had come out and pushed aside the last cloud of her ridiculous doubts.

Anna clapped her hands to silence the general hum of pre-rehearsal chatter filling the room.

'Look, he came.' Rosey pointed towards the door. 'I wasn't sure he would.'

A hush fell and heads swivelled to stare at Roland Stephens. He looked uncertain as to whether or not to step inside.

Zach was as disbelieving as anyone when their vandalism culprit had turned out to be this innocuous looking grey-haired man with a pronounced stoop and thick glasses.

Anna swept through with her kingfisher-blue caftan wafting behind like a jet trail. 'Roland, come in.'

There were a few angry grimaces and he caught the hum of muttered conversations. Although he felt sympathetic towards the old guy, he understood where the doubters were coming from too. Rosey's mother kept her hand on Roland's arm; whether it was to reassure him of her support or stop him from walking out, Zach couldn't be sure. Anna led him to the front of the room and her uncompromising gaze swept around them all.

'I'm not going to beat around the bush because that'll waste everyone's time and we've got a rehearsal to get on with. Most of you know Mr Stephens, Roland, and the sterling work he's done for the pantomime in the past.' Her mouth tightened. 'You also know he was responsible for the recent attempts to sabotage our production. He asked me for the opportunity to apologise so I'll turn the floor over to him now.'

A deer-in-the-headlights look flared in the man's pale eyes and the little colour he had drained away.

'Thank you.' Roland cleared his throat. 'I'm sorry.' His reedy voice was barely audible. 'I could make excuses for my behaviour but, at the end of the day, there aren't any that matter. I was jealous, mean and resentful.' He straightened his shoulders. 'Anna and Rosey have been gracious enough to accept my apology but I don't expect that from everyone, and, frankly, I'm not sure I deserve it.'

'You're bloody right there.' Saul Goudge, one of the cave spirits, glowered down from the stage. 'You were one of us for years. Bloody disgusting 'tis.'

'He's not talking for us all, Mr Stephens.'

Zach was taken aback when Jago stepped forward.

'We all make mistakes.' His skin reddened and he shuffled from one foot to the other. 'You've been good enough to have me back after I messed up.' He nodded at Samira. 'If this lady can forgive the way she was treated by more people here than just me and Mike, surely we can get past what Roland did?'

'You nailed it there.' Zach spoke up. 'We all need to search our hearts for some compassion.'

'Who're you to tell us what to do?' Saul folded his arms over his thick chest.

'Someone who's been on the receiving end of enough gossip and judgement to last me a lifetime.' He took Rosey's hand. 'I'm also a lucky man who's found love and a new home here with y'all. It doesn't take anything away from me to show a little kindness to a guy who's done something he deeply regrets.'

'I'm a newcomer too, and probably always will be to many of you.' Samira joined in. 'I've never met Mr Stephens, but I'm in a hundred per cent agreement with Zach … and Jago.' Her fleeting glance at her former adversary made him turn bright red. 'Nothing Mr Stephens did was insurmountable because we came together to solve the problems. I suggest we put this behind us and concentrate on putting on a good show.' Samira smiled at Anna. 'Before the last shreds of our lovely producer's patience run out, perhaps we should get on with the rehearsal?'

'Hear, hear.' Rosey clapped, and, after a brief hesitation, other people joined in until the hall rang with applause.

Zach noticed Roland pull out a ragged blue handkerchief and wipe at his eyes. He bobbed his head in an appreciative nod but couldn't speak.

'Yes, well, that's sorted then.' Anna's voice wobbled. 'I want everyone for Act One, Scene One on stage in five minutes ready to start.' She wagged her finger. 'Roland will be watching so don't let me down.' Out of nowhere, she threw her arms around the stunned old man in a bear hug and kissed his cheek before letting go.

Rosey went rigid against his side with the effort not to laugh.

'Are we likely to have any music or will we be singing *a capella* tonight, Rosey dear?'

'I'm coming.' She squeezed Zach's hand and whispered under her breath. 'A lot of help you are. I'll see you later.'

'You can bet on it, sweetheart.'

'Hey beautiful, do you mind if a cave spirit shares your piano stool for a minute to rest his weary legs?'

'I suppose it'll be okay. I don't want him putting a magic spell on me.' Rosey giggled at Zach. 'How could I forget? He's already done that.' She shifted along so he could squeeze in next to her. Her musical ability wasn't needed for a few minutes because Anna was running

Jasmine and Aladdin through their enchanted garden scene. 'So how's your day been so far?'

'Pretty damn amazing. And yours?'

'Not bad.'

'Not bad?' Zach's sexy smile turned wicked. 'Guess I'll have to work on improvin' so I can earn a higher rating than that in your tough estimation.'

'Can you come and help Fred lift the sofa out for the next scene?' Amanda appeared. 'I'd be happy to do it, but …'

'No problem. It's heavy.'

Something about her friend was nagging at Rosey, and suddenly it clicked. 'Oh my God, you're—'

'Shush.' Amanda turned bright pink. 'It's early so we're not telling anyone yet. How on earth did you guess?'

'Maybe because you normally haul scenery around quite happily, plus you've got a very satisfied look about you.' Poor Zach looked confused. 'I'll explain later.'

'Sure. I'm guessing it's one of those women things that less intelligent men don't get.'

'Something like that.' She winked at Amanda.

'I'd better go, Rosey.' Zach leaned in for another kiss. 'That sofa won't shift itself.'

It was then that a blood-curdling scream rang out and everyone stopped what they were doing. Seconds later, her mother rushed out from backstage, white-faced and clearly in shock.

'Oh dear me … I'm afraid something awful has happened. Rob has had a very nasty accident. We're calling for an ambulance. Please don't any of you go back there, you'll only be in the way.' Her mother's hand flew to her mouth and for a moment she couldn't speak. 'At least we're lucky to have our local community nurse in the chorus so

Mary is taking good care of him. There's nothing anybody else can do so you might as well go on home.' Anna carried on. 'We won't be rehearsing tonight.'

Nobody liked to be the first to leave but gradually the hall emptied. Zach disappeared to see what more he could find out, and Rosey straightened the chairs and picked up abandoned sweet wrappers.

'It's not good news. Mary thinks he's broken his leg.' Zach shoved a hand through his tousled hair. 'Rob offered to help Fred carry the sofa onstage because I wasn't around and tripped walking backwards. The heavy end landed on his leg.' He puffed out his frustration. 'If I hadn't been so keen to see you and hung around chatting, this wouldn't have happened.' Rosey didn't offer any meaningless platitudes about it being an accident and not his fault. He'd realise the truth of that when he was thinking straight again. She caught sight of her distraught mother and the reality of Rob's injury sunk in. This was worse than treacle in the piano and a few ripped costumes. Without the dame, they didn't have a pantomime.

'I'm really sorry, Zach, but I think I'd better stay home with Mum tonight. You can see how upset she is.'

'Yeah. It's lousy for Rob and the show.' He shuffled his feet. 'I could hang around too if you want?'

'It's okay. You'd better go on back to your parents.' Rosey sensed his relief. No doubt the last thing Zach wanted was to be dragged into a conversation about what would happen if Rob couldn't perform on Friday. She popped a quick kiss on his mouth then turned away and glued on a smile. 'Let's lock up here, Mum, then we'll go home and stick the kettle on.'

'You're a good girl.' Anna smothered her in a tight hug then let go and gave her a long, hard stare. 'You know the logical answer to the problem, don't you?'

If she delayed the inevitable by asking what her mum was talking about, that would be pointless. 'Zach is *not* the answer and you're well aware of that.'

'But—'

'But nothing.' Rosey crossed her arms and tried to look fierce. 'We'll have to come up with another solution.'

'Like what?'

'Maybe Saul Goudge could step in?'

Anna scoffed. 'Don't be ridiculous. He barely manages to remember the three lines he's got as a cave spirit, and I've had to tell him to mouth the words to the songs because he's always out of tune.'

'With a bit of practice, he might be all right.'

'In six days! Don't be daft.'

Rosey wracked her brains for an alternative suggestion. 'How about Jago? I know he's never had a speaking part before but he's quick to pick up directions.' Rosey watched Anna wavering. 'He's got a decent singing voice too.'

'I'll think about it tonight. We'll either have to find a substitute dame by tomorrow or cancel the show.'

The ultimatum made Rosey's heart sink.

Chapter Twenty-Nine

'Whoa, stop right there, Anna. I couldn't possibly—'

'Why not?'

Zach received the same piercing stare she normally reserved for chattering children in the junior chorus.

'You've warmed yourself up as one of the cave spirits. You'd be brilliant.'

Before he put the argument out there that a nameless spirit with no lines was a completely different scenario from taking on a crucial role that would make or break the show, Rosey interrupted them.

'Mum! I told you *not* to ask.' She glowered at her mother. 'You said you'd consider asking Jago, so what happened to that?'

'I *did* think about it, Rosey my love, but we've got to be realistic. He can't possibly learn the role in this short a time. Maybe another year we'll try him in a bigger part, but there's no way we can let the whole pantomime rest on his shoulders.' Anna rested a coy smile on Zach. 'You're a completely different story, my 'andsome.'

Before he had the chance to protest, Rosey jumped to his defence again.

'Apart from anything else, Zach won his last Oscar for playing a doomed Arctic explorer – he's hardly going to prance around our village stage in gaudy dresses and a purple wig.'

'Great actors can play any parts.'

'This one can't. Not any longer. Could you ask Mike to come back?' Heat prickled the back of his neck. 'Sorry. Stupid suggestion.'

'Yes, it is, young man. Samira would walk out and rightly so.' Anna's voice softened and a little voice in his head told him to beware. 'You know the dame's lines, don't you?'

He couldn't deny it so he kept his lips firmly pressed together.

'I've watched you following along. You know every single part.' A sly smile crept over her face. 'Surely you won't let Rosey down?'

'Mum! That is so not fair. You can't manipulate him that way.'

The twinkle in Anna's eyes said otherwise.

Zach knew if he stuck to his guns and refused to step in, Rosey would back him every inch of the way … but would she be secretly disappointed? 'If I said yes – and it's still a big *if,* so don't get your hopes up – hasn't it occurred to you some of the other cast members might be resentful?'

'That's their problem. I've got a show starting in five days and you're the only person capable of stepping in and doing even a half-decent job. If you won't give it a try, we might as well cancel.' Her eyes swam with tears. 'It's our seventy-five-year anniversary this year too. Polcarne's first panto was in 1948. After the war ended, England was struggling to recover and people's spirits needed a lift. We've never missed one since.'

He reminded himself she was a consummate actress and fought to harden his heart against her pleading. 'Wouldn't an American dame be an anomaly? There's no way I can nail a Cornish accent.'

'Oh my 'andsome, don't fret about that. Widow Twankey's suggestive lines will sound even funnier in your lovely southern drawl.'

Now he knew how an oyster felt being irritated by a grain of sand. He might as well give in and try to turn it into a pearl. 'See if you can round everyone up to come back here tonight. Explain that I'm willing to have a quick run through to see how it goes.' He fixed Anna with a hard stare. 'Afterwards, you put it to a vote.'

'And if they vote yes, you'll do it?'

'Yeah. I guess.'

'I'll start making calls.' Anna grabbed Rosey's arm. 'You can help.' She flashed Zach a triumphant grin. 'You'd better start going through Widow Twankey's lines, and later on Rosey can run through the songs with you.' Her jubilation cranked down a notch. 'I didn't think to ask if you can sing? It doesn't have to be opera quality but vaguely in tune helps?'

'He's got a lovely voice. Didn't you hear him at the carol service?' Rosey shook her head in exasperation.

'Don't worry, I can stumble through a few funny songs.' He omitted mentioning his voice training lessons at drama school. 'I'll go back to the farm and work on my lines there.' His parents would be flabbergasted. First off, he fell in love. Next, he bought a piece of land and planned to build a house. Yesterday he got a deal with a literary agent. Now he was on the verge of accepting his first proper acting role in over two years. Not a bad amount to squeeze into a couple of months.

'I'll give you a ring later and let you know what time to be at the hall.' Rosey's smile turned cheeky. 'If you've got a spare minute, you might want to practise walking in high heels.'

'Heels?' He must have sounded horrified because both women burst out laughing. 'Does Mike have anythin' I could wear?'

'Yes, but I can't see him letting us borrow them. He's built up his own collection over the years from charity shop finds – he re-dyes them if needed and tarts them up.' Anna sighed. 'The dame's costumes belong to us and I'm sure Zoe can alter them to work for you.'

'Mum, don't let's worry about that for a minute,' Rosey pleaded. 'We've got more important things to sort out.'

'I'll come up with somethin' if it comes to that.' Zach's reassurance seemed to do the trick and her mother's smile returned.

'I'll walk out to the car with you.'

Outside, he wrapped his arms around her and rested his head against hers. 'What am I doin', Rosey?'

'Being a brave, wonderful man.' She pressed a lingering kiss on his mouth. 'I'm concerned for you though.' Worry clouded her eyes. 'I tried to warn Mum—'

'It's not your fault. I could've said no and actually meant it.' He managed a faint smile. 'Maybe I need to do this to prove I still can. I've no desire to return to professional acting but perhaps I need to know I could if I wanted to.'

'I get that. I didn't touch the piano for months after I came back home. The stupid instrument sat there taunting me every day until I gave in. As soon as my fingers touched the keys again, I rediscovered the joy I felt when I first learned to play. Being an accompanist, teaching piano and composing for the pantomime – that satisfies me deeply and if I can do it for other shows too, that'd be even better. I used to see that as less than being a concert pianist but now I've come to realise it's simply different sides of the same coin.' Rosey's eyes shone. 'If you don't go soon, someone not a million miles away will be out to tell us off.' She smiled and nodded back towards the house.

He needed to block out any lingering doubts because if they crept back in, it would be fatal.

Rosey stood mesmerised. It was amazing how different it was to watch Zach acting only a few metres away from her on the stage from seeing him in one of his many film roles. She couldn't help smiling as the slightly higher voice he'd adopted for Window Twankey rang out through the hall.

'Well, la-di-da, you sure are an old tease, Abanazar. I think I should put some extra starch in your underwear to make you behave around a poor widow lady.' He instinctively shimmied his hips and fluttered his eyelashes in the time-honoured suggestive way of a traditional pantomime dame. No one would believe he had been unfamiliar with pantomimes until quite recently. From the moment he set foot on the stage, he became *the* Zach Broussard again and inhabited the part of Widow Twankey like a well-worn glove.

A wave of emotion swept through her and Rosey fought to hold back tears.

'You look as though the world's come to an end.' Her mum sidled up to her.

'How was that?' He bounded off-stage and landed in front of her with a smile stretching from ear to ear. Zach grasped her shoulders and planted a lip-smacking kiss on her mouth before beaming at her mother. 'Thank you for bullying me into this – in a good way.'

'*Humph*, it made sense. That's all.' Anna's eyes narrowed on him. 'It looks like my silly daughter's got her knickers in a twist because she thinks you'll be dashing off back to Los Angeles now.'

'Mum!' The word mortified didn't come close to covering Rosey's toe-curling embarrassment. Her mother knew her like no one else and she'd recognised the fears growing like weeds inside her head.

'I'm not goin' anywhere.' Zach frowned. 'Not unless she wants me too.'

'Oh no, she definitely doesn't.' The riff on the traditional pantomime banter brought back his smile. 'Sorry. I had a little wobble, that's all. You were so wonderful and I—'

'Panicked. I get it.' He stroked a hand down over her hair. A gleam brightened his eyes. 'I've been carrying something around for days, waiting for the perfect moment, and I reckon this is it …' He fumbled around in his trouser pocket and pulled out a small black velvet box.

Rosey pressed her hands over her mouth when he dropped down on one knee, only vaguely aware that they were now the focus of everyone's attention.

'Mama tried to insist you'd expect a fancy restaurant, champagne and red roses, but my dad reckoned simple is best and he's a sensible guy.'

'He is.' A stunning solitaire diamond ring winked at her and the breath caught in her throat.

'Marry me, Rosey. I could be poetic and give you a million reasons why I love you, but—'

'It would take too long. All I need is you.' She smiled. 'And this!' She gazed down at the ring. Rosey waggled her left hand in his face. 'Don't you want to make sure it fits?'

'Oh, I know it does.' He smirked. 'A little birdie told me your size.'

'Would that little birdie be my mum? Are all our parents in on this?'

'Maybe.' Zach turned pink.

'Well, I think that's wonderful.' Rosey smiled so hard she was surprised her face didn't crack open. 'They're important to us and it's lovely they approve.'

'Approve? One or all of them would've given me a thick ear if I hadn't got my act together.'

'Pun intended? Act together?'

'Are you ever going to answer the poor man?' Her mother's grin was wider than the Atlantic Ocean. 'We haven't heard you say yes yet, have we?' She nodded around at the rest of the watching crowd.

Rosey wrapped herself around Zach. 'Of course the answer is yes. He knew that.'

'Oh yes I did.' He kissed her and everyone burst into applause.

There was no time to savour the moment before a gaggle of excited children gathered around her, begging to see Rosey's ring. She guessed her red, shiny face could be used to power the National Grid at this point, and so many people wanted to shake Zach's hand that it would surely be throbbing later.

When there was a lull, Zach turned back to Anna. 'Right, future mother-in-law, are you ready to put me playing the dame to the vote?'

'If you seriously think it's necessary, we will.'

Rosey knew there'd been some rumblings of dismay when people first heard the proposition but no one had stepped up and said they wanted to give it a try. After the wild success of the impromptu rehearsal, the decision was in no doubt.

'And as for you, young man, you pulled my leg about your singing voice too, didn't you?'

'Maybe.'

'We've still got an awful lot of work to do before opening night on Friday.'

'Yeah, I know. But we'll pull it off.'

Rosey's throat tightened and she couldn't have spoken if someone had paid her. Three months ago, Zach had wanted nothing to do with anything connected to the stage and now he was reassuring her mother they wouldn't let their audience down. She loved this man more than anything.

'We certainly will.' Anna bustled onto the stage and clapped her hands for everyone to be quiet. 'I promised Zach we'd vote on whether you all agree he should stand in as Widow Twankey, so let's get this done.' Her fierce gaze swept the room. 'Anyone who votes "no" had better be prepared to play the part themselves. It's either that or we cancel.'

'Subtle, isn't she?' Zach whispered. 'Cornish democracy in action.'

A sea of hands went up and no one spoke when Anna asked if there were any dissenters.

'You'll be pleased to hear I've had a text to say Rob's operation went well. He should be out of hospital in a few days, but he'll be on crutches for a while.' Her mother beamed straight at Rosey and Zach. 'I think it's high time we celebrated our new dame's engagement to my lovely daughter! Let's get cleared up and out of here.'

'Amen to that,' he muttered. 'After that, I plan on taking a certain hot pianist to bed so we can enjoy our own private celebration and make sweet music together.'

'Oh for heaven's sake, turn off the Hollywood charm. You know it's wasted on me.'

They were both still laughing when her mother nabbed them.

'I've spoken to Zoe. She needs you at her house at nine o'clock tomorrow morning for a fitting.' She smirked. 'I can't wait to see you in the finale dress. It's a stunning yellow satin crinoline with purple flounces and a towering purple wig.'

'Perfect.' Zach chuckled. 'Gold and purple are the colours for Louisiana State University. My dad's alma mater. Must be fate.' His gaze locked with Rosey and she blushed all over. 'C'mon. The first round is on me. That should help win over any last doubters.'

They did a final check of all the doors and windows – Roland's tricks had left them more cautious. Arm in arm, the three of them walked into the crowded pub to loud cheers. The Hollywood gossip magazines had nothing on the Polcarne locals when it came to a well-oiled publicity machine and the news had spread already. There were plenty of ribald jokes that cast humorous aspersions on Zach's manhood and Rosey's wisdom in planning to marry a man who was being forced into dresses and high heels. She was relieved when he laughed it all off with his trademark charm. Nobody knew what a touchy subject that was.

'Oh no, what's he doing here? I thought he'd been banned.' Rosey tightened her grip on Zach's hand. Mike Blamey had risen up from a table by the fire and was giving them the evil eye. He elbowed his way through to plant himself in front of them.

'You've got everything you wanted now, haven't you, mate?' Mike jabbed Zach in the chest. 'My part in the panto. The hottest chick in the village. And guess what?' Another hard shove almost knocked Zach off-balance. 'Last week it was "suggested" I find other employment because the school doesn't want me "poisoning young minds" with my so-called racist views while I'm mopping the floors.'

'I'm real sorry you lost your job, but that's what happens when being an asshole catches up with you.' The calm rebuttal made Mike's face turn to granite and a pall of silence filled the pub. 'I thought we were safe from being hassled. Weren't you told to stay away from here?'

'I let him back in because he promised not to cause any trouble and it were a new year, like.' Jock appeared and was full of apologies. 'That's it. Get out and stay out.' He clamped a hand on Mike's shoulder and steered him outside.

'Maybe we can enjoy that well-earned drink now he's cleared off. I've gotta say, Rosey, that you and Cornwall have a unique way of helping a guy sort out his life.' Zach grinned. 'I wouldn't have it any other way though. Keeps me on my toes … and high heels.'

'About the shoes—'

'Don't fret, I'll get my mama on that. She loves a challenge. I bet she'll be draggin' my poor father around every shop in Cornwall tomorrow. Trust me, she'll come up with something.'

Rosey didn't doubt it for one moment – the same way she had no more doubts about Zach's commitment to her, the village and the pantomime. 'I'm sure she will. Now buy everyone a drink for heaven's sake.'

'Yes, ma'am.'

Who wanted a quiet life anyway?

Chapter Thirty

'Can I get a make-up check?' At the previous night's dress rehearsal, Zach had teased Rosey about being pretty sure she'd never expected any fiancé of hers to ask that question.

'Overexaggerated eyebrows – check. Mile-long fake lashes – check.' She touched his cheek. 'Enough rouge to make you visible from space – check.' Her eyes sparkled. 'And lips so red and luscious they could be a bunch of cherries.'

'Yeah okay, enough of the flattery.' It was a challenge to sound tough and macho while wearing a gaudy red-and-white checked mini dress and rompers, white lace stockings and sparkly red shoes. The latter addition was courtesy of his mother, who'd taken to her new role as fashion coordinator to Widow Twankey with an unhealthy glee.

'You look perfect, but I'm sorry – I've got to go. They'll let the audience in any minute now and I play a medley of the show tunes while they're getting seated. We're sold out and there's a waiting list for tickets since the word got out you were performing.' A touch of concern sneaked into her smile. 'You'll be okay?'

If he admitted he was on the verge of throwing up and had to ask Beth to do his lipstick because his hands were shaking, Rosey would fly into a panic. This was normal for him. As a young actor, he'd tried to hide his stage fright until he saw a mega-star, now a household name, retch into a plastic bucket before going on stage. No one made any comment and he'd come to the conclusion most other actors had their own nervous quirks before performing.

Some demanded their costumes were hung up a certain way, and others needed complete silence and isolation from the rest of the cast. Turning into a mess of jangling nerves seemed mundane in comparison.

'Yeah, I'll be fine.' He'd barely slept for the last five nights and would no doubt crash after Sunday's final performance. Poor Rosey had been driven half crazed by his insistence that they go over the script and the songs time and time again until they became second nature. If he was going to make a fool of himself, it would be the right sort – one that had the audience laughing *with* him not *at* him. 'I'd ask for a kiss but I don't want to smear Beth's good work. Joe caught me dressed out in all this rig a couple of days ago and I thought he'd die laughing.'

'I'm not surprised. I won't say the usual good luck phrase. I saw Rob hobbling along the road today so it might be a bit tactless.'

'Yeah, it kinda makes "break a leg" take on a whole new meaning. I'd better go too or your mom will be on the war path.' Making a dignified exit wasn't possible so he launched into the swaying provocative walk he'd perfected for the dame, leaving Rosey convulsed with laughter.

Backstage the usual chaos ensued with missing costumes, burned out light bulbs and a stubborn plywood model of a clump of trees that refused to stay upright. By the time Beth called the five-minute warning, a cloud of nervous anticipation settled over everyone. Abanazar, the evil magician, waited in the wings ready to stride out in front of the curtain and launch into the monologue that kicked off the show. The chorus of villagers stood around the colourful market place ready for the opening scene. After a lively song, the chief of police would appear and then Aladdin would make his entrance before it came to

Zach's big moment. Widow Twankey arrived in a rickshaw pulled by Jase, a teenage girl. He made her giggle when he expressed his doubts over whether she could manage someone of his size.

'Don't 'ee be so daft. Mike Blamey's no light-weight and I've been hauling bales of hay and driving a tractor since I were ten years old.'

Rosey stopped the preliminary music, the lights dimmed, and she launched into the dark theme she'd composed for Abanazar. After the first monologue, the curtains creaked open to rapturous applause and Zach's heart raced. In his head, he sang the opening number along with the chorus and recited the lines leading up to his own entrance. Jase glanced over her shoulder and gave him a nod.

It was time.

The very first time the audience responded with 'Oh no he isn't' after Widow Twankey boasted that Abanazar was bewitched by her beauty – with a sly eyebrow wiggle and shake of the purple wig – the last of his nerves fled. He was hooked. By the time he kicked off the second act, the traditional hilarious scene set in the laundry loaded with suggestive jokes and slapstick routines, he and Ernie Sampson, who was acting as the chief of police, played off of each other as if they'd been doing this forever. Ernie had given up his Monday evening to rehearse this scene until Zach felt fairly comfortable they could pull it off. By the time he waltzed off stage, he'd sweated off half his make-up and the tight-fitting dress was stuck to his body, but his exhilaration was off the charts. The audience whooped and cheered until the curtain came down.

'Awesome job, mate.' Joe chased after Zach as he headed for the dressing room. 'You bloody know what you're doing, don't you?' A touch of awe sneaked into his voice.

'It's my job. I've trained for years to do this, remember? Well … not exactly this.' He chuckled. 'The Juilliard School doesn't have classes on being a British pantomime dame in its curriculum. It's actually bloody hard work. I saw Mike play the part before he quit and, for all his failings, he nailed it.'

'Yeah, I know. I'd better go and see to the lighting, or the assistant stage manager will cut off my oats.' Joe grinned.

'You love her really.'

'Yep. She's all right.'

Before he knew it, Zoe was helping him into his dress for the finale. This scene was the highlight of the pantomime and where a big chunk of the costume budget was spent. It was always colour coordinated and as spectacular as they could afford to make it. No doubt his father was out there wearing his LSU sweatshirt to match the cast. After one last rousing song, they took their final bows and Zach experienced an inordinate rush of pleasure when Widow Twankey got a decent number of cheers and more than a few wolf-whistles.

He retreated to the dressing room – a cramped space shared with all the other men – and picked up a bottle of baby oil and pad of cotton wool to remove his heavy make-up. Zach stared in the mirror and made a swipe through his over-rouged cheeks.

'Admiring yourself?' Rosey appeared behind his shoulder and leaned in to kiss his sweaty forehead. She touched his dress. 'Thank goodness we're not the same size or you'd be raiding my wardrobe.'

'I hardly think so, honey.' He slipped into the dame's high-pitched voice. 'Your clothes are too sedate for the glamorous Widow Twankey.' Zach tugged her down on his lap for a kiss. 'Now your mother's wardrobe is another story. The gold outfit she's stunning everyone with tonight would be perfect for date night with Abanazar.'

'You've got a hoard of fans out there waiting to see you so hurry up and change so you can come and greet them.'

He froze. He should have been able to laugh it off with a joke but couldn't make his mouth form the words.

Rosey watched his countenance change and wanted to kick herself for being thoughtless. 'There aren't too many, and I'm sure they'll be happy with a quick autograph. We couldn't keep all of the press out so a few are hanging around to take pictures.'

'It's okay. Honestly. It wouldn't be fair on your mom and everyone else who's worked so hard if I don't man up and do my bit.'

'Are you sure?' She stroked his cheek. 'I'll be by your side if that's enough to keep the wobbles at bay?'

'Enough doesn't begin to describe you, and, yeah, I'm sure …' The rasp thickened his deep rich drawl. 'I—'

'Rosey Teague, you'd better bugger off before we all start stripping and you see something you shouldn't.' Ernie ripped off his policeman's coat and threw it on the chair.

She eyed him up and down before standing up. 'I doubt it would be that exciting but I'll go anyway.' Rosey bent down to whisper in Zach's ear. 'I'm looking forward to getting to know the charming Widow Twankey far better … intimately, in fact … later when I get her on her own.'

'Oh, she'll be ready,' he growled.

The other men started to troop in so she made a strategic withdrawal and hurried out to help clear up the hall. She made a start on stacking the chairs, but was distracted and stood still for a moment as she watched several excited members of the junior chorus being shepherded home by their long-suffering parents. It would be an uphill struggle to calm them down this late in the evening but tomorrow was Saturday so they could all enjoy a lie in. That might bolster their energy enough to survive two more evening performances and a Sunday matinee. She pitied their schoolteachers on Monday morning.

Rosey rubbed a finger over her ring.

'You're probably hoping for a genie to appear but will a deconstructed dame do instead?' Zach slipped his hands around her waist and pulled her close. He gazed in the direction of the noisy children too. 'Sweet, aren't they? I'm sorry I can't grant the one wish we'd both love more than anything.'

The wistfulness in his voice made her throat tighten. 'Remember what we talked about?'

'Yeah, and you're an awesome woman. If I tell you so every day for the rest of our lives, it'll never be enough.'

'Yes. It will.' Rosey leaned against his broad, warm chest. 'How about we go to face your adoring public together now and get it over with?'

'Perfect.'

She didn't comment on his strained smile because her own was equally forced. 'Come on then.' Glancing towards the back of the hall, she noticed the crowd had grown considerably. Her confidence wavered and she felt Zach's fingers tighten around her hand as they made their way down the narrow aisle between the rows of chairs. One young woman noticed them approaching and screamed with excitement, and before Rosey knew what was happening, they were surrounded and bombarded with questions and pleas for autographs and pictures. She was fascinated to see Zach switch into the calm, professional manner he was known for, and watched in admiration as he signed pantomime programmes and posed for photos. Anyone would think this was his favourite thing in the world to do. After a while, he pulled her away and held up his hand, asking for silence.

'We sure do appreciate y'all coming out tonight. This has been the best experience for me and I'm eternally grateful to the Polcarne pantomime group. Any help I've been able to give them has been a small repayment for everything they've done for me.' He drew Rosey closer. 'I won't be answering any questions so please don't waste time asking them. I'm extremely happy for you to spread the news that Rosey and I are engaged and I'll be making my home here with her.' He flashed a broad grin. 'Now Widow Twankey is in need of a stiff whisky and her beauty sleep in order to be ready for tomorrow's performance.' Zach leaned down to whisper in Rosey's ear. 'Let's head for the back door.' He swivelled her away and they walked towards the stage.

They hadn't seen his parents since the show finished, but now they were standing there waiting to see him.

'There you are, son. We wondered where you'd gotten to. Your mama and I were looking for you.' Pierre's smile couldn't be any wider.

'C'mere, *cherie*, and let me hug you.' Marie wrapped her arms around Zach. 'Your father tried to tell me but I wouldn't listen. I was wrong.'

'What do you mean?'

‘You *were* right to come here.’ A twinkle bloomed in her eyes. ‘Of course I’m not convinced you could’ve known that.’

‘I guess it was a bit of a gamble but I reckon it paid off.’ He winked at Rosey.

‘If I say anything more, I’ll bawl – and I don’t know about you, but I’m ready to party. There’s a glass of wine at the pub with my name on it.’

‘Hear, hear.’ Anna came to join them. She turned her smile on Zach. ‘What do you think about you and Rob being the Ugly Stepsisters in Cinderella next year?’

‘Next year?’ Rosey and Zach both burst out laughing. ‘Oh yes we will!’

Chapter Thirty-One

Eleven months later – Christmas Eve
'A little more to the right. It's crooked.' She scrutinised the holly wreath Zach was attempting to hang on their bright blue front door. 'What do you think, Molly, is it pretty?' The shy four-year-old nodded and buried her face back in Rosey's dark red corduroy skirt.

'Are my girls ready to hang up their stockings tonight?'

'Well, I definitely am and I think someone else might be too.' It tugged at Rosey's heart when Molly gave Zach a wary nod. Her father's mistreatment had left the little girl distrustful of all men so she refused to go near Zach or speak directly to him

After their quiet spring wedding, a few weeks after Joe and Beth's, the first thing they did was apply to the local council to start the process of becoming foster parents. Their social worker understood Rosey's reservations about becoming too attached to the children they wanted to help but convinced her that, although giving a child from a troubled home unconditional love before letting them go again would be painful, it would be a precious, possibly life-changing, gift. It turned out there was a dire need in Cornwall so Molly was already their third placement. The first two were both babies, who only came for weekend stays as respite for their parents, but Molly had been with them for over a month now.

'Our first Christmas in our new home.' Zach stepped back beside her.

The house wouldn't have gone up this quickly without Beth's intervention. Her family were builders so they'd hired her uncle and his sons to build Hayfield House. It seemed the obvious name to choose because it was built on what used to be Joe's hay field. They settled on a square, traditional design made of Cornish stone and topped with a slate roof to blend in with the older farm buildings.

'Happy?' She didn't really need to ask because her new husband was night and day different from the guarded, bruised man who'd arrived in Polcarne. He spent his days working on their house, writing his children's books – the first of which had come out in the summer to rave reviews – and doing occasional voiceover work that Cody put his way. He'd also run drama workshops in a couple of the local schools and was set to tread the boards again in next month's pantomime.

'Yeah. I sure hope you are too, Mrs Broussard?' His electric-blue eyes bored into her. If Molly hadn't have been there, he'd have kissed her but any physical contact between them distressed the little girl so they had to be careful. 'Have you nailed the Fowey panto's finale yet?'

As soon as she'd put out feelers to other village shows, she'd been inundated with more offers of work than she had the time for. 'It came to me about two o'clock this morning. I almost sneaked out of bed to write it down but I didn't want to wake you so I hummed it in my head until you woke up.'

'I've come with an invitation.' Joe strolled up the path. 'Beth's been baking again so we've got warm mince pies on offer.' He patted his stomach. 'I'll be as fat as she is soon.'

'Who're you calling fat? I'm a voluptuous pregnant woman.' Beth joined them, resting her hand on her swelling belly.

Before Rosey and Zach got married, he'd decided to pre-empt the inevitable questions and be upfront with her mother, Joe and Beth about his fertility problems. There was a brief wobble in the closeness between the two young couples when Beth discovered she was pregnant and they held back from sharing the news for fear of hurting Rosey and Zach's feelings. When Joe finally blurted it out, they both assured him that they couldn't be happier. That was the truth, but still they hugged extra hard in bed that night, wordlessly comforting each other.

'I can't believe you're keeping the restaurant open over Christmas.'

'With a business this new, we can't afford to lose the goodwill we've built up. We're only serving lunch tomorrow and again on Boxing Day. No evening meals.' Beth beamed. 'It does Joe good to get worn out running around after me. He's getting in shape for all the sleepless nights ahead.'

The Old Hay Barn, where Zach started off his Cornish life, now hosted diners instead of overnight guests. Its remote location and limited seating for twenty-four people had somehow become a plus rather than a deterrent.

'Are you excited about Father Christmas coming tonight, Molly?' Beth crouched down and smiled at their foster daughter.

'We are, aren't we, sweetheart?' Rosey squeezed the little girl's hand. 'Mama Marie made a red stocking with your name on and I'm sure it'll be full in the morning.' That coaxed a fleeting smile from the child. Who would fill Molly's stocking next Christmas? Anyone or no one? She blinked before tears blurred her eyes. The latest update from the social worker was that Molly's dysfunctional parents looked unlikely to be considered fit to ever parent their daughter again, but it was still a possibility.

'The mince pies will burn if we stand here talking any longer,' Joe complained.

'Don't be daft. I took them out of the oven before I came up.' Beth stroked Molly's tight black curls. 'We don't want them too hot for tiny mouths, do we?'

They soon piled into the warm, welcoming farmhouse and made straight for the kitchen. Christmas carols played on the radio and a miniature artificial tree on the counter twinkled merrily away.

'Your mum's back to her usual mood this year, I see. Bah Humbug and all that.' Joe chuckled.

'True.' Anna's flirtation with celebrating Christmas in a big way had waned faster than the few flakes of snow that were the closest thing Cornwall usually got to proper winter weather. 'She's coming up to us tomorrow for the day.' She wiped a few crumbs from the little girl's mouth. Molly had eaten her mince pie while they were all chatting. 'That's enough now before bed. We'll have plenty more tomorrow, I promise.'

'When do Marie and Pierre arrive?' Beth asked.

'The week of the pantomime.' Zach said. 'They're determined not to miss seeing me in a selection of gaudy dresses and high heels again.'

Molly had snuggled back in Rosey's lap, sucking her thumb and now her eyelids were drooping. 'I think someone is ready for bed.' She pushed back her chair and hoisted the sleepy child up in her arms. 'Come on, let's go home.'

Home. Zach's heart swelled. He'd done nothing to deserve this good fortune but was trying his hardest to pay it on.

The anguish he'd gone through trying to cope with his failing marriage and Laura's tragic death had faded. Time couldn't wipe out the past but it did soften the impact and allowed him to live with it. His fervent hope for Molly was that her bad memories would disappear to be replaced by good ones. The sweet little girl deserved nothing less.

'We need to put out milk and cookies for Santa.' Zach strolled alongside Rosey and smiled over at Molly, who was fighting to stay awake. This morning he'd baked a large batch of his mother's traditional snickerdoodle biscuits and Molly made his day when she'd come close enough, albeit with Rosey nearby, to add the red and green sugar sprinkles. She flung them around with cheerful abandon, and he'd been happy to sweep up the floor afterwards and clean down all the surfaces where they settled like a sugary cloud.

Inside the house he turned on the tree lights while Rosey took Molly with her to the kitchen. When they returned, the little girl's expression was serious as she carried a snowman shaped plate full of biscuits, frowning as if the objects entrusted to her were unexploded bombs. Rosey followed close behind with a glass of milk, and once they set everything down on the hearth, they sat together on the sofa. Zach perched at the far end and took out the worn copy of *The Night Before Christmas* that his mother had sent at his request the previous week. He began to read the timeless story and noticed Molly craning her neck to see the pictures. Keeping his focus on the book, he sensed her edging closer, and by the time he was halfway through her leg pressed against his and a tousle of her black wiry curls lay on the arm of his red sweater. He glanced over at Rosey, her face flushed with heat from the wood burning stove, and she smiled right back. This was what Christmas was all about. Zach reached the end of the book but didn't move, afraid of startling Molly.

'It's time for bed, sweetie. Shall I carry you up?' Rosey's offer made the little girl shake her head.

'I want Zach to.' She held out her arms, and as they latched around his neck, he smelled the gentle lavender shampoo Rosey had used on her in the bath tonight. His heart swelled. No other Christmas present would match this.

After they'd tucked the sleepy child into bed, he took Rosey's hand and led her across the hall to their own bedroom. 'Merry Christmas, my love.'

'Oh yes it is.'

* The End *

Thank You

As always I'm grateful to the lovely Tasting panel members who fell in love with Rosey and Zach's heart-warming story with its festive and fun celebration of the great British pantomime. If you would like to help spread the word about *A Little Christmas Panto* and have a minute to leave a review where you bought the book that would be amazing.

Angela

x

About the Author

Angela was born in St. Stephen, Cornwall, England. After completing her A-Levels she worked as a Naval Secretary. She met her husband, a US Naval Flight Officer while being based at a small NATO Headquarters on the Jutland Peninsula in Denmark. They lived together in Denmark, Sicily, California, southern Maryland and London before settling in Tennessee.

Angela took a creative writing course in 2000 and loved it so much that she has barely put her pen down since. She has had short stories and novels published in the US. Her debut novel, *Sugar & Spice*, won Choc Lit's Search for an American Star competition and is her UK debut.

Follow Angela:

Twitter: www.twitter.com/AngelaBritnell

Facebook: www.facebook.com/angelabritnell

More Choc Lit from Angela

Summer at Seaspray Cottage

What would you do if you inherited a Cornish cottage by the sea?

If you're Thea Armitage, sell it as soon as possible. Whilst there's no denying that Seaspray Cottage has its charm, it just holds too many bad memories for Thea to consider keeping it – although at least spending the summer preparing it for sale gives her a distraction from troubles back home in Tennessee.

What Thea didn't count on was her worst Cornish memory moving in right next door. Local bad boy Harry Venton played no small part in Thea's decision never to return to Cornwall twenty years before – and now he's her neighbour! Could things get any worse?

Except Harry isn't the boy he was, and as Thea comes to realise that her opinion of him was built on lies and misunderstandings, perhaps things will start looking up for her summer at Seaspray Cottage ...

A Cornish Summer at Pear Tree Farm

Book 1 – Pear Tree Farm

Cornish charm and a Tennessee twist – the perfect pair?

Nessa Vivian is determined to keep her parents' business afloat, but Pear Tree Farm near the backwater Cornish village of Polgarth didn't do well as farm, and it's not faring much better as a camp site. Maybe it's due to Nessa's habit of taking in troubled runaways, like ex-soldier Crispin, for next to nothing. Or perhaps her highly-strung sister Lowena is right – caravans named after Beatles' songs and homegrown pears are not enough to turn the farm into a tourist haven.

Then another troubled runaway turns up, posing the greatest threat yet. Ex-musician Ward Spencer from Tennessee is certainly intriguing, but could his plans to put nearby Tregereth House on the map mean Pear Tree Farm is finished – or does his arrival signal a second lease of life, and not just for Nessa's business?

A Cornish Christmas at Pear Tree Farm

Pairing up at Pear Tree Farm in time for Christmas …

Pear Tree Farm in Cornwall, owned by the kind-hearted Nessa Vivian, is known for taking in lost souls, and ex-soldier Crispin Davies is certainly one of those. But the once sleepy caravan park is now a thriving business, and far from the peace and quiet Crispin was craving, he soon finds himself roped into helping out with a short-notice Christmas festival, organised by Nessa's force-of-nature sister, Lowena.

But despite Crispin's initial reluctance, his involvement in the festival serves to throw him together with Ashley Spencer, an American woman and fellow lost soul, who works at the nearby Tregereth House.

Could Lowena's ambitious scheme result in a more hopeful Christmas and New Year for them both – with a few surprises along the way?

Sequel to A Cornish Summer at Pear Tree Farm.

Visit: www.choc-lit.com for details

More Choc Lit from Angela

Visit www.choc-lit.com for more details.

More Choc Lit from Angela

Visit: www.choc-lit.com for details

Introducing Choc Lit

We're an independent publisher creating
a delicious selection of fiction.
Where heroes are like chocolate – irresistible!
Quality stories with a romance at the heart.

See our selection here:
www.choc-lit.com

We would love to hear how you enjoyed *A Little Christmas Panto*. Please leave a review where you purchased the novel or visit: **www.choc-lit.com** and give your feedback.

Choc Lit novels are selected by genuine readers like yourself. We only publish stories our Choc Lit Tasting Panel want to see in print. Our reviews and awards speak for themselves.

Could you be a Star Selector and join our Tasting Panel? Would you like to play a role in choosing which novels we decide to publish? Do you enjoy reading romance novels? Then you could be perfect for our Choc Lit Tasting Panel.

Visit here for more details:
www.choc-lit.com/join-the-choc-lit-tasting-panel

Keep in touch:
Sign up for our monthly newsletter Choc Lit Spread for all the latest news and offers: www.spread.choc-lit.com.

Follow us on
Twitter: @ChocLituk
Facebook: Choc Lit
Instagram: ChocLituk

Printed in Great Britain
by Amazon

31884741R00152